WHEN TWO HEARTS MEET

JANELLE MOWERY

HARVEST HOUSE PUBLISHERS

EUGENE, OREGON

All Scripture quotations are from the King James Version.

Cover design by Left Coast Design, Portland, Oregon

Cover photos © Corbis / iStockphoto

The author is represented by MacGregor Literary Inc. of Hillsboro, Oregon.

When Two Hearts Meet
Copyright © 2011 by Janelle Mowery
Published by Harvest House Publishers
Eugene, Oregon 97402
www.harvesthousepublishers.com

Library of Congress Cataloging-in-Publication Data
    Mowery, Janelle.
    When two hearts meet / Janelle Mowery.
       p. cm.—(Colorado runaway series ; bk. 3)
    ISBN 978-0-7369-2810-6 (pbk.)
    ISBN 978-0-7369-4162-4 (eBook)
    I. Title.
    PS3613.O92W49 2011
    813'.6—dc22

2011007474

Printed in the United States of America
      11 12 13 14 15 16 17 18 19 / LB-SK / 10 9 8 7 6 5 4 3 2 1

To my Lord Jesus Christ.

And to my husband, Rodney,
for all his patience, love, and support.

ACKNOWLEDGMENTS

I want to thank Rod Morris for his patient guidance throughout this series.

I would also like to thank my family and friends for their encouragement.

Special thanks go to Nancy Toback. I am truly grateful for your help and reassurance. You are a special blessing.

✳ ONE ✳

March 1874 Colorado Territory

Warned by the clatter of breaking glass, Luke Mason flung himself from his saddle. Seconds later the sound of a gunshot reached his ears. The bullet splintered a branch behind his head. He pulled his pistol and rolled toward the protection of a large pine tree.

Crazy Sally wasn't so crazy after all. Her ravings during the past week about strange smells and noises didn't come from an overactive imagination but from the cabin in front of him.

The strong odor of cooking mash proved the presence of a working still inside. Luke stood and peeked from behind the tree. A shadow passed in front of a window followed by more shattering glass and clanging. A string of curses drifted toward him as two men argued. Time to establish some kind of communication with those inside.

"Hello in the cabin!" Silence. "This is Deputy Mason. I'd like to come in and talk."

Two quick, successive shots were his answer. Luke fired back and moved to another tree to get closer. A bullet landed a foot over his head. Chips of bark pelted his hat. Luke took a deep breath and plunged toward a boulder as he fired several rounds. A thin stream of smoke drifted skyward from the cabin.

Luke hunkered down and reloaded as he prepared to dash toward the structure. He couldn't believe they would burn their still on purpose. The fire must have started by accident or else they were planning their escape.

With a tug on his hat, Luke spun around ready to make his move. The thunder of horses' hooves and wagon wheels coming down the trail made him freeze. He squatted lower and waited.

Luke gaped at the stagecoach coming around the bend. He always thought the driver was a few spokes shy of a sturdy wheel, but now it was stamped as fact in his mind. Why would Frank drive this far off the main road? Luke stalled his attack, hoping the stage would hurry past. A feminine voice called for the driver to stop. Disbelief and the first spark of anger coursed through him when Frank obeyed.

The coach stopped between him and the cabin. Luke heard the click of the door latch, and he jumped from his shelter and lunged toward the stage. He slammed the door shut and heard a gasp as it thumped against the person inside.

Luke craned his neck to see the driver. "What are you doing, Frank? Get out of here!"

"The lady said—"

"I don't care what the lady said." Luke glanced in the window of the carriage. The young woman inside sat slack-jawed, rubbing her elbow. Some hair had come loose from her bun and bonnet and hung in tangled curls along the sides of her face. Her eyes were wide, possibly from fear, but she also looked outraged...and pretty.

Luke tore his gaze away and slapped the side of the coach. "Get moving, Frank."

The woman slid to the window. "But sir, I can help if someone's hurt. That's why—"

Luke stuck his face through the window. She leaned back and put her hand to her mouth.

"You haven't helped. You've hindered." He stepped toward Frank. "Get her out of here."

Frank gave a shrill whistle and slapped the reins against the rumps of the horses. Luke used the moving coach to get closer to the cabin. He ducked behind a tree and peeked around the side. Flames licked out of the structure's windows.

Luke ran toward the rear. The back door hung open. The absence of horses lent proof to his assumption that the men were gone. He shoved his pistol into his holster, then turned and glared in the direction the stagecoach had disappeared. He hoped the young woman didn't plan to get off in Rockdale. He didn't think he could handle any more of her type of help.

Rachel Garrett's heart pounded and nerves tingled as her eager eyes took in the sights. She stuck her head out the stagecoach window and received a face full of dust. She ducked back inside and laughed as she coughed and sputtered. *Well, that's one way to be greeted into my new home.*

The incident didn't quash her excitement. Nothing could, although she had to push away the memory of tears falling down her mother's cheeks as she said good-bye to her parents. Rachel clung to the knowledge that her arrival marked the beginning of her new lifework, the fulfillment of a dream, and the end of the trouble that had haunted her the last four months.

She wiped her face and swatted at the dust on her coat. The fine powder clung much like the cloying scent of excrement from the cattle outside the coach. Rachel waited for the stream of cows and cowboys to pass before she dared peek out again. She'd never been farther west than her home in Missouri, and everything she saw held her spellbound, from the plains of Kansas to her first glimpse of the glorious Rocky Mountains.

As the coach entered Rockdale, Rachel craned her neck, hoping for a glimpse of the building where she would spend most of her time. The town looked bigger than she expected, and she wanted to see it all. While many of the buildings they passed gleamed with new lumber, some structures looked rough, as though left over from the earlier years and kept patched together. The bleak sight caused her to wonder about the proprietors. Another bout of apprehension struck, but she tamped it down. Her teacher and mentor, Dr. Freeman, assured her he was sending her to the best town and doctor in the west.

They left a small church behind. Rachel's gaze remained fixed on the whitewashed spire long after the rest of the building faded from view. Once she left the doctor's office, she would make it a point to go back and meet the pastor. Maybe he could use someone to help out around the place when she wasn't working. The surroundings lacked flowers and shrubs, minor touches that would make it welcoming to strangers like her. She learned while away at nursing school that no matter where she was, she would always feel at home in church.

The sound of clanging brought her attention back to the scene in front of her. They passed by a livery and other buildings. A general store flashed past, as well as a hotel and eatery. Several women bustled down the boardwalk, and men lingered outside the feed and hardware store. Rachel held fast to her seat, wishing the coachman would slow down so she could take in more of the scenery.

As though the driver read her thoughts, the stagecoach slowed and then stopped in front of the depot. Within seconds, he opened the door and held out a dirty, calloused hand to help her step onto the platform. She smiled and thanked the man, then looked down the street to see what she'd missed.

Music from a couple saloons in the middle of town drifted toward her. She knew they were inevitable, but it didn't mean she had to like that they appeared in every settlement. They tended to keep people in her profession quite busy. Thankfully, the sheriff's office stood nearby to help keep most of the ruckus to a minimum.

Rachel scanned the street looking for her new place of employment. Dr. Barnes wrote that his main office stood next to the barbershop. She looked the direction they'd come, but didn't recall seeing a barbershop. She took a couple steps before her travel bag rushed past her head and hit the ground in front of her feet. Dust billowed up around her skirt bottom.

"Sorry, ma'am." The driver didn't look a bit sorry as he shrugged. "Watch the head and feet, little lady. Your trunk's coming next."

Rachel backed up to wait for her trunk to descend in the same manner as her bag.

"Hold up, Frank."

A young man appeared from the shipping office next door and hurried across the boardwalk toward them. He climbed on the back rail of the coach and helped the driver ease the heavy chest onto the platform. When he straightened, he tipped his hat and smiled as if helping damsels in distress were an everyday occurrence.

The young man wiped his palm on his trousers before offering his hand. "Afternoon, Miss. I'm Chad Baxter."

Rachel examined Mr. Baxter's face as she shook his hand. Merriment danced in his brown eyes as well as a hint of interest.

"Thank you, Mr. Baxter."

"Oh, come now." He placed his other hand over hers, and she gave a gentle tug to pull her hand free. Mr. Baxter allowed it, though his expression let it be known he wasn't used to rejection. He tucked his fingers into his pockets and leaned toward her.

"Mr. Baxter is my father's name. Call me Chad, Miss…" Chad raised his eyebrows.

Rachel studied him a little longer. He seemed harmless enough, like a young pup eager for attention. "Rachel Garrett."

He grinned and rocked back on his heels. "Ah, Miss Garrett. I hope you'll call me Chad. I wouldn't want things too formal between us."

Rachel held her even expression although she was intrigued. Her mother had been right. People were more forward in the west. Funny. Their bold ways didn't startle her as much as she expected it should. She fought the laughter that bubbled inside her at Chad's boyish attempt at charm.

Chad tapped the trunk with the toe of his boot. "Do I dare assume this means you'll be staying in town awhile?"

"Chad?" An older gentleman stepped out of the shipping office and walked toward them. She could see where the young man received his good looks. "Is my son being a pest, Miss?"

"Not at all. I think he was welcoming me to town in his own unique way."

The man's brows rose. "Unique, huh? Well, knowing Chad, that's a mighty diplomatic way to put it." He held out his hand. "Richard Baxter. Welcome to Rockdale." His handshake was brief but courteous as he looked her in the eye. "Can my son and I help you with this trunk?"

Rachel glanced down the street. "I'm supposed to be staying in a small house near Dr. Barnes's home."

"Oh, so you're the new nurse we've heard so much about," Chad said. "I expected someone much…"

"Older?" Rachel said.

Pink blotches stained his tanned cheeks.

"I can see I have more training to do." Richard put his arm around his son's shoulders. "And that you're more than capable of keeping him in his place. If you can wait, I'll have Chad deliver your trunk for you after work. Doc's house is two streets over on the left. It's the big white one with black shutters. You can't miss it. His office," Mr. Baxter gestured the opposite direction with his thumb, "is halfway down and across the street."

"You're very kind, Mr. Baxter. Thank you."

"Not a problem." Richard squeezed his son's shoulder. "Chad, those crates aren't moving themselves." He turned back to her. "Nice meeting you, ah—"

"Rachel," Chad said, his gaze never leaving her face. "Rachel Garrett."

Richard winked at her and bowed slightly at the waist. "Miss Garrett."

Chad gave her a sheepish grin, stooped to pick up her trunk, and followed his father into the office.

Rachel stared after them, unable to wipe the smile from her face as she grabbed her carpetbag and headed down the boardwalk. Maybe their manners were less polished compared to those of her friends back home, but such friendliness was endearing, and she was already beginning to feel at home.

She passed the hardware store and met the stares of the men sitting on the benches as she offered a greeting. She nodded and smiled to the women who gazed at her through the dress shop window next door, hoping they would one day become friends. She hurried past the swinging doors of the saloon, her gaze locked on the white sign boasting Dr. Barnes's name. She wasn't supposed to start work for three more days, but hunger to see the office and love for her work carried her feet across the dirt street and up the steps.

She glanced through the window of the barbershop next door. Men waiting their turn sat chatting, their feet dangling off the bottom rung of wooden stools, some with newspapers held high. What did the men do for a living and how would they fit into her new life? A sign propped inside the grimy window informed her the shop doubled as a dentist office. The dark stains on the floor circling the spittoon caused a shudder to run through her. She sent up a silent prayer that she'd never have trouble with her teeth.

Screams assaulted her ears before she reached the doctor's door. She hesitated, then grabbed the knob and held tight as the shouts from inside the office intensified. The nameplate nailed to the door read *Jim Barnes, M.D.* Dr. Freeman proclaimed Dr. Barnes was one of the best. She prayed he was right.

Another shriek from inside made her take a deep breath, turn the knob, and enter. The man standing closest to her yelled that his wife was about to have a baby and the doctor needed to come right away.

Next to the man, a woman held a young boy with blood stream-ing from his nose. His tears made clean tracks down his grimy face. Another man pounded on a doorframe, begging for the doctor's help, though he didn't look hurt. Others with no visible signs of ill-health occupied the few chairs lining a wall.

Rachel peered through the doorway that led into the examining area. Before moving that direction, she instructed the young mother to tip her son's head back and handed her a small white towel off a nearby washstand.

"Just gently pinch his nostrils closed."

She edged toward the examining room and around the man beating on the frame. The sight of numerous shiny instruments made her pause. Doctor Barnes had spared no expense on his office equipment. Was his practice that lucrative or did the money come from another source? Either way, the tools would make her job easier.

A man bent over a padded examining table. A woman stood next to him. *Did the doctor find a replacement nurse before I could get here?* A scruffy-looking man stood at the end of the table wringing an already mangled hat. The patient on the table bellowed and tried to sit up.

The doctor, with his sleeves rolled up, stood over him and pushed him back down. "Lay still, Walt. You're only making it worse."

"But Doc—"

The doctor beckoned toward the man with the hat. "Hold him down, Patch. I gotta put him under so I can fix this leg."

Patch clamped his hat on his head and leaned down to press on the patient's shoulders. The injured man fought against him.

Rachel dropped her travel bag in a corner and approached the doctor. The patient he worked on writhed in pain. Rachel glanced at his leg, bent at an awkward angle below the knee.

"Dr. Barnes?"

The doctor didn't look up as he grabbed the uninjured leg swing-ing toward his head. "Yes?"

His patient hollered and almost rolled off the table. Rachel moved to his head and stood next to Patch. She grabbed the mask and ether from the small stand next to the table, placed the mask over the patient's face, and administered the ether. In moments, the man fell unconscious. The doctor looked up. Rachel couldn't tell if the expression on his face was shock or anger.

She pointed toward the patient's leg. "I suggest you get started. He won't stay unconscious long."

"Who are you and what do you think you're doing?"

"I'm just putting into practice some of what Dr. Freeman taught me."

Dr. Barnes glanced at her as a slow grin spread across his face. "How is that old pain maker?"

"As ornery as ever. He sends his regards." She eyed the other woman who had tears running down her cheeks, then turned back and applied another drop of ether. "I believe I'm your new nurse, Rachel Garrett. Would you like me to help you here or get to work out in the waiting room?"

The doctor gave her a look of relief. "Do you know how to deliver a baby?"

Rachel nodded.

He jerked his thumb over his shoulder. "Go with Henry there. His wife is having a baby and needs help. Give Mrs. Cagle the ether. She can take over that job. My medical bag is behind my desk in the next room. It should have everything you'll need. When you're finished there, come on back."

"Yes, Doctor."

A look of relief crossed Henry's face as he whirled and headed out the door without waiting for her. Rachel skirted through the waiting patients to get the bag, then rushed out the door and ran into what felt like a wall. Her arms were gripped in a firm grasp. She pushed away. When she opened her eyes, a shiny badge met her gaze. She looked up into the scowling face of the deputy she'd met earlier. His intense eyes, much like before, made him all the more intimidating.

"You?" His brows rose then folded into a scowl. "You all right?"

"Ah, yes, fine."

"Excuse me." He brushed past her and continued down the boardwalk. He seemed in a mighty big hurry. *He'd be handsome if he smiled.*

"Miss?"

Rachel spun at Henry's voice. He took her by the arm and pulled her toward his wagon. She discovered what a sack of feed felt like after Henry all but threw her onto the seat. He scrambled up next to her, grabbed the reins, and gave them a hardy flick. Rachel shoved the doctor's medical bag between her feet as the horse and wagon picked up speed. She needed both hands to hold on if she wanted to remain in the seat.

"Uh, the doctor said your name was Henry?"

"Yep."

"Can I ask your last name?"

Henry glanced at her. "Moeller. Henry Moeller. My wife's name is Patricia. She was screaming like she'd been shot when I left. I hated leaving her, but I was too scared to stay. It's our first young'un, ya know."

Rachel wanted to look around for the cork that unplugged Henry's mouth.

"I got a lump in my gut the minute she told me she was with child. That knot's been growing right along with her own belly till I thought I'd be sick." Henry veered the horse onto a narrow path. "Then when her pains started this morning, I swear I felt 'em too."

"What has you so upset, Mr. Moeller?"

Henry looked at her as though she were daft. Or maybe he questioned her ability to deal with the task that lay ahead.

"Well, how'm I supposed to know if I'll be a good pa? I don't know what to do with a young'un. Them squallers don't come out talking, ya know."

Rachel patted him on the back. "I'm sure you'll do just fine. Anyone this concerned is bound to be a good father."

Henry brought the horse to a stop in front of a small, unpainted cabin. The weathered boards holding up the sagging roof were ill-fitting, as though patched together from discarded odds and ends. How long had the cabin been standing—and how much longer would it continue to stand?

Henry jumped down and pulled her from the seat. He held on to her hand and dragged her toward the door. She wrested her hand from his grip and rushed back for the doctor's bag, then gestured for Henry to lead the way. She quickened her pace to keep up with him.

The kitchen, dining, and living area, all contained in one large room, were clean. Shelves lined two walls near the cookstove arranged with pots, pans, and various foods. A crude but functional table sat in the middle of the room surrounded by four small, simple benches. Two well-used, overstuffed chairs were placed near the fireplace with a table and lamp sitting between them. The only item that looked new was the handcrafted cradle positioned near a door at the back of the cabin.

Henry cleared his throat then opened the door and disappeared through it. She rushed to follow.

Three lamps lit the room. The labor pains must have started before daylight. One lamp ran low on oil. A sheen of perspiration and damp strands of hair clung to the forehead of the woman writhing in the bed. One blanket lay in a tangle on the floor.

Rachel shed her heavy coat, draped it across a scratched wooden chair, and sat beside her. She felt for a temperature with one hand while checking Mrs. Moeller's pulse with the other. Behind her, Henry paced the room like a caged animal.

"Mr. Moeller, would you get some clean towels? I could also use some warm water for washing."

Henry scurried from the room.

"He's been fussing over me since I told him about the baby," Mrs. Moeller said. "Now I can't get him to stand still." The last word came out in a grunt as pain gripped her.

"Do you know about how far apart the contractions have been coming?"

Mrs. Moeller looked at her in confusion.

"How often do your pains come?"

"Every—few—minutes." The woman clutched at the sheets and moaned through the pain.

A sound behind her made Rachel turn in time to see Henry's knees buckle. She pushed the chair toward him, grabbed the towels from his arms, and turned back to his wife.

The laboring woman panted. "Henry...where's the warm water?"

Henry jumped to his feet and ran from the room. Moments later, he returned with a steaming pot and poured some into the washbasin. He flopped back down on the chair, and Rachel scrubbed her hands clean, then turned back to his wife.

"My name is Rachel Garrett, and I'm the doctor's new nurse."

Mrs. Moeller eyed her from the bed, her brow wrinkled. "How old are ya?"

"Old enough to have assisted in many births. In fact, this is my favorite part of the job. I delivered twins not two months ago. Now, I'm going to lift the covers and examine you."

Rachel rolled the blanket and sheet back and went to work. Henry slipped out of the room, peeking in from time to time at his wife. Rachel lost track of how many minutes went by before she held a new baby girl in her arms. The newest Moeller let out a lusty squall to announce her arrival.

Henry appeared in the doorway and then moved to hover behind Rachel while she cleaned the infant. He reached out and touched the tiny toes, then stepped beside Rachel and stroked the miniature hands of his daughter.

"Henry." Mrs. Moeller laughed. "I'm over here, Henry. You remember me, don't you?"

He sent a sheepish look at Rachel before heading toward the

bed. He sat beside his wife, enfolded her in his arms, and gave her a smacking kiss on her cheek.

"Ya done good, woman."

Rachel continued cleaning the baby, and soft ringlets of downy hair appeared. The cute rosebud mouth opened and then pursed when Rachel ran her finger along the bottom lip. She couldn't help but smile before kissing the tiny forehead.

After wrapping the baby in a blanket that Henry pulled from a small chest near the bed, Rachel placed the infant in her mother's waiting arms. Henry sat beside his wife and stared at his daughter's tiny face. Rachel enjoyed the tender scene.

With Henry's help, she exchanged the soiled bedding with clean sheets. She perched in the chair Henry had vacated and watched the family. He must have forgotten she had no way back into town. She waited several minutes and then cleared her throat. The young couple looked up at her.

"I must get back to town."

"I'm sorry." Mrs. Moeller turned to her husband. "Give her a ride back, Henry. Then be sure to stop by the store and tell Granny. The news is sure to spread through town by morning about our new little Elizabeth."

Henry fidgeted on the bed as if he wanted nothing to do with leaving. His wife patted his arm. "I'll be fine, dear. Just hurry on back." She turned to Rachel. "Thank you so much for your help, Rachel. I have no doubt the doctor will be pleased with you as his new nurse."

"Thank you, Mrs. Moeller. I'm sure the doctor will be out soon to examine you both to make sure everything's fine."

Mrs. Moeller struggled to sit and put her hand on Rachel's arm. "Please, call me Tricia. Mrs. Moeller makes me feel so old."

Rachel couldn't resist taking one more look at the sleeping infant. She caressed the baby's cheek, then donned her coat and bid Tricia good-bye.

Henry opened the front door, but this time he allowed Rachel to precede him. She stepped out, only to bump into a chest and have her arm grasped for the second time that day. Again, she found herself staring at the deputy's shiny badge.

"Are you Rachel Garrett?"

Rachel looked up into that same handsome, scowling face. "Yes."

"You have to come with me."

He took the medical bag from her hand and pulled her toward a waiting buggy.

TWO

Deputy Luke Mason couldn't believe his eyes. The nurse Doc sent him after was the same woman who had slammed into him earlier. Worse, she was the same woman who had kept him from catching the two criminals he had tried to arrest.

He climbed into the buggy and pulled her in behind him. When she settled onto the seat, he placed the medical bag between them and flicked the reins.

Luke noticed she was staring at him, and he turned to meet her gaze. Her eyes were wide with fear.

"Am…am I being arrested?"

He flicked the reins again to get the horse moving faster. "No, you're not under arrest. My mother fell. I went for the doctor, but he was busy. He sent me for you."

The nurse's hand went to her mouth, and Luke heard a muffled chuckle. He turned to find her amber eyes sparkling.

"I'm sorry. I'm not laughing at your mother's injury. I've only been in town a few hours, and I didn't know what I'd done to get in trouble with the law." She sobered in an instant. "How long ago did your mother get hurt?"

"Evidently, right before I ran into you in front of Doc's office."

"Oh, so that explains your…"

"Explains my what?"

"Well, you seemed in a hurry, that's all. Is your mother all right?"

"You can ask her yourself when we get there."

He checked her out of the corner of his eye. She looked stiff, her back straight, giving her a professional appearance. Several strands of dark hair escaped her bonnet, and he didn't need her to look at him to remember her eyes. Their gold tint would captivate many a single man in town. But she appeared too young to be a capable nurse. Could he trust her with his mother?

They rode in silence for two miles until they reached the edge of town. Luke noticed her white knuckles grasping the railing of the seat, and he slowed the horse to a canter.

"I'm sorry if I scared you." He extended his hand. "By the way, my name is Luke Mason."

"Pleased to meet you."

Her strong handshake surprised him. Most women presented only their fingertips. He dismissed the thought as he pulled up in front of his mother's home.

"Oh, how lovely. And a white picket fence!"

She sounded just like his mother when she first saw the place. "Yep, my mother moved in about six months ago."

"Where'd she move from?"

"Texas. Guess I coaxed her into moving when I landed the job of deputy in this town."

"Who'd want to be a lawman?" She put her hand to her lips. "I mean…well, it's a dangerous job."

"I'm following in the footsteps of the man I admire most." He didn't respond to her quizzical look.

Luke hopped to the ground and grabbed the medical bag before leading her up the steps and into the house. He moved into the living room and dropped to his knees next to his mother. She reclined on the couch with her left foot propped on a pillow. She looked too pale.

"I returned as quickly as I could, Mother."

"I told you I was fine, Luke. You didn't need to rush." His mother didn't even look at him. Her gaze remained glued to their guest. "You must be the new nurse."

Rachel smiled and removed her coat. "Yes, ma'am. My name is Rachel Garrett. Your son told me you fell."

Luke didn't move as Rachel examined his mother, who winced when Rachel carefully manipulated her ankle.

"May I ask how you hurt yourself?"

His mother didn't answer and looked everywhere but at them.

"Go ahead, Mother. Tell her."

Rachel rose, nudged him out of the way, and knelt in his place. Luke moved down to his mother's feet without a word. Rachel picked up his mother's hand and held it while her fingers pressed on the wrist.

"I guess it doesn't matter how you did it," Rachel said. "What's important is that you're not hurt anywhere else."

Luke's mother patted the nurse's hand. "I'm fine, dear."

"No bump on the head?"

"No."

"Good. Well, your ankle isn't broken, but it is badly sprained. I'll wrap it to help with the swelling, but you should stay off it for a few days. After that, you should be on it only for short periods of time until it becomes more comfortable for you. Soaking it in some Epsom salts should help with the pain."

"What about fixing meals for my son? I need to be on my feet for that."

"Your son appears to be big enough to take care of himself for a few days, Mrs. Mason. I noticed a restaurant on my way into town. He can pick up enough food for both of you while you're off your feet."

Luke's mother looked at him and her lips twitched. For some reason, he felt annoyed that she seemed to like Rachel.

"If that's not possible," Rachel continued, "then I'll come and cook supper the next few days."

"Am I included in that offer?" Luke said.

"I guess I could manage a few extra bites for you if need be."

"You won't need to come and cook for us, dear," Mrs. Mason said. "Luke is capable of picking something up for his old mother."

"You're not old, Mrs. Mason. But this ankle will slow you down for a bit." Rachel's professional manner returned as she tended to the swollen ankle.

"Will it keep me from playing the piano at church this Sunday? I play every Sunday and I certainly don't want to miss the next service because of a bad leg."

"Well, tomorrow is Saturday so I wouldn't want you walking on it that soon. But maybe your son could carry you to the piano. You do use your right foot to work the pedals?"

Mother hesitated a moment and then ducked her head. "Yes, but my son doesn't attend church with me."

"Oh." Rachel cast an almost imperceptible glance at him. "Well, then I guess I'll have to look for a wheeled chair and attend your church with you."

"You would do that?" Luke wished he hadn't said the words out loud.

"Of course. If your mother desires to work for the Lord by playing the piano even through her pain, then I intend to help her do just that." She turned back to his mother and took her hand in her own. "I'll check with the doctor about a wheeled chair and get back to you tomorrow. Maybe he'll have some other ideas if I can't locate one."

His mother looked at the young nurse with a loving gaze. "You're a believer, aren't you, Rachel."

Rachel nodded. "I'll be looking for a church to attend now that I'm living here. Helping you on Sunday will allow me to look into yours first."

"Well, since there's only one church, you won't have to look far."

"Oh." Rachel's brows rose as she stood. "I need to get back to the office, but I'll be back to check on you tomorrow. I hope I'll have the needed chair with me. It was nice meeting you, Mrs. Mason, though I wish it could have been under better circumstances."

"Call me Sadie."

Rachel smiled as she donned her coat. "Thank you, Sadie."

"Give her a ride back to the office, Luke. Then plan on bringing back some supper for us." Sadie sent him a playful wink.

"Yes, Mother," he said with a bow.

"We'll also plan to eat at a restaurant after church on Sunday. Would you join us, Rachel? I would like to get to know you better."

"I would love to, Sadie. Thank you for the offer." Rachel bent and patted her shoulder. "I'll see you tomorrow."

"I look forward to it." Sadie turned back to Luke. "See that she makes it back to the office safely."

Luke forced a smile. He knew his mother was sizing up the nurse to see if she would be good enough for her son. When would she learn that he could make his own decisions about women? He knew the type he liked and this little nurse didn't meet his qualifications.

He motioned for Rachel to precede him. Once her back was turned, Luke sent his mother a scowl and shook his head at her when she winked. He waited for Rachel to button up her coat and retrieve the doctor's bag before opening the door.

He had just enough time to see her step outside before the barrel of a shotgun was shoved under her nose.

❊ THREE ❊

Luke grabbed Rachel's arm and pulled her back next to him while he reached for his sidearm. The move made the man swing his gun toward Luke's chest.

"Don't do it, Mason." The gunman pulled the hammer back. "Just toss your gun aside."

Rachel gasped and dropped the doctor's bag to the floor. Luke did as told and threw his pistol onto a chair on his mother's porch. Rachel trembled, and he wished he could comfort her, but he didn't dare take his eyes off Joe Farris. What had gotten into the man?

"Put the gun down, Joe. You don't want to do this."

"Yes, I do. I been waiting long enough. This little lady's coming with me." The barrel of the gun moved back to Rachel. "Let's go."

Luke took a step forward. Joe growled low in his throat and aimed at Luke's chest. "Don't make me shoot you, Mason. I don't wanna, but I will."

Luke held up his hand. "What's this about, Joe? Why the gun?"

"To show I mean business."

"About what? Why do you need the nurse?"

Moisture welled in Joe's eyes. "It's my Clara. She's bleeding."

Rachel saw the man's tears and knew he spoke the truth. A closer look at his face helped her recognize him as the man pounding on the doorframe at the doctor's office. She stooped to grab the medical bag.

"Lead the way, Mr. Farris."

She managed to take two steps before Luke pulled her back. She struggled to free herself, but he held her tight. *What does he think he's doing?*

"Don't you realize how dangerous this could be?" Luke whispered close to her ear.

"Hey!" Joe said. "Step back, Luke. The lady wants to come with me."

Rachel's gaze moved to the weapon in Joe's hand. She could still smell the gunpowder from when he held the barrel under her nose. She took a deep breath and tried to calm her queasy stomach and whirling mind.

"I'm going with him." She glanced up at Luke and then looked into Joe's eyes. "He won't hurt me, Luke. Isn't that right, Mr. Farris?"

Their gazes met and held. His eyes flickered with surprise and then relief.

"Uh…that's right, I guess."

The barrel of the gun dropped. She nodded and moved forward, only to be pulled back by Luke again.

"Give me the gun, Joe. Then I'll let her go."

She tugged her arm from Luke's grip. "It's all right, Deputy. He said he won't hurt me." She stepped away from Luke before he could grab her arm again and headed toward the buggy. "Is Clara your wife, Mr. Farris?"

A glance over her shoulder let Rachel know her move surprised both men. She kept walking, afraid that if she stopped, she wouldn't get her feet moving again. Joe took one last look at Luke before he raced down the porch steps to catch up to her.

"Uh, yeah, Clara's my wife. Nigh on fifteen years now."

Rachel heard Luke clomp down the stairs, and she expected him to try to stop her again. Instead, he helped her into the buggy and climbed in beside her. He didn't look at her, just flicked the reins and turned the horse around, though muscles twitched along his jaw line. Joe Farris sat astride his horse waiting for them. His shotgun lay across his lap.

"Do you think sometime today," Luke growled between clenched teeth, "you can let *me* handle a situation? It's what I get paid to do."

"Sorry." Rachel clutched the handles of the medical bag in her lap to hide the shaking of her hands. Not once in all the years of training did anyone warn her nursing could be so dangerous. She chose the occupation because she enjoyed helping people. She never dreamed those same people might turn a gun on her. She glanced at the deputy next to her and thanked the Lord she had met some kind people or she would have wondered if the whole town was like these two testy men.

Luke stopped the horse in front of a small but well-kept cabin set in the midst of several trees. Joe didn't allow her time to look around. He held the front door open and waved her over with his rifle.

"Clara?" he shouted over his shoulder while watching Rachel. When she reached him he grabbed her arm and propelled her inside. "Clara?"

A soft moan came from behind a curtain. Joe pulled the checkered fabric back to reveal a ghost-like woman lying on a bed. Rachel rushed to Clara's side and took her wrist in her hand. A weak pulse feathered below the woman's translucent skin. Joe dropped to his knees beside his wife and kissed her forehead as quiet sobs escaped his throat.

Rachel peeled back the covers and gasped at the amount of blood pooling around Clara's hips.

"Is she pregnant, Mr. Farris?"

The man continued to hold Clara's head.

"Joe!"

He looked up at Rachel in surprise, his tears leaving streaks down his cheeks.

"Is your wife pregnant?"

He nodded. "Fourth time. She lost the first three."

"Does Doctor Barnes know about this?"

Joe shook his head. "Clara wanted to wait and see what happened." His look pleaded with her. "Is she gonna be all right?"

Rachel looked around and found Luke standing near the door with Joe's shotgun in his hands. "Get me some water. Lots of it."

Luke placed the gun on the mantel and moved to do Rachel's bidding. He brought a large bowl filled with water, spilling half the liquid over the side in his haste. Rachel pushed Luke out of the room and pulled the curtain closed. She rolled up her sleeves and turned to dip a rag into the water.

"Joe."

"Clara?"

Rachel turned back to the woman in bed and saw her mouth hanging open as she gazed at Joe. Tears ran down Clara's temples and dampened her hair as she attempted to reach for her husband. Joe took her hand in his.

"No, Clara. You can't leave me. You're a strong woman. Please, Clara." Joe kissed her fingers as he spoke.

The woman's bottom lip trembled as she attempted to take a deep breath. "I'm…sorry…Joe." The words were barely audible.

Rachel heard a long sigh hiss from Clara's mouth. She checked for a pulse and found none. Rachel said a silent prayer as she pulled the blanket up to Clara's chest.

"I'm sorry, Mr. Farris."

"No! She's not dead. Do something." He reached across the bed and grabbed her arm. "I said, *do something*! Help her."

Rachel winced at the pain his grip inflicted. "I can't, Mr. Farris. It's too late. She's gone."

"Noooooo!" Joe released her arm and dropped on top of his wife. "Clara. Please, Clara." Sobs wracked the man's body and shook the bed.

Rachel tried to fight her tears, a losing battle. Luke pulled back the curtain and met Rachel's gaze. She shook her head and wiped the moisture from her cheeks. He motioned her out of the room, and she followed him to the door.

"Let me get you back to Doc's office," Luke said as he held her coat out to her. "You can tell him about this while I find some help for Joe."

"But someone needs to stay with him."

"Not you. He's too upset. I can't leave you here alone with him." He opened the door to let her know the conversation was over.

Rachel shoved her arms into the coat sleeves to ward off the cool of the late afternoon. She wished she could stay and help the poor man, but the look on Luke's face let her know she wouldn't get her wish.

They made the trip back to the office in silence. Rachel said a quiet thank you as she stepped from the buggy. Fatigue weighted her feet as she stumbled up the steps to the door. She entered to find it much calmer than when she'd left. She forced a smile at the woman sitting in one of the chairs. The little boy next to her appeared to be fine. Rachel nodded to them as she entered the examining rooms to find the doctor.

"Dr. Barnes?"

"Right here." His voice came from behind a curtain on the left. She pulled it back and stepped inside to find him stitching a gash on a man's hand. "Did you get a chance to check on Mrs. Mason?"

"Yes, sir."

The doctor glanced up. "Is she all right?"

"Yes, she's fine. I wrapped her ankle and told her I'd check on her again tomorrow."

"Great." He continued to examine her face. "Is there anything else?"

"I need to talk to you about something when you have a minute."

"All right." He motioned toward the waiting area. "Why don't you check on the young man in the other room while I finish stitching up this gentleman's hand? Then we should be finished for the day and can have that talk. If you need any help, let me know."

Rachel closed the curtain and took a deep breath. She removed her coat, placed it and the medical bag on a chair, and then called the child and his mother into the other examining room. As she helped the young man climb onto the table, she tossed the mother a quick smile and a soft hello before turning back to the boy.

"So, what's your name, young man?"

"William."

"Well, William. My name is Nurse Garrett. What can I do for you today?"

He glanced at his mother, who gave him a nod. "I have a rock stuck up my nose."

Misery shone from William's face as he made his announcement. Rachel had to bite her bottom lip to keep from laughing. She resisted the urge to give him a hug.

"I guess that explains the bump I see on the side of your nose. Let's take a look, shall we?"

Rachel pulled open a few drawers before finding a small, mirrored lantern. She lit it and moved back to William's side, then tipped his head back and took a quick peek.

"How did you manage to get the rock stuck up there so far?" Rachel set the lantern aside and leaned against the table to look into William's eyes. He stared right back at her.

"I had the help of two friends."

"It appears to be in there pretty tight. Does it hurt?"

He shook his head. "It just doesn't feel very good."

"I can imagine." She patted him on the shoulder. "I'm going to get that out of there for you, William, but I need you to lie back on the table for me. Would you like your mother to come and hold your hand while I do this?"

The boy nodded, and the mother moved to her son's side. Rachel looked around the office to locate the instruments she would need.

"How old are you, William?"

"Eight."

"So you've been going to school for a couple of years. How do you like it?"

"It's all right. The teacher's really nice."

"Well, that makes school even better, doesn't it?"

Rachel finally found everything she needed and returned to the boy's side.

"Now, William. I'm going to do this as carefully and painlessly as I can, but it will probably make your eyes water a little. I'm going to give this cloth to your mother, and she can wipe them if need be. Are you ready?"

He had a look of fear in his eyes but nodded anyway. Rachel gave him her biggest smile, hoping to calm his nerves. She began the procedure only when he returned her smile with a trembling one of his own.

The rock sat snug in his nose, but it took her only a few moments to work it loose. When she had it out, she held it up for William to see.

His eyes grew large and he grinned. "Can I keep it?"

"If your mother doesn't mind, I don't see why not." After receiving a nod from the mother, she dropped the rock into the boy's waiting hand. "Before you sit up, I want to put some drops in your nose. That rock may have made it a bit raw inside, and the drops will help it feel better."

With that done, she had William off the table and ready to leave. "You were very brave, William. And an excellent patient, I might add."

Rachel ruffled his hair as she walked them to the door. She received an adoring look from him as he stepped outside.

"Thank you." The mother spoke for the first time as she held out some money. "You were very good with him, Miss Garrett. You put him at ease and I appreciate that."

"You're quite welcome. You've got a good boy."

Rachel turned around and found the doctor leaning on the

doorframe watching her. His patient stepped past both of them and left the office holding his bandaged hand up in the air.

The doctor took a couple steps toward her. "I agree with Mrs. Baxter. You were very good with her son."

Rachel handed the cash to Dr. Barnes. He took it and slipped it into his pocket.

"I have someone waiting in my office who wants to talk to me," Dr. Barnes said. "We can discuss whatever you needed when I'm finished. Then I'll take you to see your house."

"That would be fine. Is there anything I can do to help?"

"No. This won't take long. Why don't you sit and relax a bit. I'll be right with you."

The doctor turned away, and she busied herself cleaning up the two examining rooms. She hadn't eaten since that morning, and a quick look out the window revealed that the sun was about to set.

When she finished setting the two rooms to rights, she seated herself on the softest chair she could find in the waiting area. Exhaustion swept over her, and she laid her head back and closed her eyes, hoping to unwind a few minutes before the doctor could see her.

The sound of shouting grabbed her attention. She stood and peeked into the doctor's office. A man held a rifle pointed at the doctor's chest, and her heart jumped to her throat.

It's happening again!

FOUR

Rachel prayed she'd find some kind of weapon to help Dr. Barnes out of his predicament. She moved to the other side of the doorway where the man couldn't see her and leaned against the wall. Several deep and calming breaths later, she spotted the end of a broom handle poking out from behind the counter. She tiptoed over to it and took a practice swing and poke at the air. The slender piece of wood was better than nothing at all.

The voices continued to rise in volume. Rachel used the noise to slip up behind the man holding her boss at gunpoint. As she lifted the broom handle in the air, she saw the doctor's gaze flash toward her. The gunman turned. Rachel gasped as she recognized Joe Farris. The gun was now pointed at her.

Joe sneered as he pulled the hammer back. "It's Nurse Garrett."

The barrel of the gun rose until she could see down the black tunnel.

"Wait." Rachel dropped the broom and held her hands in front of her. "No, wait. *Please!*" The last word came out a ragged whisper as she started to sob.

"Nurse Garrett?"

"No. Don't. I'm sorry." Rachel closed her eyes so she wouldn't see the blast that would end her life.

"Miss Garrett?"

Rachel felt someone grasp her arms. She struggled to pull free.

"Rachel!"

She opened her eyes. Dr. Barnes sat next to her, gripping her wrists. He released her and smiled.

"Bad dream?"

She sat up and looked around. They were alone. "Where's the man from your office?"

"He left." Dr. Barnes leaned forward to catch her eye. "You all right?"

Rachel lifted a trembling hand to smooth her hair. She forced a laugh. "Yes, of course. I…you were right. I was dreaming."

"I'm sure you had a long day. I think we're finished here. Are you ready to go or do you want to have that talk?"

"Ah…" Rachel stared down at her shaking hands. "Maybe in the morning?"

"Sure." He stood. "Let's get your things and head home."

The doctor grabbed her travel bag and his medical bag while she slipped on her coat. He led her to the buggy out front—the very same buggy she'd been in so many times that day with the deputy. She hoped this next ride would be more pleasant than the last. She thought of Mr. Farris and shuddered.

"Are you cold?" The doctor's gaze examined her face as he would a patient.

She tried to smile. "No. It's just been a long and somewhat harrowing day."

"All right, tell me about it. You looked upset when you returned. What happened?"

Rachel turned away and looked at the stores as they passed. She had no idea it would be this difficult to say the words. She'd already said something similar not too many months ago.

The doctor nudged her with his elbow. "Hey, it couldn't possibly be that bad, could it?"

"Clara Farris died today while in my care." Tears welled in her eyes as she recalled the scene. "She lost her baby and bled to death."

She pulled her kerchief from her sleeve and dabbed at her eyes.

The doctor turned left off the main street before he reined his horse to a stop. Rachel glanced at him. He opened his mouth as if to speak, then clamped it shut again. He turned and faced her.

"I sent you to help with the Moeller baby. How did you end up in the home of Clara Farris?"

Rachel told him everything that happened from the time she and Luke opened the door to find Joe with his gun. She ended with the news that Luke planned to find help for Mr. Farris.

Dr. Barnes gave a low whistle. "How sad. I wish they would've told me about the baby. If you aren't in a hurry to get home, I'd like to swing by there and check on Joe."

"I think that's a great idea."

The house stood empty when they arrived. The doctor called out but received no answer. He shrugged and climbed back into the buggy. "I'll check on him tomorrow."

He turned the horse back toward home. They ended up on the same street as Luke's mother's residence. At the end of the street, the doctor pulled to a stop in front of a large house. Off to the side stood another small home and a tiny stable.

The front door swung open as the doctor helped Rachel from the buggy. A beautiful woman stepped onto the porch carrying a little boy on her hip. The face of a young girl peeked out from behind the woman's skirt.

"Sorry we're late, Beth. It was one of those days."

"I can tell. You two look about ready to drop." She shifted the boy to her other hip. "Come on inside. I have supper waiting. The only thing you have to do the rest of the night is chew."

"Thanks, honey." The doctor turned to grab both bags from the buggy, then motioned Rachel to go ahead of him. "Beth, I'd like you to meet my new nurse, Rachel Garrett. She arrived a day early, but as far as I'm concerned, she was just in time."

Rachel climbed the three steps to join Beth on the porch. "Hello, Mrs. Barnes."

"Call me Beth." She bounced her son. "This is Tanner, and this," she stepped aside to reveal their daughter, "is Emma."

Emma scooted back behind her mother but stole another look. Rachel bent to peer into the little girl's face.

"That's a mighty pretty name for a very pretty girl."

The compliment didn't bring Emma out from her hiding place, but she blessed Rachel with a wide grin. Rachel stood upright and groaned as her back felt every minute of her time on the stagecoach and buggy. Beth put her arm around Rachel's shoulders.

"Come inside and get a quick bite. Then I'll show you to your house so you can get some rest." She glanced over her shoulder. "I'm not sure which one of you will last the longest, but I'm so thankful you're here. My husband's needed help for longer than he'll admit."

"He did look like a drowning man when I walked in this afternoon."

"I looked that good?" Dr. Barnes winked and set the bags inside the door. "I'm going to put the horse in the stable. I'll be right back."

By the time he returned to the kitchen, Rachel and Beth had everything on the table. Dr. Barnes kissed the cheek of each member of his family, then sat and rubbed his hands together.

"Let's pray so we can eat."

Rachel appreciated the prayer as the reverence in the doctor's voice revealed his deep love for his heavenly Father.

As they ate, Jim and Beth plied Rachel with questions about her trip and also the well-being of Dr. Freeman. Jim's obvious respect for their mentor warmed her to her new employer even more.

After the meal, Beth cleaned up Tanner's face and handed him to his father. Tanner immediately stuck his thumb in his mouth and reached up to play with his father's earlobe, never taking his eyes from Rachel. She smiled at the accuracy with which he found the lobe.

Rachel stood to help clean up, but Beth waved her back. "I know you two have some business to discuss, so just sit down, Rachel. I can do this."

Emma shoved her chair next to her father and leaned against him. Jim put his free arm around her and pulled her close. Then he gave Rachel his full attention.

"We've discussed Clara, but what about the Moeller delivery? How did that go?"

Rachel filled the doctor in on the new member of the Moeller family, telling him it was a healthy little girl and that she had stayed long enough to make sure the mother was comfortable with her new role. "I also told her you'd be by soon to check on her and the baby."

"Very good. Now, what about Sadie Mason? I'm assuming that since you didn't bring her in to the office, it was only a sprain."

"That's right, but it was a bad sprain. I told her to stay off her feet for at least three days. She didn't like that idea because she couldn't cook for her son. I suggested that he bring food home from a restaurant until she was back on her feet."

The smile that spread across the doctor's face and the chuckle that came from Beth made Rachel nervous.

"Did I do something wrong?"

The doctor shook his head. "No. But I can just about imagine the look on Luke's face when you said that."

"Actually, I didn't even look at him, but his mother was trying to hide a smile."

"I'll bet. She has him spoiled."

"I also promised to try to locate a wheeled chair. She was rather adamant about wanting to play the piano at church on Sunday. I told her I'd attend with her and wheel her to the piano and back. Do you know if there's a wheeled chair to be found in this town?"

"Indeed. I keep one at the office. I'll go with you tomorrow to bring it to her." He shifted Tanner to his other leg. "And everything went fine with young William?"

"Yes, but I imagine his nose will be sore for a day or so. That was a good-sized rock, and he had it up there pretty far."

He shook his head. "Trust me, that won't be the last time you'll have a chance to nurse that boy to health. Now, let me explain how I run my offices as well as mention a few of your duties. First, on Mondays, Wednesdays, and Fridays, I work at the office in town. On Tuesdays, Thursdays, and Saturdays, I open the office here at the house. I'd like you at the office about half an hour ahead of time to make sure everything is set up and ready for the day's work. I work Saturday mornings. You'll only need to work if there's an emergency."

"I can work Saturday mornings as well."

"There will be times I will need you for emergencies, not only on weekends but also during the night. I would rather you plan to take all weekends off to rest up if such occasions arise. Any questions?"

"Dr. Freeman always wanted me to wear a white blouse and dark skirt during business hours."

"I'll expect the same, if you have them."

"I do."

"Good. Any other questions?"

"I don't think so. I believe we covered most everything in our correspondence."

"Great! I don't know how to thank you enough for being so willing to jump in and help today, Miss Garrett."

"I was glad I could help. And I hope you'll call me Rachel, at least when we're away from the office."

"All right, Rachel it is. Now, my earlobe is getting sore so I'm going to get this young lad off to bed. You too, Emma." The doctor stood then paused. "Dr. Freeman gave you his highest recommendation. I can see why."

"Thank you. He spoke just as highly of you."

Jim nodded and left the room. Rachel turned to Beth. "I guess I should find my way to the house so you and your family can finally be alone. Thank you for the meal."

Beth sat on the chair next to Rachel. "You didn't get a chance to go to the house and get it settled. Why not stay in our guest room for the night? I'll help you get settled tomorrow."

"I accept your offer."

"Would you like a bath before you turn in?"

"It sounds wonderful, but I don't think I could manage to stay awake long enough to accomplish that."

"Well then, I'll just plan on fixing one for you in the morning."

"Thank you, Beth. You've been so kind."

Beth smiled. "Come on. Let me show you to your room."

Fifteen minutes later, Rachel managed a quick thank you to the Lord before sleep overtook her.

FIVE

Something tickled Rachel's fingers. She moved her hand. Moments later, the tickle returned. She opened her eyes. Emma Barnes stood next to the bed, and she jerked her hand back.

Rachel wiggled her fingers. "Good morning, Emma."

Emma stepped back and eyed her with misgiving.

"How old are you, Emma?" The little girl held up four fingers. "My, but you're a big girl for being four years old. How old is Tanner?"

"He's gonna be two soon." Emma relaxed against the bed. "Mama's cleaning him up from breakfast. He gets a messy face when he eats."

Rachel sat up and glanced at the window. "So has your father already started working this morning?"

Beth Barnes entered the room with Tanner in her arms. "I'm sorry, Rachel. I asked Emma not to disturb you."

Emma ran to her mother and wrapped her arms around one of Beth's legs.

"She was fine. I enjoyed waking up to such a pretty face." Rachel winked at Emma, then motioned to the window. "I slept too late."

"It's not that late. We've only just finished breakfast. I kept a plate of food warm if you're hungry."

"That sounds great. I'll be down in a few minutes."

Rachel scrambled from the bed when the trio left and entered the kitchen a few minutes later.

Beth set the plate in front of Rachel, then sat across from her. "Jim and I thought maybe you'd like to spend the rest of the morning getting settled into your new home. Chad Baxter dropped off your trunk yesterday. I had him put it inside the door. After dinner, I could take you shopping for any supplies you need while Jim watches the children. He said when we returned, you and he could take the chair to Sadie and check on her ankle. How does all that sound?"

"That's fine, but I hope you don't think you have to help me or entertain me."

"Not at all. I'll enjoy the chance to get to know you better. Would you like your bath right away or would you rather have a look at your new home first?"

"Actually, a bath sounds wonderful. I haven't had one since I left St. Louis."

Beth rose and started warming the water. "You're welcome to use our tub anytime. Your house is on the small side, and there's not much room for a tub. I also thought it would be nice if you'd have a couple meals a week with us. I know you'll be tired after working all day and won't feel like fixing anything."

Rachel waited for Beth to turn around. "Do you have a younger sister?"

"As a matter of fact, I do. How did you know?"

"It seems you're used to taking care of someone, and I don't mean your children." They exchanged a smile. "Are you certain your husband will be able to stand seeing that much of me each week if I eat here with you?"

"Jim and I have already discussed it, and he said it was fine."

"Then I'll accept."

Beth sat at the table again. "Would you like to join us for church tomorrow?"

"I would, but I already promised Sadie I would help her tomorrow."

"We attend the same church. We could help you with Sadie. And how about dinner afterward? Have you already made plans?"

"Sadie invited me to join her and her son at a restaurant."

"Ha, I wish I could've seen the look on Luke's face when you said he should pick up some food from town while his mother's recuperating."

"Is he a difficult man?"

"No, not really. He's actually rather sweet. But his mother's been spoiling him since she arrived a few months after he did. Probably because he's following in his father's footsteps. He was a lawman too."

"Was?"

"Sadie told us he was killed about nine years ago while going after some bank robbers. They got the drop on him and he couldn't escape. Luke still can't talk about it without growing angry and bitter." Beth stood and checked on the water. "It's hot. Are you ready?"

An hour later, Beth led Rachel to the small house next door. They walked directly into the kitchen and dining area, the sink, counter, and cabinets off to the right with a small stove next to the counter. A table and four chairs sat near the middle of the room with a blue-and-white checkered cloth covering the table. To the left of the door was a small living area with a couch, chair, and small table, which supported one of the two lanterns in the house. The walls had been painted white, and curtains that matched the tablecloth hung from the windows. A short wall divided the living area from her bedroom, with a small changing area across from her bed.

Rachel turned to Beth. "It's beautiful. I love it. I couldn't have asked for more. Thank you."

Rachel hung the few dresses in her travel bag and emptied her trunk, then returned to the main house to help Beth with dinner. Jim joined them at twelve thirty. Once they'd finished eating, the two women headed into town to take care of Rachel's shopping.

"How did you and Jim meet, if you don't mind me asking?" Rachel asked as they walked together.

"I don't mind. We met in St. Louis. While Jim studied to become a doctor, I was studying to be a nurse. We married just before he finished his schooling. The plan was for me to be his nurse when he settled in a town, but my pregnancy with Emma put a halt to that. I didn't even get to finish my schooling."

"Were you disappointed?"

"I thought I would be, but I haven't regretted it a bit. I can't imagine that nursing could be anywhere near as much fun as raising Jim's children. I still help him now and then when someone comes to the office at the house, but my first love is raising the children. Jim acquired the business from an old friend of Dr. Freeman when he wanted to retire."

They had arrived at the general store, and Mr. and Mrs. Ashton, the proprietors, greeted them as they walked through the doors. Rachel wandered the aisles and was amazed at the well-stocked and clean store. Almost finished with her shopping, she rounded one of the aisles and found herself face to face with Luke Mason.

He sure had a way of making her heart thunder. Rachel took a breath and searched for something to say. "How's your mother?"

"I think she's all right. She said she slept fine."

Why didn't he ever smile? "I hope I didn't offend you yesterday, Mr. Mason, when I suggested that you bring some food home for your mother."

Luke's brows rose. "Not at all. I know you were just looking after my mother's best interests."

"Did her ankle seem any better this morning?"

"She moaned a couple of times as I helped her down the stairs. I think I'll suggest she sleep downstairs tonight. Are you still planning to check on her today?"

She nodded. "The doctor and I will be by a bit later this afternoon."

"Good. Maybe I'll see you then. Otherwise, I'll see you at the restaurant after church."

"You're meeting us there?"

"Just as soon as the sheriff relieves me. I work Sunday mornings because he enjoys going to church. The other deputy has the day off."

"Oh." Rachel paused a moment. "But don't you miss getting to attend church?"

Luke's eyes narrowed. "No." He tipped the brim of his hat. "Good day, Miss Garrett. I hope you find this town suitable as your new home." He stepped around her and strode out the door.

Beth approached Rachel and motioned after Luke. "What happened? He looked upset."

"I asked him if he missed attending church. I guess I said the wrong thing again."

"Luke has never entered the church doors since his father died. Sadie said he blames God for all of it. It breaks her heart."

"Is he a believer and just mad at God?"

"I'm not sure. That's something you'd have to ask Sadie."

Rachel raised her brows. "I'd better wait till I know them better before I go stepping on my tongue or their toes again. Twice in two days is more than enough."

An hour later, Rachel looked over Dr. Barnes's shoulder as he examined Sadie's sprained ankle. After a quick check, he leaned back. "Rachel's right. Your ankle isn't broken." He wrapped it again. "All right, Sadie. We'll be by in the morning to pick you up for church." He slapped his hands on his knees then stood.

"I know you planned to eat at a restaurant after church tomorrow, Sadie, but Beth wanted me to invite you, Rachel, and Luke to our house instead. It would be much easier to get you home and settled again, rather than Rachel trying to get you home from the restaurant."

"That sounds wonderful. Thank Beth for me, Jim."

"I'll do it. We'll see you tomorrow, Sadie."

Rachel trailed the doctor home. Luke never made an appearance while they were there. She hoped he didn't stay away because of her and her knack for asking the wrong questions.

Morning came all too soon for Rachel. After staying up late to unpack her trunk, she fell into bed exhausted for the second night in a row. She sped over to the doctor's house. Beth entered the kitchen moments later.

"Good morning. Sleep all right?"

"I don't think I moved all night, so I guess I did."

They all climbed into Jim's wagon and rode to Sadie's house. Luke stood waiting to help Jim get Sadie into the wagon. Then with a quick nod to Beth and Rachel, he climbed on his horse and disappeared down the street. Rachel sat next to Sadie's chair to help steady it for the ride.

Once they arrived at church, Jim had several men help him lift Sadie and the chair from the wagon. Sadie took it all in stride and with good humor, teasing the men that she'd have to sprain her ankle more often if that was the only way she could get hugs out of them.

Rachel trailed behind Jim as he pushed Sadie toward the church. She stopped when something tugged on her skirt. William Baxter smiled up at her.

She crouched and touched his arm. "Hello, William. How are you today?"

"Fine."

"Any more problems with your nose?" When William shook his head, she smiled. "Good."

Before she could stand, two other boys approached and stopped a few steps away. William glanced at them and then spun back around with a gleam in his eyes.

"That's Mickey and Alex, my friends."

"Hi Mickey. Hello Alex. You two wouldn't be the friends that helped William with that rock the other day, would you?"

The two boys elbowed each other and laughed.

"I figured as much. How about we go inside. I'm getting cold." Rachel stood and found William's mother waiting on him. "Hello, Mrs. Baxter. It's good to see you again."

"Hi, Miss Garrett. I'd like you to meet the rest of my family. This is my husband, Richard."

Rachel's mouth dropped open. "We've met." She reached to shake his hand. "I met both your husband and son when I arrived in town."

"Oh my. You must've had your fill of Baxters Friday." Mrs. Baxter touched Chad's shoulder. "Chad is twenty. Our daughter Robin is sixteen. Next is my second son, Myron, who is fourteen, then my third son, Steven, who is twelve, and you've met William."

Rachel greeted each of the children, ignoring the stare of their eldest son and focusing on their only daughter. "Do you ever feel outnumbered?"

The girl gave her a shy nod and smile. "All the time."

Mrs. Baxter motioned for them to head to the church. "Why don't you join us for dinner after the service?"

"I'd love to, Mrs. Baxter, but I've already been invited to eat with the Barnes family."

"Maybe next Sunday then. And please call me Cora."

"Thank you, Cora. I'd love to join you next week."

Rachel spotted the Barnes family near the front of the church with Sadie, and she excused herself and moved down the aisle. The way Chad eyed her made her nervous. Next Sunday ought to be interesting.

The service started when Dr. Barnes pushed Sadie in her wheeled chair to the piano. Sadie made it obvious she enjoyed playing the piano. Energy radiated from her, though she wore a serene smile.

Rachel took the opportunity to look around at the faces in the room. How many of the parishioners would soon be patients? Not that she wanted any to be sick or hurt, but she couldn't contain her curiosity about the residents of her new home. She spotted a couple women who would be having a baby soon, and several others held small bundles in their arms. She reined in her interest when the doctor wheeled Sadie back to the pews.

Pastor Robbins stood and began a message about prayer that kept Rachel engrossed. He began in Matthew 6, where Jesus taught His disciples how to pray. The pastor ended by having the congregation turn to John 17, where Jesus prayed to His Father before He was arrested.

"The verses in Matthew tell us that we need to praise God, ask forgiveness for our sins, thank God for all things, and make our requests known to Him. But here in John, verse 22 reads, 'And the glory which thou gavest me I have given them; that they may be one even as we are one.' Jesus likened the unity of fellow believers to the unity between Himself and God. He prayed for all believers, not only for their protection but also for their unity. Jesus showed us how to pray for each other.

"Lastly, 1 Thessalonians 5:17 says, 'Pray without ceasing.' God wants to be uppermost in our minds so that we can be in constant communication with Him. Setting aside a specific time to pray is great, but we can pray at any time throughout the day.

"I would like each of us to leave with the intent to pray daily for those you see here today. Plan to spend some time praying, not only for your own needs but also for those of your fellow believers. You may be surprised to find that when you spend time praying for a person, you will come to love that person."

As Sadie played the final song, Rachel knew that if Pastor Robbins's messages were always that good, she'd love her new church. She couldn't wait to meet the man and tell him how much she enjoyed her morning and his message.

Beth was a step ahead of her. She had invited the pastor and his wife to join them for dinner along with the banker Pete Wallace, his wife Annie, and their three children Ben, Sarah, and little Samuel. Rachel had a good time getting to know her new friends a bit better. She went to bed that night praising God for her wonderful first two days in her new hometown.

❊ SIX ❊

Rachel inhaled the fresh scent of her pillow cover, then moaned as she rolled over. The shard of sunlight stabbing her eyes made her gasp. She threw off the covers and leapt from the bed. Minutes later, she dashed out the door with a quick prayer that she'd remembered everything. Her first day on the new job and she'd be fired first thing because she couldn't get to work on time.

A gunshot wiped all thoughts from Rachel's mind. Another shot turned her steps to her left toward the outskirts of town. If someone was hurt, she'd be on hand to help. The thin grove of trees she neared looked familiar. She paused at a tree when another shot went off. She peeked around the tree and spotted a house on the other side of the woods and recognized the Farris home.

Motion drew her attention. Luke Mason hid behind one of the bigger trees close to the house. She scooted from one tree to the next and was about to duck behind a tree near him when she stepped on a small limb. Luke spun around, his gun pointed at her. Shock registered on his face.

Another shot rang out. Luke grabbed Rachel and held her arms in a bruising grip.

"What are you doing here?" He sounded just as angry now as the day she arrived on the stagecoach and ran into him outside of town.

"I heard the shooting and thought that someone might be hurt. I came to see if I could help."

"If you're not careful, you'll be the one who's hurt." He pushed her toward the tree. "Sit down here so you'll be safe."

Rachel ignored him and peeked toward the house. "Isn't that the Farris home?"

"Yes."

"So it's Mr. Farris doing the shooting?"

"I believe so."

Rachel stepped back in front of Luke. "Have you tried talking to him?"

"Of course!"

"I mean something besides telling him to throw out his gun."

"Are you trying to tell me how to do my job, Miss Garrett?"

"No, I'd never presume to do such a thing. But since I was with Mrs. Farris when she died, maybe I could talk Mr. Farris into turning over his gun. He's probably still upset over losing his wife."

Another shot rang out. Luke again grabbed Rachel and pushed her against the tree.

"Bullets don't listen to talk, Rachel. I don't know what he's shooting at, but you could be hit by a stray bullet. Sit behind this tree and stay out of sight. Someone will be here soon enough to help me. You can talk to Mr. Farris once things are under control. Until then, sit tight."

Sheriff Taylor arrived moments later. After a quick glance at Rachel, he looked at Luke with a scowl.

Luke shrugged. "She just showed up, Morgan. Said she wanted to help anyone who might be hurt."

The sheriff turned his glare back on Rachel, then spoke to Luke. "Go over there and come up alongside the house. I'll do the same on this side. He has another way into his house on your side. See if you can get in while I distract him at the front door."

Luke nodded, then squatted in front of Rachel. "Don't move from that spot. I want to talk to you when we're done here."

He didn't wait for an answer. Rachel knew better than to move, yet she couldn't stop from peeking after him. Luke ran from tree to tree to get in position alongside the house. Sometime later she heard the sheriff hollering.

"Mr. Farris, throw out your gun." The sheriff paused. "Just open your door nice and slow and throw your gun on the ground."

Rachel heard a muffled response but couldn't understand the words. Then some scuffling echoed through the trees.

"I got him." There was more thumping before the door opened. Luke stood in the frame. "I got him, Morgan."

Rachel jumped to her feet and ran toward the house. Joe Farris was talking when she arrived, slurring his words.

"I wasn't shooting out the window or anything. I was just shooting at different things in the house."

The sheriff leaned over the table, his face only a foot from Joe's. "What were you thinking? Any one of those shots could have hurt someone passing by your house."

Sheriff Taylor stepped around the table, pulled Mr. Farris to his feet, and handcuffed him. He motioned toward Rachel with his head and spoke to Luke. "You take care of this problem. I'll see you back at the jailhouse."

Rachel waited until the sheriff and Mr. Farris were several steps away before looking up. "I'm sorry, Luke. I was wrong to show up and especially wrong to try to tell you how to do your job. I see that now."

"That's the second time, Rachel. You can't just show up at a gunfight."

"I know. I'm truly sorry. I only wanted to help, but I won't do it again."

He examined her face for several seconds then nodded. "Thank you." He motioned toward the door. "Let me walk you to your office."

Luke couldn't think of a thing to say to the nurse, and the trip to her office was made in uncomfortable silence. The doctor yanked the office door open and stepped out, his expression one of concern.

"Everything's fine, Doc. I'll let your nurse explain what happened."

He ignored the look she flashed at him, tipped his hat, and strode to face the sheriff's wrath. The trip to the jailhouse didn't take nearly long enough. Rachel had begun to haunt his thoughts, especially after she'd stared at him with those big amber eyes. Try as he might, he couldn't wipe her from his mind. At times she was charming, but most of the time she managed to get under his skin and rile him, and he wasn't sure why.

Luke was still rolling it all over in his mind when he walked in the door of the sheriff's office.

"Did you talk to Miss Garrett?"

"Yes, sir."

"And she understands not to put herself in danger or get in our way again?"

"She understands."

But Luke couldn't promise she'd never do either one again. Rachel couldn't seem to control that part of her character. Her kindness didn't stop at being a nurse; it went all the way to her heart. Last night she had arrived at their front door, her arms laden with their supper. She left everything on their table without saying much except to announce she'd be back the next night to retrieve the dishes.

Luke ran his hands over his face and began filling out the paperwork the sheriff always wanted after any arrest. He hoped that getting back to work would help get Rachel out of his mind.

SEVEN

Luke Mason led his horse down an alley next to the sheriff's office, then rode out of town on the next street over. He'd managed to avoid Rachel for three days by using that technique. He knew he'd have to face her again, probably sooner than later, but he'd do what he could to put that off as long as possible. Time and distance hadn't done much to make her fade from his thoughts.

Luke tried instead to focus on the mission Morgan had just handed him. Rancher Jace Kincaid's report that someone was firing shots in the mountains to the east of his ranch needed to be checked. His gut told him the shots were coming from the same men he'd almost caught the day Rachel arrived in town, that they'd just moved their still to a new location. But without knowing the reason for the gunshots, Luke didn't have any idea what he'd be riding into.

For the most part, life around Rockdale was simple and quiet. Except for chasing the elusive makers of corn whiskey, he'd spent most of his time arresting drunks, Joe Farris being the latest. But that was Joe's first offense, and who could blame the poor man after losing his wife. Even Morgan seemed to understand and sent him home with only a scolding once he'd sobered.

Luke slowed his horse and eased through the trees while listening for any sound that was out of place. He expected the two men to build

52

another still somewhere nearby. He sniffed the air for that odd sweet smell now so familiar.

The scent of cooking meat drew Luke to his left. Voices floated toward him. He dismounted, tied his horse to a branch, and crept through the trees. He knew of a small clearing with an even smaller cabin that had been abandoned, with good reason. Near the opening to the clearing, he stopped behind a tree for a look. Two women wandered in and out of the cabin, one hauling out trash while the other swept. They looked dirty but innocent enough.

"Hello in the cabin."

The woman with the stick broom dropped it and reached inside the door. She pulled out a shotgun and pointed it his way. The other woman stayed inside.

"Hold up, ladies. I'm Deputy Luke Mason."

"Show yourself."

The woman looked like she knew how to use that gun. He yanked his badge from his shirt and stuck it on the outside of his coat.

"All right. I'm coming out. Don't shoot."

The woman with the gun squinted at him when he emerged, his hands held chest high.

"Come closer."

He made it halfway to the fire and recognized a rabbit on the spit.

"That be far enough."

She stared at the badge several seconds, then lowered the gun. The other woman appeared and hid behind the first, who continued to hold the shotgun in a way that she could use it in a hurry if needed.

"Why you here? We ain't done nothing."

Luke lowered his arms and took a few more steps. Juice dripped from the meat and sizzled in the fire. Rabbit wasn't his favorite, but the ladies had it smelling rather tempting. He tipped his hat.

"Ladies. I was told of some shooting up this way. You know anything about that?"

"Only thing we shoot is food."

He nodded. "Good. But have you heard any other shooting around here?"

The second woman stepped out from behind the first and pointed. "Up yon way. They's been lots of shooting and noise up there."

"Have you seen anyone?"

"Not a soul. Just got here our own selves."

Luke tucked his thumbs in his gun belt. "You figure on settling in?"

The first woman took a step forward. "That's the plan. Ain't no one living here no ways."

"No, ma'am. It's been abandoned for some time now."

"I ain't no ma'am." She jerked her thumb toward the other woman. "This here's my sister Sue. I'm Sylvia. We be the Manning sisters. Leastways that's what we're called most times."

"Nice to meet you ladies. You need anything or see something that doesn't seem right, you'll find me in town. Just ask for Deputy Mason." He tipped his hat again. "Good day, ladies."

He retraced his steps to retrieve his horse, smiling and shaking his head. No telling where they'd come from or how long they'd traveled, but a good bit of trail dust clung to their faces, hiding their true age. If he were to guess, they were in their forties or fifties.

Before he could swing onto the saddle, one of the ladies hollered followed by something like a screech. Luke raced back to the clearing. A man stood over one of the women, their shotgun in his hands. Luke never slowed his steps and tackled the man before he could swing the barrel around and fire a shot. He ducked the fist coming at him and threw a punch of his own. The man moaned and quit struggling.

Luke stood and pulled the man to his feet. He reached for the handcuffs, then swung around when he heard a shriek. One of the women had the stick broom in her hands and whacked the man upside his head. The man howled and ran for the trees. Luke had just started after him when the shotgun blasted. Pellets stung Luke's left arm, but the majority of them spun the man around and landed him on the ground.

Luke sat on him, then turned to the women. "Put that gun down."

"Why? I ain't letting him get away. Not after the way he hit my sister."

"He won't get away. And I don't want you shooting me again."

The woman lowered the barrel. Luke pulled the man's hands behind him, making him howl again, and snapped the cuffs on him. He pulled him from the ground once more and led him to the cabin before shoving him down and squatting to face him.

"Who are you?"

The man just smiled.

"You got a horse out there?"

The smile remained and he added raised brows.

"If you have a horse, you'd best say so or you'll be walking into town."

The man's smile disappeared. He motioned behind the cabin with his head.

Luke stood and examined Sylvia's swollen lip. "You all right?" When she nodded, he peered into her eyes and saw she spoke the truth. He turned to Sue. "If he moves, shoot him again. I'm going for his horse."

Half an hour later Luke and the man rode into town. The offender had yet to say a word. Luke hoped Morgan would know who he was or at least get him to talk. He spotted Chad Baxter unloading a wagon and reined to a stop.

"Do me a favor, Chad?"

"Sure. Need help bringing that man in?"

Luke bit back a smile. Chad wanted to do anything other than work for his father. "Not this time. Would you go tell the doctor I need him at the jail? This man needs some patching up."

A grin on his face, Chad leapt from the boardwalk. "You got it."

Luke nudged his horse, ready to get this man behind bars. Then he could start picking the pellets from his arm.

Rachel turned when the door opened and cringed at the sight of Chad. He found every and any reason to cross her path if for nothing more important than to say hello.

"Swab."

The doctor's command gave her an excuse not to greet the young man. Any word from her seemed to encourage him.

"Uh, Doc?"

Jim Barnes blew out a sigh. "What do you need, Chad?"

"It's not me." Chad strolled into the room and crossed his arms. "The deputy sent me. Said he needs your help with that man he arrested. I saw blood."

The doctor took a deep breath. "I can't go. I've got to finish stitching up this gash." He looked up at Rachel. "Grab your bag and head over there. I'll catch up when I can."

"Yes, sir."

Chad stepped out of the way. "I'll walk you over there. Wouldn't want anything to happen to you."

"I'll be fine."

"I know, because I intend to make sure of that."

She let him trail along. Once they reached the sheriff's office, she stopped him at the door.

"Thank you, Chad. Tell your parents hello for me."

She slipped inside and quickly shut the door. She turned and discovered another cause for tension sitting at the sheriff's desk with his shirt off. Luke Mason scrambled for his shirt. She averted her eyes.

"I thought the doctor would be coming."

"He was too busy and sent me instead." Rachel peeked over her shoulder and found Luke covered. "Where's the patient?"

Luke held up his hand. "Let me cuff the man before you go back there. Just wait here and I'll let you know when we're ready."

When he turned, she noticed the blood spots on his shirt sleeve. "Wait, Luke. What's wrong with your arm?"

"It's nothing."

She patted the chair next to her. "Let me decide that."

"I didn't ask for the doctor to come see me but my prisoner."

"Everyone makes mistakes."

He tilted his head and narrowed his eyes for several moments. "I'll wait for the doctor."

She returned his stare. "Are you trying to get me fired?"

"What? No. Why would you think that?"

"Because if you won't let me do my job, that's what will happen." She tapped the chair again. "Let me at least look at it."

He blew out a sigh, unfastened the buttons, and slid his left arm from the sleeve. He dropped onto the chair. Rachel pulled the lamp to the edge of the desk for a better look. Three small holes.

"What happened?"

"I was shot."

"What'd your prisoner shoot you with?"

"Ah, well, it wasn't the prisoner. How's it look?"

She frowned. "Who shot you?"

"Is knowing that going to fix my arm?"

"No, but these don't look like any gunshot I've ever seen before." She pulled the forceps from her bag and cleaned it, then Luke's skin. "Hold still. I'm going to try to retrieve one. Would you like something to deaden the pain?"

"No. Just do it."

She took a deep breath and went to work. In seconds, she removed the first object.

Luke let his breath out. "Ouch. Hurry up and finish."

Rachel placed each oddly shaped ball on the small piece of cloth she'd laid on the desk. When finished, she cleaned the wounds, making Luke gasp again.

"I thought nurses were supposed to be gentle and sensitive."

"I thought deputies were supposed to be tough."

Luke barked out a laugh. "All right. I deserved that."

Once the wounds were bandaged, Rachel rinsed the objects she'd removed from his arm and held them close to the lantern. "They look like…small rocks?" She held them out to Luke. "Who did you say shot you?"

Luke scrutinized the small pieces. "We'd better get to the prisoner. He has more in him than I did."

Rachel stood to follow him to the back. He stopped her again. "Let me get him cuffed. Morgan will have my hide if that man hurts you in any way."

"Is the shooter a secret?"

"What?"

"Who shot you?"

He huffed and looked away. "A woman, all right? A woman shot me. Now wait here."

"I'd love to hear the story."

He peeked back around the corner. "And give another woman ammunition to use against me? Not on your life."

Rachel bit her lip to keep from reacting, then waited with as much patience as she could muster.

"Come on back."

What she saw almost made her forget to control her tongue and opinion. The prisoner had been handcuffed from behind, shirtless, but only after sticking his arms through the bars. He looked very uncomfortable, but Rachel bit her lip to keep from saying anything.

Luke waved her into the cell, and she sat next to the prisoner. She tried not to wrinkle her nose at the strong smell of alcohol and sweat. She started cleaning the head wound first. The prisoner groaned before letting out a string of swear words.

Luke moved his face close to the prisoner's. "Watch your mouth or she'll be bandaging another bump on your head."

The prisoner didn't say another word, but Rachel couldn't finish the job soon enough after he began to leer. Relief filled her when Dr. Barnes entered.

"I got this, Rachel. Why don't you head back to the office in case anyone else shows?"

She was about to leave the jailhouse when she realized Luke trailed behind her. She stopped and turned to see what he needed.

"You didn't ask me how or why he was injured."

"It wasn't any of my business."

Luke's eyebrows rose. "That never stopped you before."

Rachel felt a spark of anger but tamped it down and smiled instead. She deserved that where Luke was concerned. "I came to realize you had a bad opinion of me, and I decided to show you that I'm not usually like that."

Rachel wished him a good day and left him with his mouth hanging open. Her smile melted the moment she recognized the man on the boardwalk near the doctor's office.

❈ EIGHT ❈

Rachel stared from the middle of the street until a horse and rider passed by too close for comfort. With a deep breath, she finished crossing the street knowing she couldn't avoid the man any longer. Dread filled her as she stepped onto the boardwalk. How did he find her and how much trouble did he plan to cause this time?

"Hello, Mr. Dunlavey. How'd you know where to find me?"

"Why? Were you trying to hide?"

That was too close to the truth. She motioned around her. "This was much too good an opportunity to pass up."

"Because no one around here knows about your past?"

"As I said before, Mr. Dunlavey, I'm sorry for how things turned out. I wish things could have been different." She could feel tears forming. She had to leave. "Have a good day."

She ducked inside the doctor's office gasping for air and fighting the pain in her chest as the tears started to fall. She peeked out the window. Mr. Dunlavey stared inside for several moments before he turned and strode down the street.

Rachel dropped onto the nearest chair and sobbed. *When, Lord? How long will I have to pay for my mistakes?*

Rachel helped the little girl down from the examining table and held out the jar of peppermint sticks. Eve peered up at her mother for permission and received a nod. Dr. Barnes wiped his hands on a towel looking as tired as she felt. With no one else in the waiting area, they might get to go home early.

Jim tousled the top of Eve's head, then looked at her mother. "Bring her in again next week so I can see if her ear is healing."

The door slammed open. A man Rachel had seen only in church stood in the frame, his chest heaving. Jim strode toward him.

"What's wrong, Jace. Bobbie in labor?"

Jace Kincaid shook his head. "It's Lyle Phipps. He's been gored by a bull."

Jim raced into his office and returned with his bag. "I'll need you on this, Rachel."

Jace launched from the boardwalk onto his horse and raced out of town leaving behind a cloud of dust. Jim helped Rachel into his buggy and they followed as fast as possible.

They arrived to see Mrs. Phipps leaning over her husband. Their four children gathered around them like a fragile wall. Mrs. Phipps held her apron on her husband's abdomen in an attempt to staunch the blood flow. With her other hand, she covered another wound on Lyle's ribs.

Rachel gently took the woman by the shoulders and leaned close to her ear. "I'm sorry, Mrs. Phipps, but we need you to move so the doctor has room to work." She motioned to Jace. "Would you take her and the children to the house?"

Jace put his arm around the woman and led her away. Rachel knelt across from Jim. She tried not to react to the gaping holes in Lyle's ribs and stomach. They worked together trying to repair the wounds and stitch the man together, but he'd already lost so much blood. The internal damage was massive.

Jim paused in his work. She glanced at him and read the hopelessness on his face. He took a deep breath and leaned in to continue, but moments later they heard Lyle take his last breath having never opened his eyes.

Jim looked at Rachel, and his shoulders slumped. "I'll go talk to Norma."

Jim's steps were slow and heavy. Rachel stood to follow but stopped when she spotted Luke Mason. He met her gaze for several moments, then he turned and removed the bedroll from the back of his saddle. He moved to Lyle's side and covered the body.

He continued staring at the blanket. "How's Norma?"

"I'm not sure. I was about to go in and check."

He nodded. "Let me know if I'm needed."

Rachel could hear the pain in his voice. She squeezed his arm, then headed inside. She wasn't prepared for the looks in the children's eyes. The tears flowing down their faces caused her own to start.

Jim sat near the table with the wife, his knees almost touching hers as he held her hands. Quiet sobs shook her shoulders. She waved her children over and pulled them close. Jim patted Norma's shoulder then strode outside.

Rachel approached and wrapped her arms around the woman. Her body quaked, though not a sound escaped her lips. With the door standing open, Rachel saw the doctor, Luke, and Jace place Lyle's body into a wagon. The children wailed. Rachel scooted them from the door, glancing back to see Jace drive the wagon away while Jim had a short conversation with Luke.

Moments later, Jim returned inside and motioned her over. "I've asked Luke to give you a ride home in my buggy. I'll use his horse to get home when I feel Norma's ready to be alone. I hope she'll allow me to give her some medicine to help her sleep."

"What about the children? Maybe I should stay here with her."

Two buggies rolled into the yard. A couple women hurried inside, one to Norma's side, the other pulling the children into her arms.

"Looks like she has all the help she needs right now. Go on back. Tell Beth I'll be home as soon as I can."

Rachel found Luke leaning on the top rail of the corral staring at a bull. She moved next to him. "That the one?"

"That's what Jace said." He motioned to the buggy. "You ready?"

She accepted his help onto the seat. "How did it happen?" The look he gave her reminded her he didn't like her asking those questions. "Sorry."

He let out a long breath. "Jace was here looking to buy the bull. Lyle climbed inside to retrieve his hat he'd dropped. The bull attacked. Jace managed to drag Lyle out, but it was too late."

Luke looked so tense she didn't think it would take much to make him snap. The poor family. What would they do now? Accidents like this always confused her. Why did people have to go through such sorrow and hardships?

For my thoughts are not your thoughts, neither are your ways my ways, saith the LORD.

The verse Rachel's mother often quoted ran through her mind. God, in His infinite wisdom, knew what was best for His people and His ultimate plans. Human minds could not even fathom the depths of God's thoughts, methods, and purpose. She bowed her head and said a brief prayer for the family.

Luke looked at her. "You're praying? Why? What kind of God would take a man from his family? Can you answer me that? How could a God who claims to love us do such a thing?"

"God *is* a loving God, Luke." Rachel paused when Luke snorted in disbelief. "I can't claim to understand all of God decisions, but I know that He does love us. Days like today sometimes cause me to question Him, but God is so much wiser than we could ever hope to be. We just have to keep trusting Him."

"Yeah, well you go right ahead, Rachel. But I have no intention of trusting someone who will allow so much pain to happen in the world."

The remainder of the trip was intense silence. Luke stopped in front of Beth's house so Rachel could relay Jim's message. Beth and Sadie sat on the porch.

"Would you like me to take you home, Mother?" Luke said.

She sat quietly, looking at him for several moments. "No thanks, Luke. I'll sit with Beth and Rachel a bit longer."

He nodded, then turned the horse toward the stable behind the house. Rachel climbed the few steps to join them and dropped onto a vacant chair.

"You look done in." Sadie leaned to pat her arm. "Why don't you go on home and get some rest?"

"I will. I think I just need a moment to relax." She put her hand over Sadie's. "But maybe you should go with Luke. He's rather upset."

Sadie sat back. "I figured as much. There's no talking to him when he's like that. I'll have more of a chance to get through to him after he's had time to calm down."

Rachel ran her conversation with Luke through her mind again. "At least he believes in God, right? I mean, the way he's so angry with God, he seems to believe in Him."

"Oh yes, he believes there's a God," Sadie said. "I was with Luke when he gave his life to the Lord at the age of twelve. But he was so hurt and angry when he lost his father, he turned his back on God. He said he couldn't trust Him any longer. Just mentioning God makes him grow hard and angry. I thought time would help him get over the loss, but he's just as angry today as when he lost his father."

Tears had come to Sadie's eyes as she spoke. The three huddled together and spent time praying for Luke and the Phipps family.

Luke stood in the shadows waiting for Doc to return and watching the three women with their heads bowed. A feeling of longing washed through him, but he shoved it away. They could trust a God who offered nothing but pain, but he'd had his fill. He turned away and walked home. He could retrieve his horse in the morning.

NINE

S now started falling as the funeral for Lyle Phipps ended. Rachel stood at the back of the crowd feeling like an intruder. Most of the town turned out for the ceremony, but she knew only a handful of them.

Norma thanked everyone for their prayers and support, then announced she and the children would be leaving on the Sunday morning stage to live with her parents until she could decide what to do, but they wouldn't be back. Banker Pete Wallace would oversee the sale of the land.

Rachel hurried home so she could warm her feet, but her mind remained with Norma and the children. Sometimes time and distance had a way of easing troubles and pain. Other times, they followed like unwanted shadows. Maybe the Phipps family would be more fortunate than she'd been.

The snow still fell the next morning as Rachel readied for church. She peeked out the window and shivered at the foot of snow on the ground, even as she admired winter's tenacity as well as its beauty.

She hadn't taken many steps toward the church when Jim Barnes, his family, and Sadie Mason pulled next to her.

"Hop in. It's bound to be warmer than trudging through the snow."

Dr. Barnes helped Rachel into the back of the wagon. She scooted under the blanket and squeezed as close to Sadie as she could.

"You'll join us for dinner after the service, won't you Rachel?" Beth said.

"I'm afraid I can't. I've already accepted an invitation to join the Baxter family."

As soon as they arrived at the church, the Baxter children claimed her attention and insisted she sit with them. Somehow, Chad managed to occupy the place next to her on the pew. Rachel took a deep breath. This had the makings of a long day.

The snow had stopped falling by the time the service was over. Rachel rode home with the Baxters in the back of their sleigh, a treat since she'd never ridden in one before. She snuggled with Robin and William beneath a blanket. When they arrived at the house, she discovered they lived only one street over from the Barneses, putting them on the outskirts of town. Behind their large house was a good-sized barn to house their livestock.

"Your kitchen is beautiful, Cora," Rachel said as she entered the large kitchen painted a pale yellow with lavender flowers and green vines.

"We have Robin to thank for that. She's the artist in the family. After dinner, you should have her show you her bedroom. It's beautiful too."

The ladies turned to the task of getting dinner finished. William perched himself on a chair and entertained them with chatter about his and his friends' latest exploits. Myron and Steven were busy setting the table in the dining room and took turns pestering young William. Richard and Chad joined them in the kitchen after getting the horse and sleigh put up in the barn.

Soon the meal was ready and on the table. After the blessing, Rachel had to stifle a laugh as the boys wasted no time digging in. Once she tasted the food, Rachel could see why. Cora Baxter was an excellent cook.

Chad monopolized the conversation, bombarding Rachel with so many questions, she was afraid she'd walk away from the table still hungry.

"Chad, honey, let Rachel eat," Cora said.

Over the course of the meal, Rachel learned that the Baxters owned and ran the shipping office next to the stage depot. Chad helped his father every day, and the other children helped when they could after school and on Saturdays. The children were polite, not interrupting each other and apologizing if they did as they each took turns speaking or asking questions.

When the meal was finished and the dishes cleaned and put away, William tugged on Rachel's arm. "Come see our puppies, Miss Garrett."

Rachel pulled on her coat and followed all the children to the barn. The temperature inside was surprisingly warm. William handed Rachel a wiggly puppy. The fuzzy little critter shoved its icy nose against her cheek and started licking. Rachel laughed, pulled it away, and tickled its belly and ears. They stayed inside, chatting a little longer before Rachel grew restless.

"I think it's time I head home. Thank you for sharing your puppies." She led the way outside. "I'm going to tell your parents good-bye."

She didn't take three steps before something hit her in the back. She turned in time to see William throw a snowball, this time hitting Rachel in the arm. His wide grin almost made her laugh.

Rachel shrieked with feigned outrage. "Now you've gone and done it."

She bent down and threw some snow back at William. In no time, an all-out snowball war began. Robin stayed off to the side refusing to join the battle until Rachel threw a well-aimed snowball and hit her just below her neck. The shock on Robin's face made everyone laugh.

"All right, you asked for it," Robin said as she scooped up a fistful of snow.

Chad, Robin, and William teamed up against Rachel, Myron, and Steven. After several minutes of warfare, it was difficult to determine who was winning the fight. Finally complaining of being cold, the laughing group called for a truce and made their way inside the kitchen. Cora met each of them with a cup of warm cider. Rachel ended up staying most of the afternoon, and Robin showed Rachel her room as well as several paintings she had done.

"They're beautiful, Robin. You're a talented artist."

Robin dipped her head. "Thank you."

They returned to the kitchen, and Rachel gave Cora a hug. "I've had a wonderful day, but I think it's time I head home. Thank you for the invitation."

"You're welcome any time." She turned to Chad. "Why don't you give her a ride home?"

"Oh, no. That's not necessary. I don't live that far from here."

But Chad was already putting on his coat as he raced out the door. He returned with a cutter hitched to one of their horses. He helped her onto the seat, dropped next to her, and flicked the reins. They hadn't gotten far when he leaned close and bumped her with his shoulder.

"How about you allow me the pleasure of taking you out to the restaurant tomorrow night? Just you and me."

Rachel had dreaded this moment. "I don't think so, Chad."

"Another night then. How about Friday?"

She clasped her hands together and asked God for the right words. "I'm sorry, Chad, but I'm not interested in any relationships right now. I just want to focus on my job and get to know the people in and around town."

He didn't look at her but nodded. "All right, but don't be upset if I ask from time to time. Eventually you'll say yes."

Nothing more was said until he stopped in front of her house and helped her from the cutter. "Hope you have a good week, Rachel."

"Thank you, Chad."

She hurried inside, praying it would be a great many months before Chad asked to see her alone again. She liked the Baxter family and didn't want anything to happen to damage the new friendship.

Luke Mason slowed the buggy at the sight of Chad and Rachel sitting side by side in the Baxter's cutter. He couldn't put his finger on just what was wrong with that picture. All he knew was that he didn't like seeing them together. He flicked the reins wishing he was on his way home instead of on his way to pick up Cassie Chatham. Maybe before he arrived he could come up with a good reason not to go out tonight. She wouldn't accept that he was tired. He'd tried that once before and endured an hour of sulking before he finally coaxed a smile.

Cassie must have been watching for him out the window. She had the door open before he had come to a complete stop. The sight of a blanket in her arms ruined the excuse of it being too cold to ride in an open buggy. She all but skipped down the steps.

"Hi, Luke. I've been looking forward to this all day. I've been so bored."

Luke offered his hand to help her inside the buggy, then helped her cover her legs with the blanket. "Ready?"

"Haven't you been listening? I've been waiting for this moment. Longing for it." She wrapped her hands around his arm and leaned close. "I always enjoy spending time with you, Luke. Don't you know that?"

All the way to the restaurant Cassie chattered about all the sitting around she'd done throughout the day. Luke wanted to tell her to get a job or volunteer to help at the church, anything but sit at the house, but he didn't want to endure more pouting or a temper tantrum. The question he should be asking was why he continued seeing her.

Inside the restaurant, he helped her sit and scoot closer to the table. He nodded to a few of the townsfolk before he took a seat. The pleasant smell of pot roast and yeasty bread should have had his mouth watering. *Oh to be home reading a good book.*

The waitress brought them glasses of water and took their order. Luke took a drink and leaned back. He had to admit Cassie looked very beautiful tonight. Her long blond curls framed her creamy face and draped her shoulders in a way that reminded him of the posters he'd seen of performers back in Dallas. Maybe that's why he continued seeing her each week. After all the evil he saw, beauty was a welcome change.

Rachel was pretty too, but in a different way. Her beauty went all the way to her heart, obvious by the way she cared about people. All people, evidently. What did she possibly see in an immature young man like Chad? And what was he doing comparing Cassie and Rachel?

"Hello!" Cassie rocked side to side, then leaned across the table. "What's wrong with you, Luke? You haven't heard a word I've said. Aren't you glad to see me? Or did you have a bad day? You know you can talk to me about it. I'm a good listener. Everyone says so. Especially Grandmother. She's always telling me I'm a great listener, and you know how much she likes to talk." She sat back in her chair. "So tell me about your day."

Luke stared. How could a woman talk so much and yet say nothing? She wore him out. His ears wouldn't stop ringing until morning. "My day was fine. The usual."

"Hmm. So you were bored too. You poor thing. You should stop in for a while every day. We could be a bright spot for each other. And I know Grandmother would love to see you. She goes on and on about you whenever you've spent time with her." She took a sip of her water. "And if you came by, I could show you the new dress I'm working on for her birthday. I hope she likes it."

The food came just in time. Luke tucked into the roast, mashed potatoes, and bread rolls while Cassie pushed hers around on the plate as she gave him the details of the dress material as well as the small party for her grandmother's birthday. This wasn't the first time Luke wondered if Cassie ate before he picked her up. Whenever he'd eaten with Rachel, she ate as though she enjoyed every bite, as if the food was the best she'd ever had. Rachel always voiced her approval and appreciation.

He stopped chewing. Why did Rachel keep popping into his thoughts?

"Bite your tongue, darling? Or does the food not appeal to you?"

"No, the food is great." He finished the rest of the meal quickly.

The waitress returned. "Would either of you like some dessert? A piece of pie or cake maybe?"

"No, just the bill please."

Cassie's mouth dropped open. "I wanted some chocolate cake."

"Why? You didn't take a bite of your meal."

"My, but aren't you a grouch. I think it's you who needs something to sweeten you up." She smiled. "Maybe I can take care of that."

"No need. I'm fine."

"No you're not, but you will be."

Luke paid the bill, led Cassie from the restaurant, and helped her back into the buggy. He turned the horse toward her house.

"Don't take me home yet, Luke. I want to spend some time alone first."

"I don't think that's a good idea."

"Why not?" She put her hand on his leg. "Just a little while?"

He lifted her hand from his leg and placed it on her lap. "I'm taking you home."

Cassie huffed and leaned away from him. "What's wrong with you? You've never been so distant before."

He didn't answer. He couldn't. He didn't have an answer to give her. They passed under one of the oil lamps along the street, revealing Cassie's wrath. He remained quiet until they arrived at her home, then helped her out of the buggy and climbed the steps with her. At the door, she reached and took his hand.

"I'll see you again next week?"

He looked in her eyes. "I don't think so."

"Why not? You used to enjoy our time together, even laughed a lot. What happened?"

"I don't know. I just…" He shook his head. "I don't want to be in a relationship right now."

"We can just be friends. Just spend some time together once in a while. It doesn't have to be anything more until you're ready. I promise I won't push or keep asking if you're ready. We'll just enjoy each other's company."

"Look, Rachel—"

Luke's heart stopped at his mistake at the same time Cassie's mouth dropped open.

"Cassie. I'm sorry. I didn't—"

Her hand met his cheek with a loud crack. "How dare you. You've been seeing another woman at the same time?"

"No!"

"You…you…" She swung at him again. He sidestepped the second hit. She shook her finger at him. "I'll make sure you regret this."

"Cassie, I didn't do it."

But she waved him away. She opened the door and stepped inside, took one last look at him, and slammed the door in his face.

❋ TEN ❋

Rachel trailed Dr. Jim Barnes up the porch stairs, her interest and curiosity growing with each step. Who were the Chathams and how were they able to afford such a magnificent house? Jim wanted her to take over his weekly visits to check on the matriarch of the family, but he had yet to fill her in on any information about them.

The door opened before Jim had a chance to knock. No doubt the large front window allowed the residents a great view of all potential visitors. The thought gave Rachel an uneasy feeling. Yet the middle-aged woman who opened the door wore a wide, welcoming grin.

"Hello, Doctor. We've been expecting you."

Jim moved inside. "Edna. How's your mother today?"

"The usual. Her mind is razor sharp, but her body continues to betray her."

Jim nodded. "I'll take a look in a minute, but first I want you to meet my new nurse, Rachel Garrett. She'll be making weekly checks on your mother and let me know if I need to make a visit of my own."

"Oh, but Mother always looks forward to your visits."

"And I'll still be by every month unless Miss Garrett thinks I need to check on her sooner."

Edna Chatham examined Rachel's face then smiled. "Miss Garrett, it's a pleasure to meet you."

"Please call me Rachel," she said as she accepted Mrs. Chatham's hand.

"Very good. My mother is in the salon." She led them through the house and into a room at the end of a short hall. "Doctor Barnes is here to see you, Mother."

"Wonderful. I'm ready for a visit from a handsome man." The elderly lady looked up from her book and the smile dissolved. "Oh dear. Now, Jim, don't tell me you've replaced me with a much younger and prettier woman."

Jim strode across the room and leaned to kiss the woman's cheek. "You know there's not a more beautiful woman in Rockdale than you, Mrs. Munroe."

Mrs. Munroe's face beamed. "I won't tell your wife you said that as long as you keep saying it and start calling me Lucille."

Jim laughed. "Deal." He waved Rachel over. "I'd like you to meet my new nurse, Rachel Garrett. She'll be making my weekly visits to check on you."

"Oh good. Fresh ears for my old stories."

"And I'm looking forward to hearing them."

Mrs. Munroe's eyes sparkled. "I think we'll get along just fine. Let's get on with this examination, Jim, so I can learn more about this pretty girl."

"Yes, ma'am."

Rachel's heart broke for the poor woman and her gnarled joints. *Her days must be filled with pain.* Jim shed his coat and began a thorough check, having Rachel do the same before he sat back in a nearby chair when he finished his assessment.

"Having trouble breathing, Lucille?"

"Not all the time."

"How about the pain?"

"About the same."

Jim rubbed his chin. "Are you holding anything back from me?"

"Now, Jim, you know me better than that."

"I do, that's why I'm asking."

Mrs. Munroe laughed then coughed. "Nothing has changed since the last time you were here."

"Except that cough."

"It rarely happens."

Jim leaned his elbows on his knees. "If it gets any worse, send someone to let me know." He took her hand in his. "I want your word."

"You have it. I'll send the message through your new nurse. Send her often."

"So you can tell your stories." Jim stood. "You're in for a treat, Rachel. Lucille tells great tales." He dug some medicine from his bag. "Here's your pain medicine for this week."

"Grammy, have you seen my—" A pretty blond girl stopped in the doorway. "I'm sorry. I didn't know you had company."

Jim pulled on his coat. "We were just leaving, Cassie. Good to see you again."

"You too. Is this the new nurse I heard about?" Cassie stepped forward with her hand out. "I'm Cassie Chatham."

"Rachel Garrett."

Cassie dropped Rachel's hand as though she'd been burned. "Right. Rachel." She peeked around Rachel. "I'll be back later, Grammy."

Rachel stood wondering what had just happened. Mrs. Chatham rose from the corner chair she'd occupied since her mother's examination had begun.

"I apologize for my granddaughter's manners. I'm afraid I didn't have the heart to discipline her. I thought she'd been through enough after seeing her father die." She wrung her hands. "Her mother ran off and left her for me to raise."

Rachel waved away her comment. "That's all right."

"No, it's not. I'll speak to her."

Rachel touched Mrs. Munroe's shoulder. "I'll be back soon, ready to hear my first story."

"Looking forward to it, dear."

Mrs. Chatham saw them to the door. "Thank you for your visit."

Jim helped Rachel into his buggy. "That was awkward. Cassie's always been spoiled, which makes her act peculiar at times, but I've never seen her quite like that before."

"So it was me?"

"Who knows, but don't let it bother you. Make sure you pay special attention to the sound of Lucille's lungs. If it gets any worse than today, I want to know about it."

"She seems sweet. Wish I could have known her when she was younger. I would imagine she was a handful."

"She still is."

Rachel laughed and couldn't wait for her next visit. Before they could drive away, Jace Kincaid galloped up to them. Though his eyes looked wild, there was a slight curve to his lips.

"It's time, Doc."

"Hang on, Rachel. We've got a baby to deliver."

She had to clamp her bag between her feet so she could hang onto the side bar. Jim drove as though his life were at stake as he tried to keep up with Jace. They rolled down an embankment, across a creek, and up the other side before stopping in front of a large ranch house.

Jace had left the front door open, but he was nowhere to be seen. Jim helped her from the buggy, then hurried inside. He looked up the stairs.

"You up there, Jace?"

Footsteps thumped, then Jace's face appeared at the top of the stairs. "Hurry!"

Rachel hiked up her skirt and trailed Jim up the steps. They entered a large room and rushed to Bobbie's side. Jim began to check her pulse.

Bobbie pulled her arm away. "It's still beating, Doc. Just get this baby out."

Jim moved to the foot of the bed. Minutes later, Bobbie gave a loud groan, and Jim held a newborn in his hands. He looked up at Bobbie, then at Jace.

"Do you have a boy's name picked out?"

Tears ran down Bobbie's face though she wore a wide grin. "His name is Jacob."

Jim handed the baby to Rachel. She hurried to clean him up, and then wrapped him and handed him to his mother.

Jace sat beside his wife, and the couple couldn't take their eyes off their new son. Rachel smiled. She'd seen the same sight many times but couldn't get enough of it. Jim bumped her and motioned with his head to leave. She doubted Jace and Bobbie even noticed.

On the ride back to town, Jim filled her in on when and how he first met Bobbie, and he soon had Rachel laughing at Bobbie's spirited personality. They arrived back at the office to find Luke Mason pacing in front of the door. He jumped from the boardwalk.

"Where have you two been?" He all but dragged Rachel from the buggy, then grabbed Jim by the arm and hurried them inside. "These ladies need help."

Two older women sat inside the room at opposite ends, both with bloodied faces. Rachel rushed to one while Jim strode to the other. Rachel examined the woman's face. Her eye and lips were swollen as though someone had beaten her with their fist. She helped the woman to her feet and led her to one of the examination rooms.

"What happened?"

The woman pursed her lips.

Rachel tried again. "What's your name?"

"Sue."

"She and Sylvia are sisters." Luke stood leaning against the hallway wall where he could easily see into both examining rooms. "I was up checking on some reported shooting and found them like this. Took some doing, but I talked them into letting Doc look them over." He motioned her over and whispered, "I can't get them to tell me who did this. Maybe you can?"

"I'll try." She returned to Sue's side. "I'm going to clean up the blood on your face so I can see what needs to be done."

"Just give me a rag and some water and I'll do my own scrubbing. Ain't the first time I done it."

Luke moved inside the room. "What do you mean? This happened before? Who did it?"

"You don't need to be yapping so much in there." Sylvia's yell echoed through the office. "No one needs know our business."

"What? You don't want them to know you threw the first punch?" Sue hollered back.

Rachel raised her brows toward Luke. He returned her stare, then frowned at Sue.

"Hold on, let me get this straight. You two did this to each other? More than once?"

Sylvia stomped into the room. "I always told Mama she shoulda stopped with me."

"If she'd done that, you'd a died of loneliness years ago, and you know it."

"Least I wouldn't hafta mop up my face so much."

Jim stepped between the sisters. "Ladies, how about we hold off on the argument at least until we get you cleaned up from the last one." He motioned toward the door. "Sylvia?"

Sylvia jumped onto the table next to Sue. "Here's fine. Don't need to go separating us. I don't aim to let her get the first strike again."

Before the two women could continue their squabble, Rachel dipped the cloth into the water, wrung it out, and wiped Sue's cheek. Sue snatched the cloth from her.

"I can do it."

Rachel exchanged a quick look with Jim. He shrugged, dampened another cloth, and handed it to Sylvia.

Luke stood with his arms crossed, then shook his head. "I gotta ask. What caused you two to get so mad you'd hit each other?"

Sylvia pointed her thumb at Sue. "She called me dumb."

"Well ya were. Everyone knows ya don't plant a garden under shade trees." Sue looked at Jim, Rachel, and Luke in turn. "Ain't that right? Plants grow best in the light."

Sylvia stopped scrubbing her face. "You know full well that when it comes time to be working in that garden, it'll be much nicer in the shade than full sunlight."

"Course it would, but there won't be no garden to work if ya plant in the shade." Sue looked at Rachel. "Tell her."

Jim reached for Sylvia's cloth and touched up the areas she'd missed. "Where'd you ladies come from?"

Sylvia pushed Jim's hand away. "From our parents." She scowled and squinted one eye. "You sure you're a doctor?"

Rachel suddenly found the floor fascinating, while Luke turned away and coughed.

"No, I meant where you moved from."

"Oh. We was up in the mountains further, but the cold ain't much fun now that we're getting old."

Sue nodded. "Yep, thought some warmer weather might keep our bones from hurting so much." She handed Rachel the bloody cloth. "This seems like a nice enough place. Got the law checking on us all the time." She motioned toward Luke. "And he ain't bad to look at while he's doing it."

Luke adjusted his hat and cleared his throat. "I may have a solution to your garden problem."

"Yeah?" Sylvia leaned closer. "I'm listening. I'm up for anything that'll keep me from getting whomped again."

"Why don't you both just plant your own garden? You each pick your own spot and plant the way you want."

Sue and Sylvia eyed each other for a moment, then Sue turned her scowl on Luke. "Why, that's just dumb. We work and eat together. Why'd we want to do something so dumb as to have separate gardens?"

The two women shook their heads, then slid from the table. Sylvia shook her finger at Luke. "You can check on us all ya want, but keep your ideas to yourself." She headed for the door. "Come on, Sue. We got work to do, and it ain't getting done jawing with these folks."

Jim followed them. "What about your faces? We haven't patched up your cuts yet."

"They'll mend. Always have."

The ladies climbed onto the back of an old, worn-looking mule. They waved and heeled the mule into a slow gait.

Jim looked at Rachel then Luke and shrugged. "I have no words."

He entered his office, leaving Rachel and Luke staring after the women. Rachel finally turned to Luke.

"That was fun. Let's not do it again anytime soon." She started to follow Jim, then stopped. "Just so you know, I didn't think your idea was all that dumb, considering the circumstances."

"Well, all the same, I think I'll follow their advice and keep my ideas to myself."

She turned to watch them continue down the street. "Curious, aren't they?"

"That's one way to describe them."

"Almost makes me want to go out and see their place."

"Don't." Luke gripped her elbow and made her look at his face. "I mean it, Rachel. Don't go out there. You could get hurt. I have a feeling they shoot first, then look to see what they get to eat for dinner."

"Surely they're not that bad."

"Don't bet your life on it." He crossed his arms. "Besides, you promised you'd stay out of my business and not try to do my job, and trust me, keeping an eye on them to make sure they stay out of trouble has become a part of my job."

She didn't exactly see it the same way, but the serious look on his face told her to agree or get another lecture. "All right, I'll stay away, unless—"

"Great. Have a good evening."

He tipped the brim of his hat and strode down the boardwalk to the sheriff's office. Rachel watched for several moments. She'd been told by her mentor that this was an interesting little town. She shook her head. He had no idea.

ELEVEN

Luke Mason strolled to the sheriff's office fighting the urge to rub his overstuffed belly. Pearl may not be as good a cook as his mother, but she knew how to put on a spread for her customers. He would have tried to pack a piece of pie next to his roast beef and potatoes, but Rachel Garrett had arrived for her own dinner. Rather than run the risk of her sitting with him, Luke decided it was time to leave. He hadn't seen her for days, but she still managed to climb into his thoughts.

The office door opened just as he reached for the knob. "There you are," the sheriff said. "We gotta go. The stagecoach was robbed."

Luke jerked the reins to his horse free from the post and climbed onto the saddle. "Anyone hurt?"

"Not that was said."

They were joined by Cade Ramsey, owner of the local livery, who pulled next to them on a wagon. "I'm coming along, Morgan. I got word they need a new wheel. One of theirs broke when they were run off the road."

"All right. Let's get moving."

When they arrived, the passengers rose from the ground, and Morgan began to interview each one about what had happened. Luke spotted a man sitting in the coach doorway holding his head, and he dismounted and made his way to him. He saw blood on the man's hand, temple, and cheek.

"You the driver?"

"Yep."

"You get a look at the men who did this?"

"Nope. They had their faces covered."

Luke glanced around the hills and then at Morgan. His hands were still full with the frightened passengers. "How many were there?"

"I saw six before one jumped on the coach and knocked me out."

"Would you recognize the horses if you saw them again?"

The driver wagged his head. "Not a chance. You'll have to ask them." He motioned to his passengers.

Luke sighed. "All right. Why don't you take my horse into town and have Doc look at your head." He took a closer look at the driver's face. "Maybe I should give you a ride to town in Cade's wagon. He can ride my horse back."

"Don't need no nursemaid hovering over me. 'Specially no man. I'm fine."

"All right. I'll help Cade fix the wheel and get the coach to you there."

The driver squinted up at him. "You know how to drive a team like that?"

"If I have any trouble, I'll let Cade take over and I'll drive his wagon."

"I heard that," Cade said. "Do as he says, Barney. We'll take care of this."

Barney stood and wavered. He took a moment to get himself steady, then pulled himself onto Luke's horse and started off at a slow walk.

Half an hour later, Luke drove the coach team and passengers into town trailing Morgan with Cade following behind to keep an eye on the repaired wheel. Barney strode from the doctor's office, then all but shoved Luke from the seat. Doc Barnes followed but stayed on the boardwalk.

"I'm telling you, Barney, you need to rest a day. You took a bad thump."

"I don't have time, Doc. I'm already hours behind schedule." He turned to Morgan. "You got all your questions answered so I can get moving?"

At Morgan's nod, Barney slapped the reins against the horses' rumps and left in a cloud of dust. Morgan motioned to Luke's horse.

"Mount up. Let's see if we can find a trail."

For over an hour, they tracked several hoofprints leading away from where they'd found the stagecoach. When the trail disappeared, they searched another hour through rocks and bushes to try to locate any other signs of the outlaws.

Luke reined to a stop. "It's as though they just vanished."

"They probably brushed out the trail." Morgan lifted his hat to wipe his sleeve across his forehead. "Let's head back, and I'll send out some wires. I'm guessing other sheriffs have dealt with this bunch."

"If you don't mind, we're not all that far from where Jace thought he heard those shots. I'd like to go up that way and check the area again."

Morgan turned his horse toward town. "Sure. Let me know if you find anything."

Luke first headed toward the Manning sisters. He rode into their yard and found them working up some ground. "Looks like you ladies finally agreed where to put your garden."

"Afternoon, Deputy." Sylvia dropped her hoe and rubbed her lower back. "Sue came up with the idea of putting it right between the two spots we'd picked." She smiled at her sister. "Sounded like the best plan."

"Brilliant." He dismounted. "You ladies doing all right?"

"We'd be doing better if you finished this for us." Sue stopped chopping long enough to send him a look and stretch her back. "Either that or keep moving so Sylvia will get back to work."

Luke ducked his head. If Sue saw his smile, she might chase him down with her hoe. "How much bigger do you plan to make this thing?"

"Only another five feet wider."

Five feet! How many people do you plan to feed?

He picked up Sylvia's hoe and went to work. Sue dropped her hoe and joined her sister on the porch of their shack. An hour later, sweat dripping down his chin, Luke propped the hoe against the house.

"There you go. All set."

Sylvia handed him a glass filled with amber-colored liquid. He accepted it, hoping it wasn't water from their well.

"Thought you could use a sip of cider as a thank you. We made it ourselves."

He took a big swallow...and choked. He coughed until he could catch his breath. "How'd you make this?"

"With corn and potatoes. It's a long-time family recipe. Except we didn't have enough sugar to sweeten this batch right. You like it?"

Luke took a deep breath. "I've never had anything like it." He swirled the glass. "Have you ladies heard any more shooting or other noise up the mountain?"

Sylvia leaned against the post and stared that direction. "No shooting, but we did hear some banging and clanging up that way days ago. Lots of racket, but it didn't last long."

He followed Sylvia's gaze. "Lots of noise, huh?" He handed the glass to her. "I need to get going. Thank you for the drink." He retrieved his horse and tipped his hat. "Ladies, it's been a pleasure."

He climbed onto the saddle and headed up the mountain. He reached into his saddlebag for a piece of jerky so he could get the taste of that cider from his mouth. Who ever heard of using corn and potatoes for cider? He shuddered. If they made that stuff very often, it's no wonder they ran out of sugar. It'd take pounds to sweeten that drink.

Luke zigzagged up the mountain. The brush grew thicker the

further he climbed. He finally had to stop when the shrubs formed a wall. He dismounted and tied his horse to a branch, then walked along the brush looking for an opening.

About to give up, he spotted a hole. The limbs and twigs tore at his shirt and denims and scratched his hands as he scrambled through. The hedge came to an abrupt end, and Luke found himself in a clearing the size of a large building. Strewn around the ground were several tubes and pots, most of them bent and dented.

Luke circled the clearing and found no sign of who'd left the mess or that they'd been there recently, though the tracks he did see looked to be made by several men. The mangled equipment led him to believe the group either had a fight amongst themselves or they'd been shut down by rivals. At the very least, he'd found the place and could keep an eye on any further activity. Morgan would be happy about that.

Once Rachel finished cleaning the doctor's office, she locked the door behind her and headed down the boardwalk toward the general store. As usual, Michael Dunlavey sat across from the office. He stood when she started down the street, matching her step for step. He had yet to approach her again, but just knowing he was always nearby unnerved her. She'd briefly considered talking to the sheriff about him, but that would require telling Morgan and possibly Luke what had happened in Missouri, and she wasn't ready for that yet. And other than watching her, Mr. Dunlavey hadn't done a thing to require any involvement of the law.

Rachel tried her best to ignore him and entered the store. The bell jangled only moments after she'd entered. She looked at the door, and just as she suspected, Mr. Dunlavey had followed her inside. Basket in hand, she moved up and down the aisles. At the back of the store, she looked over the thread for the right color to repair one of her skirts. Mr. Dunlavey stopped next to her.

"Have you told the doctor about me yet?"

"I haven't seen the need."

"No need, or just afraid to?"

"The doctor is a good man. I have no need to fear telling him any-thing." She dropped the thread into her basket and moved away. He trailed her. She turned to face him. "Can I help you with something?"

"I don't want you to help me with anything ever again. And I don't want anyone in this town to go through anything like I've had to."

His words hurt more than she expected. Tears weren't far away. How many times did she have to apologize? Without saying a word, she finished finding the items on her list and took the basket to the counter.

Purchases in hand, Rachel left the store. In moments, the door jangled again, but she didn't look back. She'd soon be leaving the main street and there wouldn't be many, if any, witnesses if he decided to exact revenge.

She hesitated, then dashed down the alley to the next street. Hurried footsteps followed in her wake. She increased her pace. Her arm was grabbed. She shrieked, dropped the basket, and swung at her captor. Her hand was caught. She struggled harder to get free.

"Rachel, stop. It's Luke."

"Luke?" His badge was the first thing she saw. "Oh, thank good-ness."

"What's wrong?"

"Nothing."

"It's almost dark. Why are you out here alone so late? I thought Doc always brought you home."

"He does, but I needed some things from the store. I thought I'd be all right."

He looked down at his feet, then knelt and gathered her items back into the basket. He stood, and she reached for the basket, but he took her hand in his.

"You're trembling." He took a step closer. "Did I scare you that badly or is something else wrong?"

Tears threatened. She could only shake her head.

"Come on. I'll walk you home."

His voice was so tender, and she was so thankful for his protection she wanted to hug him. Instead, she nodded and kept pace with his long strides. He must have noticed. He slowed and swung the basket to his other hand, allowing him to walk closer.

"I'm sorry if I scared you."

"It's all right."

"No, it's not. I should have warned you of my presence. I guess too much time around the Manning sisters has made me forget my manners."

She looked up at him. "I don't understand."

"I get the feeling that if I don't sneak up on them and just appear, they'll have too much time to shoot at me if they hear me coming."

Rachel laughed.

"It's not that funny."

"Probably not, but I can just picture you stalking them. So have they been nice to each other or had they been in another fight?"

"They actually were agreeable today, but they outsmarted me."

"How's that?"

Luke told her about working up their garden for them and about the refreshing drink they offered.

"Oh, that's too funny. They seem like such sweet ladies."

"Sweet? They shot me and beat each other up, not to mention getting me to work for them. How can you call that sweet?"

She shrugged. "I get the feeling they really care for each other. They just weren't brought up knowing good manners."

"No, but they're good shots and smart enough to trick me."

"I'll bet they're a lot of fun."

"Yeah. About as fun as a rattlesnake."

"Aw."

He lifted his hand. "I'm just playing. I wouldn't keep going to check on them if I didn't care."

She cocked her head at him.

"Don't give me that look. I can be nice if need be."

Rachel stopped when she saw Chad leaning against her house.

Luke stopped too. "Hello, Chad."

"Deputy."

"Just seeing Rachel safely home."

"Well, I'd consider that right noble of you...if it wasn't your *job*." Chad pushed away from Rachel's house. "Or is it more than that?"

Luke took a step forward, but Rachel moved between them. "It's as he said, Chad. I was scared and he walked me home."

Chad's gazed switched from Luke to Rachel. He jammed his hands into his pockets. He looked as though he wanted to say something, then thought better of it. "Have a good night."

Luke stayed until Chad was out of sight. "Why's he hanging around your house?"

"I don't know. He's never done that before that I know of."

He continued staring down the street, then nodded. "Let's get you inside."

She dug the key from her satchel and unlocked the door. "Thank you for your help tonight, Luke."

"Not a problem. Just promise me you won't be out this late again."

"I'll do my best."

He narrowed his eyes. "At least not alone."

"That, I can promise."

"Good. I'll keep you to it." He handed her the basket. "Goodnight, Rachel."

"Goodnight."

She closed the door and leaned against it.

"I didn't hear you lock it."

She smiled and locked the door.

"That's better. See you tomorrow."

Her smile lingered. For the first time, there was no tension between them.

❖ TWELVE ❖

With mixed emotions, Rachel rode to church with the Barnes family. Sure, she'd get to spend time in worship, plus she had a plan for entertaining the children before the service started that had her excited. But Luke wouldn't be there, and today would be the first day she wouldn't see him since he had walked her home. True to his word, Luke saw her the next day. And the next. He made it a point to join her at the restaurant both days and bought her dinner. If only he'd start coming to church.

"You all right, Rachel?"

She looked up at Beth and smiled. "Yes."

"Nervous?"

"A little."

Beth was the only one who knew of Rachel's plans for the children. Rachel thought it best to get an opinion so she wouldn't chance stepping on the pastor's toes. They arrived minutes later and William Baxter ran up to the wagon.

"Hi, Miss Rachel."

"Hello, William." He offered his hand to help her out. She accepted, though he wasn't much help. She ruffled his hair until he ducked out of reach. "I see you were accident free this week."

"Aw, I'm not that bad."

"You're right. I apologize." She bent to his eye level. "Would you and your friends be interested in a little story before church?"

His brows rose as he nodded. "Let me get them."

As he rounded up his friends, Rachel moved to a nearby stump and stood on it. William ran back, trailed by his pals, and joined Beth, Jim, and their two children already gathered around her.

Rachel waved her arms above her head. "Do I look like a giant to all of you now that I'm standing on this stump?"

William squinted up at her. "Nope. Not a giant. Just a little taller."

They'd caught the attention of some other children, who started moving closer.

"Even standing on this stump, I'm still not as tall as Goliath was. That giant was even taller than I can reach. But a young boy named David had to face that giant and try to kill him with his sling." She leaned down and looked into their faces. "But what do you think was the first thing David did before he faced Goliath?"

"He went looking for rocks."

"He ran away and hid."

William and one of his friends grinned at their answers. His other friend elbowed both of them.

"He did not. He ran up to that giant and stomped on his toes."

A large group of children now crowded around Rachel and the stump. She clapped her hands to get the boys to listen.

"All three of you are wrong."

William scowled. "Am not. Mama told me this story. He got some rocks."

"Yes, he did get some rocks. Five of them to be exact. But I think the first thing David did was pray. He knew he couldn't overpower Goliath by himself, so he trusted that God would be with him and help him face and defeat the enemy. What David did first was look to God for help."

She stepped down from the stump and walked in front of all the children, looking each one in the eyes. "Did you know that we each face giants every day?"

Some of the younger children's eyes grew large. A few ran to their mothers. She didn't let that stop her.

"Sins are our giants, and we have to face them every day. Our giant might be a temptation to do or say something mean, or it might be the desire to disobey our parents. Our giant might even be the feeling that we want to lie or cheat or steal."

She sat on the stump and looked at each of them again. "But whatever the giant might be, all we have to do is call on God to help us slay that giant and trust that He will help us through each problem. With God on our side, we can defeat any sin no matter how big it may be. Just as God was there to help David, He is here with us to help us in any situation every day."

Rachel asked the children to bow their heads, and she ended the story with a short prayer. She looked up in surprise when she heard some applause coming from the parents. Emma Barnes's little friend Sarah approached and took her hand.

"Would you sit with me?"

Emma moved closer. "Nuh-uh. She sits with us."

"She sits with us too," William said.

"How about I take turns sitting with you?" Rachel said. "Since Sarah asked first, I'll sit with her today."

Pleasure washed through her, knowing the children were coming to love her just as she loved them. She could hardly wait for next week.

Rachel sat in the buggy staring at the horse's rump. Go make his rounds and check all the newborn babies, Jim said. Just like that. As if it were no problem at all. Didn't he know how terrified she was of horses? She'd been working for him a month now. How was it Jim didn't know that? It shouldn't matter that she never told him, right?

"She usually moves when you flick the reins." Luke sat on his horse beside the buggy with a wide smile. "Or are you lost already?"

"Oh, ha ha." She fought a smile and lost. "I...was just...thinking."

"Is that what they call hesitating now?" He heeled his horse behind the buggy, dismounted, and moved to her side. "Have you ever driven a buggy before?"

She looked at her hands and shook her head. "I've seen it done a hundred times. It doesn't look that hard."

"It's not. Let me show you." Luke stepped onto the buggy. "Go on. Move over."

She slid over and handed him the reins.

"Oh no. If I drive, you'll never learn." He leaned back on the seat. "Just flick the reins. The horse will do the rest."

She stared, expecting him to change his mind. He didn't. He didn't even look at her but kept his eyes forward. She flicked the reins and the horse started forward.

"This really is easy."

"Just as I said it would be. Now, turn right at the end of the street."

"Turn right. Sure." She looked at the reins in her hand. "And I do that by...?"

"By pulling on the right rein only."

"That makes sense." She did as he said, and the horse turned to the right. "Oh, this is so easy."

"But you wouldn't have known that if you hadn't done it yourself. All right, now take me back to my horse so we both can get to work."

Rachel leaned over and bumped him with her arm. "I'd be offended if I wasn't so thankful for your help."

"You're welcome, but you should trust yourself more. You'd have done fine."

Two more right turns and they were back to Luke's horse. With a tip of his hat, he jumped from the buggy and sent her on with a wave.

She went to the end of the street and turned left on her way to her first stop of the day. She'd seen Joseph and Belle Kline at church but had yet to spend much time with them. She looked forward to getting to know them better.

She found their little house right where Jim described. Another horse and buggy sat out front. She grabbed the doctor's bag and knocked on the door. It swung open.

"Come on in." The woman stepped back. "I've heard so much about you. I'm Grace Ramsey. Belle and little Caleb are right over there."

Grace shut the door too fast and caught Rachel's skirt. Rachel would have fallen except for the chair close enough to grab for support.

"Oh goodness, I'm sorry." Grace opened the door and pulled Rachel's dress free. "It's just been so long since I've gotten a visit with Belle, I guess I'm too excited."

"It's all right. I understand." Rachel moved to Belle's side and touched Caleb's cheek. "He's adorable. How old is he now?"

"A month."

"Goodness, he's big."

"Takes after his daddy." Belle stood and laid Caleb on the bed. "Doc said you'd be by. Go ahead, check him out."

Rachel did a quick examination and pronounced him healthy. She wrapped him back up in the blanket and handed him to Belle. "All babies should be as strong and fit as he is."

"Thank you. Do you have time for a cup of coffee? Grace and I have been looking forward to getting to know you better."

"Sure. One cup, then I need to go."

She joined Belle at the table while Grace offered to get the cups and coffee pot. Rachel poured while Grace returned for the forgotten sugar bowl.

"Oh, no."

A bee hummed about Grace's head, dipping and diving around

her as she frantically swatted at it. When it came too close, Grace swung the sugar bowl at it. The lid flew off the bowl and sugar spewed everywhere, covering the table and floor.

Belle laughed, much to Rachel's surprise. Grace pulled her apron off and flung it at the bee, and Rachel didn't see it buzzing around any longer. Grace dropped onto the chair.

"Whew. That was close."

Rachel leaned toward her. "Are you all right?"

"Course she is," Belle said. "It's everyone else around her needs to look out." She swatted playfully at Grace. "Tell her, girl."

"Tell me what?"

Grace rose and grabbed the broom. "It's nothing really. Belle has a wild imagination."

"Do not. Go on. Tell her or I will."

Grace stopped sweeping. "Some tend to think I'm accident prone, but it's not true. It's just that animals don't like me." She pointed at her apron. "Just like that bee didn't like me."

"It's more than that and you know it."

Belle told Rachel several tales about Grace's accidents since the two met. By the time she finished, Rachel had tears in her eyes and sore stomach muscles.

"After all that and Cade married you anyway? He must like challenges."

"Now don't you start too." Grace smiled. "Life's been interesting, that's for sure."

Rachel stood. "If I don't get going, my own life will get interesting when I have to start looking for a new job. It's been fun, ladies, but I'm running late. Thanks for the laughs. And Grace, I'll get the door myself."

Grace threw a rag at her as Rachel ducked out the door.

She turned the horse and headed out of town toward her second stop at Henry and Patricia Moellers' house. They weren't home, so she continued on to her third and last stop with a family she'd never seen or met, though according to Jim, they'd been at church at least once.

She had no trouble finding the home of Layton and Katie Woods. They lived close to where the man had been killed by the bull. She knocked and didn't wait long before the door opened. A thin young woman motioned her inside.

Rachel entered and quickly swung her skirt out of the way. "The doctor wanted me to check on your son. We understand from your husband your little one's been sick for a few days."

"He has but he's better. The fever is gone and the vomiting has stopped. But he's right over here if you'd still like to see him." She led the way across the room. "My name's Katie."

"I'm Rachel. It's good to meet you, Katie." She knelt next to the little boy playing on the floor near the fireplace. "And who's this young man?"

"That's Tommy."

Tommy looked at Rachel a few moments, then pushed to his feet and ran to Katie. Once safe in her arms, he turned to see Rachel again. She pulled a toy from the medical bag, and Tommy smiled as he reached with his pudgy hand.

"He certainly looks healthy." She touched his hand as he took the toy and felt no fever. "Has he been eating again?"

"If he eats much more, he'll outgrow his father in no time."

The door opened again. "I heard that." The man strode toward them and ruffled Tommy's hair before kneeling next to his wife. "I'm Layton."

"Rachel. You've got a beautiful family."

"Thank you." He patted Katie's belly. "And it's still growing."

Katie playfully slapped at Layton's hand. "Stop that."

"How've you been feeling?" Rachel asked.

"Good. I'm just hoping I don't get what this little guy had."

"Send your husband to let us know if you do. We might be able to help you get through it."

Katie put Tommy back on his blanket near the fireplace. "Can't. He's leaving in the morning to spend some time at our claim."

"Oh. Is there someone who can get word to us?"

Katie nodded. "Jace Kincaid promised to stop in every day to check on us."

"All right then. I guess I'd better get back and let the doctor know Tommy is better." Rachel shook hands with the couple. "I'm glad we finally met."

Layton walked her out, then continued on to the barn. She climbed into the buggy, finally comfortable and even enjoying the driving. She slapped the reins down on the horse and prepared for the sudden jerk as they started forward. The horse whinnied and tugged once but didn't move any farther, though it continued to prance in place. Rachel flicked the reins harder. The horse shrieked and reared before taking off at a frantic run.

Rachel pulled back on the reins, but the horse continued to race ahead. Rachel yanked the reins past her ear. The horse reared again, shook its head, and jerked forward, wrenching the reins from her hands.

Rachel grabbed the sidebar and held on for dear life as the buggy swayed first one direction then the other. They'd gone close to a mile before Layton Woods rode past her on his horse. He leaned and grabbed the reins close to the horse's head. He pulled back on the reins to his horse, slowing the horse and buggy until they all came to a stop.

Layton dismounted and ran to the buggy. "You all right, miss?"

Rachel couldn't let go of the bar. Her body trembled and she thought she might be sick. Layton climbed into the buggy and slid onto the seat next to her.

"You're all right now. Take a deep breath and try to calm yourself."

Rachel continued to cling to the bar as she shook her head. "I know I didn't do anything to upset the horse. I didn't do anything different than the last time. I don't know why he bucked and ran like that."

Layton reached across her and peeled her fingers from the side-bar. He kept hold of one hand until her trembling calmed.

"I'm going to check the horse, make sure he's not hurt or something to make him so jumpy."

Layton slid his hands down each of the horse's legs, then checked the harness. He slid his hands down the reins and suddenly stopped when he reached the horse's hind quarters. He worked on one of the reins for a moment, then returned to her side.

"One of the reins had a problem, but it's fine now. You shouldn't have any more trouble."

Rachel looked from him to the horse. "I...I don't..." She shook her head.

"How'd you like me to lead the horse back to the doctor's office for you? That way, you can just sit back here and enjoy the rest of the ride."

Rachel didn't like the idea of riding any farther with that horse, but she nodded her agreement anyway. Layton mounted his horse and, in a slow gait, led them toward town. In no time, they were back at the office. Layton helped her from the buggy and walked with her inside.

"Thank you, Layton. I don't know what would've happened if you hadn't shown up when you did. I think I might owe you my life."

He shook his head. "Not at all. Just take care of my family."

"Count on it."

Dr. Barnes excused himself from his patient and stepped from his examining room. "Everything all right?"

Layton motioned with his head for the doctor to follow him outside. Jim turned to Rachel. "Do the usual pre-exam checks on Mrs. Hines. I'll be right back."

Rachel was more than happy to let Layton tell the doctor about the problem with his horse. Checking a patient's heartbeat was much more appealing. Several minutes later, Jim returned and waved her into his office.

"Layton tells me you had quite a ride."

"That's one way to describe it."

Jim leaned against his desk. "You all right?"

"A little shaken up, but I'm fine."

"You always shake when you're fine?"

Rachel glanced at her hands, then crossed her arms. "It was scary."

"I'm sure. Why don't you have a seat?"

"I'd really prefer to stand." Then she realized she'd been pacing and stopped.

"Layton showed me a nail he found stuck in one of the reins. Do you have any idea how it might have gotten there?"

Rachel ran the afternoon through her mind. "No. The horse acted fine until I left the Woodses' home."

"Interesting. I mean, you'd think I would have noticed a nail while hitching up the buggy, but I could have missed it. But she never acted up for me when I drove here this morning."

"Why would someone do such a thing?" Rachel looked to Jim for an answer, and he shrugged.

"Go on home, Rachel. There are only a few patients left, and I can handle them."

Rachel shook her head. "I'm fine."

Jim held up his hand. "Go home. I'll even let you take the buggy."

She shook her head again, then saw him smile.

"I was teasing. I think the walk home might do you a world of good."

"All right. And thank you." She headed for the door, then turned back. "By the way, Belle's baby is fine, the Moellers weren't home, and little Tommy is much better. Did you know Katie is expecting again?"

Jim shook his head. "Thanks for the report."

"I really am—"

"Go!" the doctor demanded as he pointed to the door.

This time, Rachel obeyed without a backward glance. By the time she reached home, she wasn't sure if the walk helped or not.

THIRTEEN

Rachel tried to keep up with Emma Barnes while tugging Tanner in the small wagon built by a friend of the doctor. The wagon looked just like a miniature buckboard. If all of Matt Cromwell's creations were as great, she'd have to see if he would make her a rocking chair.

"Slow down, Emma. I'm not as young as you."

Emma squatted to finger a budding wildflower. "You're not *that* old."

"Why thank you, Emma. I feel so much better now." Rachel turned to make sure Tanner was warm enough. "Oh Tanner, you're not supposed to eat yet."

She gently tugged the sandwich from his hands, rewrapped it, and stuck it back in the basket. By the time she started down the road again, Emma was way ahead of her.

"Wait for me, Emma."

After half an hour, Rachel was even more certain Beth would appreciate her decision to take the children for the afternoon. How Beth made it through each day and still had some energy in the evening, Rachel didn't know. She resolved to make it a monthly event, allowing Jim and Beth some time to themselves.

With such a beautiful spring day, and such a small house, a walk to a nearby pond was just what they all needed. A creek ran next to the pond, keeping it supplied with fresh water so clear they could see fish. Boulders scattered around the pond, along with several trees, made for a peaceful setting. When she had found the spot a few weeks ago, it quickly became her favorite place to relax. She couldn't wait to get there.

"Can I get out?"

Tanner had pushed to his knees, his eyes on his big sister. Rachel stopped and helped him out of the wagon. He plodded toward his sister as fast as his short legs would move. Without the extra weight to pull, Rachel had no trouble keeping up.

The kids chattered as they walked along, telling Rachel all they knew about the butterflies they saw and the wildflowers that were about to bloom. Rachel exclaimed at each item they pointed out and praised them on their knowledge, making the two children beam with pride. Once they reached the pond, she let them run around the edge. Every so often, they'd stop to throw a rock or two into the water before moving on again. She tugged the wagon under a tree and joined them.

Their exploration continued until midafternoon. Feet dragging and fists rubbing his eyes, Tanner plopped down and yawned. Rachel scooped him up, called to Emma, and led them to the wagon. She laid out a thick blanket she had brought along, then produced a book. She began to read to them, and in minutes the two were asleep.

Rachel pulled another book from the basket and climbed onto a nearby boulder with the help of some rocks that looked as though they'd been placed there for that purpose. She leaned back and opened the book she'd been reading the last few days and lost herself in the story.

"You're in my spot."

The book slipped from Rachel's fingers. Luke caught it before it slid from the boulder and handed it back to her. She stared at him as though she couldn't believe he really stood there.

"How'd you find my spot?"

"I'm sorry. I'll move."

Rachel started scooting to the edge, but Luke waved her back.

"I was only teasing. Stay there. But do you mind if I join you?"

"Not at all."

She returned to her original position. Luke slid across the rock and sat beside her, then pulled off his hat and propped it on his knee as he leaned his head against the rock wall.

"It's beautiful here."

Rachel forced herself to stop staring. "Yes, it is. How did you know we were here?"

"I didn't. I have the rest of the day off, and I sometimes like to come out here to relax. It's also a good fishing spot."

"Did you bring your pole?"

"Not this time. I didn't plan on staying long."

Luke tugged the book from her. "*Pride and Prejudice*. I would've bet you were reading a medical book. I thought with your ambitious side, you were trying to become a doctor."

Rachel leaned forward so she could look Luke directly in the eyes. "Why do you like to bait me?"

"Is that what I was doing?"

Rachel nodded. "I've also noticed that when you're angry with me, you call me Miss Garrett instead of Rachel."

Luke stared at her for a moment and then smiled. "I didn't realize. I'll be sure to call you Miss Garrett *all* the time. I also didn't realize that I was in a habit of baiting you. I'll try to tone that down a bit."

"Oh, I wouldn't want you to hurt yourself, so…" Rachel bit her lip as she saw Luke grinning at her. "I'm sorry. I guess I have the same habit of baiting you."

"I'll quit if you'll quit." He held out his hand, which she took with pleasure.

"It's a deal." Rachel turned to look at the children. "I've noticed you seem to have a way with kids."

"That's because I'm still a kid at heart."

Rachel was about to make a comment and then bit her lip.

"You were about to insult me, weren't you?" He held up his hand. "Never mind. Actually, I think kids are great. And I think the best time to mold their thoughts and habits is when they're young. If I can give them a good impression of a lawman at that age, it may help them when they're grown." Luke's eyes had drifted over the water as he spoke. "It worked for my father. I thought he was great, and so did a lot of other kids."

Rachel remained silent as she watched the familiar sadness steal back into Luke's eyes. Then she saw him almost start as if suddenly remembering he wasn't alone. Luke's gaze dropped to the sleeping children.

"How did you come to have the kids today?"

"I thought Beth would enjoy a few hours to herself, so I asked if I could have them for the day. Then she and Jim could spend the afternoon together. I used to babysit for a couple back in Missouri who would try to take at least one night a month without the children. They'd come back with their eyes sparkling and a smile on their faces that nothing could wipe away." She shrugged one shoulder. "I realized my parents always enjoyed some time to themselves. Sometimes that's hard to come by once a couple has children."

Luke was staring across the pond again. "Now that you mention it, my parents were like that. After being gone for days, my father would spend the afternoon playing with me. But when evening came, they'd find someone to watch me and he'd take Mother out to eat. I hated it when he did that because I wanted to go too. He always made up for it by taking me fishing or camping, but like you said, they would come home smiling and with eyes only for each other."

Luke turned to her with a slight frown. "I haven't talked about my father to anyone in years."

"I'm glad you feel that you can."

Luke nodded. "That was thoughtful of you...to take the kids, I mean."

"Beth's been a great friend, and I wanted to do something nice for her. I plan to take them one Saturday each month. I found this place a few weeks ago and thought the kids would enjoy playing here."

"It's one of my favorite spots. I found it shortly after I moved here and have come here ever since. Here and another place I found up in the mountains. The stream coming down is always so cool. It's very secluded. I hope to build a cabin there one day."

"I'd love to see it. I can almost picture it."

Luke sat quiet for a moment. "Let me know the next time you have the kids. If I'm not working, I'll take all of you there for a picnic."

"That sounds fun."

The children stirred, then sat up looking for her.

"Up here."

Emma and Tanner grinned when they saw her, and they ran to the boulder.

"Can I go up there?" Emma said.

"Me too."

Luke looked to her with brows raised, and she gave him a nod. Luke jumped down and handed the children up to her, then rejoined them on the crowded boulder. For the next several minutes, Luke teased and tickled the children until Tanner almost fell from the rock. Luke grabbed him just in time, set him on the ground, and jumped down next to him.

"That's enough fun for one day. I should get back."

Rachel helped Emma to the ground. "I have a snack for the kids that we'll share if you'd like to join us. It's only sandwiches, cheese, and some apple slices, but you're welcome to them."

Luke stared at her for several seconds, then smiled. "I think I will. Thank you."

Rachel led the way back to the blanket and emptied the basket of food. While they ate, Luke entertained them with stories intermingled with attempts to catch bits of cheese or apple in his mouth after throwing them in the air. Before long, both Emma and Tanner were trying to do the same. Luke even managed to talk Rachel into trying to catch a small piece of cheese he threw at her. It bounced off her nose, and the children rolled with laughter. The snack disappeared in the midst of much laughter and chatter.

"Would you like me to walk you back to the house?" Luke said as Rachel cleaned up the remnants of their small meal.

"Now how can I say no to that?" Rachel said after hearing the kids cheer the idea.

Luke pestered and chased the children all the way home. Somehow, his horse trailed along without needing to be led. Rachel hadn't seen anything like it. Maybe all horses weren't so bad.

Luke waited with the three of them while Rachel unlocked her door. She let the kids run inside before turning to Luke.

"Thank you, Luke. I'm glad you happened by. I enjoyed the company."

"As did I. I'll be looking forward to next month. Good night."

Rachel went about her small kitchen, preparing a meal for herself and the children and humming a happy tune.

FOURTEEN

Rachel stared at the horse's rump, terrified of flicking the reins. Though the doctor assured her he'd checked the entire harness for nails, that small doubt in her mind made her hands shake. But she was given a job to do. With that thought, she took a deep breath and shook the traces. The horse started off in a slow and steady gait.

Rachel flicked the reins again, sending the horse into a trot. At this rate, she'd be at the Manning sisters' place in no time…if she could find it. Jim had given her directions, but they were vague at best. She wished the doctor would have gone instead when they received word from someone who'd been riding by that it sounded like the Mannings had one of their worst fights yet. But Jace had also raced in saying one of his men had been bucked off a horse and wasn't moving. Rachel would have gladly traded jobs. At least when it came to an unconscious man she'd know what to expect.

Half an hour later, Rachel neared a fork in the road. She stopped the horse and looked both directions. Which way did Jim say to go? Frustration set in. As she ran the doctor's directions through her mind again, she heard an odd sound followed quickly by another. Though she couldn't tell if it was a laugh, shriek, or shout, she had a feeling it came from the sisters.

She tugged the right rein and clucked her tongue as she'd heard the doctor do so many times. The horse obeyed and in minutes had her entering a small clearing in the midst of all the trees. Sue and Sylvia sat on the porch rocking with laughter, their arms around each other's shoulders. They stopped when they saw her.

Rachel drove the horse toward them, stopping a short distance away to keep their shrieks from spooking the horse. She set the brake and tied the reins to the sidebar. She eyed their faces. More swelling and bruises. And their hands looked the same as their faces. She'd never understand them.

"Afternoon, ladies," she said as she stepped from the buggy.

"Well, I'll be. Look who's here, Sue." Sylvia elbowed her sister. "We must be getting popular in these parts. We ain't never had so much company before."

"Of course you're popular. Who wouldn't like two sisters who love each other enough to stay together all these years?"

"Who says we done it by choice?" Sue said with a scowl.

"Uh, did you get your garden planted?" Rachel cringed as soon as she said it. Nerves had a way of making her say the wrong thing.

But Sylvia stood and jumped from the porch. "It's over here. Come see."

Rachel followed Sylvia across the clearing. Sue trailed without a word. Sylvia led Rachel up and down several rows explaining what was planted in each. Tender shoots had broken through the surface and were opening to drink in the warmth of the sun. Rachel squatted to finger one.

"Careful." Sue stood at the end frowning at her.

"Oh hush, Sue. She ain't gonna hurt it none. She's a nurse ya know. Her hands are trained to heal not hurt."

"Well, that plant don't need no healing."

Rachel stood and stepped out of the garden. "The idea of fresh vegetables makes my mouth water."

Sylvia smiled. "Mine too. Can't wait."

"Why you here?" Sue said.

Nothing like getting right to the point. "The doctor wanted me to come check on you two, see if you needed anything."

"Bandages would be good."

"I think I can manage to leave some. Would you like me to clean and bandage your wounds?"

"Nope. Sylvia's gotten good at it. We take care of each other."

"All right. Anything else I can do for either of you?"

"Nope."

"Yep."

Rachel turned to Sylvia. "You need some help with something?"

"Sure do. We got a stray dog come wandering up. He's banged up a bit. Must have a sister."

"Oh, stop." But even Sue had a smile this time.

Rachel laughed and took the two steps to Sue's side and gave her a quick hug. "Show him to me. I can't promise I can help, but I'll sure take a look."

Sylvia coaxed the trembling ball of fur from under the porch and cradled the pup in her arms. "Done been in a fight, don't ya think?"

Rachel caressed the puppy's head. "Sure looks like it. Here, sit on the step and let me get a better look."

The poor critter's ribs were showing and it had a couple cuts, one on its ear and another on its foreleg.

"More than anything, I think this poor fella needs some food, but I'll see what I can do about patching up those cuts."

"We got some vittles cooking right now." Sylvia ruffled the dog's head. "Hope he likes possum stew."

Rachel's stomach flipped upside down. "I'm sure he will." She retrieved her bag from the buggy and returned to Sylvia's side. She ran her hand over the pup's head several times. "All right, little guy, hold still."

Other than cleaning the cuts and adding some salve, there wasn't much she could do. She wrapped the leg with a strip of cloth and tied it to keep it from moving, but from what she knew of puppies, the hound would have it chewed off before she made it back to town.

"That's about all I can do. This salve is for humans, but I don't think it'll do this little scrap of flesh any harm." She scratched behind its ears. "Cute little guy, isn't he?"

Sylvia hugged the puppy close. "Maybe this is one male who'll actually stick around awhile."

Sue snorted and stomped into the house. She returned a minute later with a small bowl full of stew and set it on the porch. The pup squirmed to be released. Once Sylvia set it down, the puppy nearly dumped the bowl in its rush to devour the meal.

Sue squatted and held the bowl still. "He needs a name."

"King."

Sue peered at her sister, then tilted her head. "Doesn't sound quite right. How about Chief?"

Sylvia smiled. "I like it."

Rachel tugged at the pup's tail. "Well, Chief, looks like you're in good hands. Time for me to get back to work."

She gathered her medical items into the bag, then handed Sylvia some bandages. "Will this be enough?"

"For a while. Thank you."

"You're welcome. But I hope you won't need them. Ladies, it's been a pleasure, but it's time for me to go."

"It's been a pleasure?"

Rachel took in the look of shock on Sylvia's face and pulled her into a hug. "Of course it has. I hope we can get together again soon."

She turned to give Sue a hug, but she was still on her knees with the dog, so Rachel knelt and did the best she could. Neither woman seemed to know what to do with her kindness.

"Good-bye, ladies."

Sylvia sat on the step again. "That's the third time she called us that."

"What?"

"Ladies."

Rachel untied the reins and waved, leaving the sisters staring at her. They weren't nearly as scary as Luke had led her to believe. They were actually sweet, in an odd sort of way.

Luke dismounted and strode to the door of Rachel's house and pounded. He waited a full two seconds before pounding again.

"Rachel!"

How dare she tell him one moment she'd stay out of his business, then turn around and do exactly what he'd told her not to do.

He hammered on the door with his fist again. "Open the door, Rachel. I know you're home!"

"I am home. Just not in the house."

Rachel stepped around the corner of her house. Beth Barnes and her two kids followed close behind. Rachel rubbed dirt from her fingers.

"What's wrong?"

"I think you know what's wrong." Luke closed the distance between them and stopped inches from her. "I thought we had a deal. You were supposed to let me do my job and stay out of the way. I told you I didn't need your help. You can get hurt."

"I don't know what you're talking about, Luke. I haven't been trying to do your job. In fact, I've been trying to stay as far away from your job as I possibly can."

"Oh, really." Luke crossed his arms in front of him. "Where did you go yesterday?"

Rachel frowned as she looked away. Then her eyes widened. "Oh. I went out to the Mannings' house."

"Yeah, oh." Luke uncrossed his arms and pointed a finger under her nose. "I warned you not to go out there. Those two women can get mean. You know they've been known to fire off a few shots from their guns. My arm is proof of that. If you would've walked in on their dispute, you could've been hurt. You're supposed to wait for us to make sure it's safe."

He could see anger rising in Rachel's eyes. Her lips tightened. He braced for her response. It never came. Beth moved to Rachel's side.

"Luke, Jim asked Rachel to go out and check on the Manning women. She was just obeying his request."

Luke stared at Rachel for several moments, a tense silence existing between the three of them. He finally let out a loud and long sigh.

"I'm sorry, Rachel. I didn't realize you'd been asked to go out there."

Rachel's breathing slowed and her expression softened. She nodded her acceptance of his apology.

"Ladies."

He tipped the brim of his hat and strode to his horse and galloped back to the jailhouse still fuming, but this time at himself. He refused to believe he had any feelings for Rachel even though she had a way of clouding his judgment. A part of him wanted to go back and apologize properly, but the other part told him it wasn't a good idea. The best idea was to forget about her.

Rachel stood in the small dust storm Luke created as he galloped away. Though out of sight, she still stared where she'd last seen him.

"So much for our truce."

"What do you mean?" Beth led the way back to the garden. "You two had a truce?"

"Sort of. I thought so." She shook her head. "I don't know."

"He's only fighting his attraction for you, Rachel."

"Ha! You're way off, Beth. He's not attracted to me. He can hardly stand to be around me. All I do is make him angry."

She dug into the garden work with a vengeance, making the dirt fly from her hoeing. She stopped to pull a clump of weeds and noticed that Beth stood grinning at her.

"Don't start, Beth."

"All right. Just remember what I said—"

"I won't have to, 'cause you're wrong."

The two went back to work, but every time Rachel checked, Beth still wore her smile.

Forgetting about Rachel proved to be more than difficult. Unknown to Luke, his mother had invited Rachel over for dinner after the Sunday service. Now she sat across the table from him, both of them trying to avoid each other's gaze. Sadie sat between the two of them, passing food and looking almost as uncomfortable as Luke felt.

"You did a good job with the lesson again, Rachel," Sadie said, breaking the silence. "The kids really seemed to enjoy it."

"Thank you, Sadie. It's been fun." A bright smile came over Rachel's face. "Especially when I get such a good response from them."

"That little William is quite a character, isn't he?"

"He really got into erasing his sins, didn't he?"

Luke paused in dishing his plate. "Erasing sins?"

Sadie reached for the dish. "Rachel's been doing short devotionals for the children before the service starts. Today she used a slate and chalk to describe to the children how God erased their sins when they asked Him to forgive them. She asked for suggestions of sins each of them could commit and was given several."

She set that dish down and reached for the next. "Rachel wrote each suggestion on the slate and told them that when they asked for God's forgiveness, He would erase them from their lives just as she erased the slate. Rachel passed the slate around so each child could write a sin on it, and then erase it. When it was William's turn, he wrote down several sins, drawing chuckles from the adults watching, especially his parents."

"The piece of hair that sticks up on William's head just adds to his personality," Rachel said. "It's almost like a signal, warning everyone of what's to come."

Luke couldn't help but smile at Rachel's description. He knew William well, and her account was right on target.

The tension between them had eased, making the rest of the meal much more enjoyable. His admiration for Rachel grew as his mother filled him in on all the stories Rachel had told the children. He'd have to sneak over to the church to watch her next Sunday.

Rachel helped clean up the kitchen, then announced she was going home. Luke held the door for her and fell into step next to her.

"You don't need to walk me home, Luke. It's not far and I can't imagine anything will happen to me between here and there, especially in broad daylight."

"I don't mind."

And he didn't, but he also didn't know what to say. Actually he did, but he didn't know how to start. Finally, as they approached her door, he simply opened his mouth and began.

"Look, I just wanted to apologize once more for my actions and words yesterday. I did a poor job of it, and I wanted to make sure you knew how sorry I am."

"Apology accepted."

"Thank you."

She unlocked her door and opened it, but turned before entering.

"I told you I would try not to interfere with your job, Luke, and I meant it. If I do happen to interfere, it would be by accident."

"I know."

She peered into his eyes for a moment, then nodded. "Thanks for walking me home."

"You're welcome."

Luke stared at the closed door before returning to work with a much lighter step.

FIFTEEN

Rachel locked the door to her house and headed down the road to her favorite place. She planned to keep the day all to herself. For the last several Saturdays, she'd given her time to help others with one thing or another. But today, she was going to be selfish. As bad as that sounded, she refused to let herself feel guilty. Everyone needed a little quiet time.

With a light snack, some stationery, and her Bible packed in a basket, she intended to relax and read for a while before writing some letters she'd been putting off. When she arrived at the pond to find the Manning sisters fishing from the edge, she knew a moment's disappointment. Maybe they'd been here awhile and would be leaving soon. In the meantime, she'd make the best of the situation.

"Hello, ladies. Catching anything?"

Sylvia swung around. "Look, Sue. It's the nurse again." She waved at Rachel. "Pulled in a couple. Enough to feed us another day."

"Good. How's Chief?"

"He's a rascal. Left him tied up back home so he wouldn't scare the fish."

"All right, I'll leave you ladies to your fun."

She continued past them, shoved her basket onto the boulder, and climbed on top. She placed her small blanket on the rock, settled into a comfortable position, and pulled out her Bible.

Only a few verses into the chapter she'd chosen to read, she heard a voice. Seconds later, the voice grew louder. Rachel looked at the ground. Sylvia stood mere yards away, her brows raised.

"I'm sorry, Sylvia. What did you say?"

"I asked what you was reading."

"The Bible."

"Oh."

Sylvia climbed onto the boulder. Rachel moved over a bit, and Sylvia scooted beside her. She looked over Rachel's shoulder, then touched one of the pages. The wind caught the paper and flipped up one of the corners. Sylvia fingered the sheet.

"Kinda thin ain't it?"

"Yes, they are."

"Them letters on there are sure small."

Rachel remained silent while watching the different expressions move over Sylvia's face as she continued to examine her Bible. Sylvia closed it and ran her hand over the cover and binding, then opened it again to examine the inside. She finally handed the Bible back to Rachel and sat back, but her eyes remained on the pages.

"Would you read some to me?"

"Sure. I'd be glad to."

Rachel scrambled to come up with the best place to start reading, something that would get and keep them interested. Since they'd been fishing, she landed on Jonah and turned to that book of the Bible.

"'Now the word of the Lord came unto Jonah the son of Amittai, saying, Arise, go to Nineveh, that great city, and cry against it; for their wickedness is come up before me. But Jonah rose up to flee unto Tarshish from the presence of the Lord, and went down to Joppa; and he found a ship going to Tarshish; so he paid the fare thereof and went down into it, to go with them unto Tarshish from the presence of the Lord.'"

She paused as Sue joined them, pulling in her legs so Sue could get around her without falling from the boulder. Once Sue was settled,

Rachel started over again. As she read, she noticed the women seemed more intent on trying to look at the words than listen to them.

Sylvia leaned even closer. "Where's them words you just said? Point to 'em."

Rachel ran her finger under each word as she read. "'But the Lord sent out a great wind into the sea, and there was a mighty tempest in the sea, so that the ship was like to be broken.'" She stopped and checked to see if they had any questions.

The women nodded. "Keep going."

She managed only a few more verses before Sue interrupted.

"How do you know how to say them words?"

Rachel scrambled to think of a way to answer her. "First, you have to learn the letters of the alphabet and the sounds that each letter makes. Then you start putting those sounds together."

The women nodded, though their faces revealed their confusion.

"Here, let me show you."

Rachel pulled out her stationery and wrote each letter of the alphabet in her neatest penmanship, saying each letter as she wrote it. Then she had the women say them with her. They repeated the alphabet several times until Rachel thought they had it down before she taught them the sounds each letter made. The excitement in the women's voices was contagious.

Then Sue huffed, leaned away from Rachel, and crossed her arms. "Oh, what are we thinking? We can't learn this stuff. We're too old."

"But you are learning, Sue. You two have been doing great. And besides, you're never too old to learn."

She wrinkled her nose. "Well, my head's tired anyway. How about you keep reading and let my old noggin rest."

Rachel read the rest of the book of Jonah, this time amazing the women when they heard that a man was swallowed by a giant fish.

"There ain't no way a fish can be big enough to eat a man. The biggest me and Sylvia caught was only yea big." Sue held her hands apart almost two feet.

"That's in the lakes around here. There are huge oceans out there that are homes to whales and many other creatures."

"Whales?"

Rachel wondered that they seemed to have so little information about the outside world.

"Whales are similar to fish, but they're huge. I'll try to find a book that will show you just how large some of them can be. But the point is, anything's possible with God."

"Now that, I've heard of. This God, I mean. He's like this thing we can't see but is there. A man told us about it years ago."

"God is more than that, Sylvia. He's the Almighty, Lord and Creator of all things. Here, let me show you." Rachel turned to the first chapter of Genesis and started reading. "'In the beginning God created the heavens and the earth.'"

Rachel finished the chapter and paused. Sue had been looking around while listening rather than trying to follow along. She squinted one eye.

"You telling me that all them things out there, the trees and water and all that, was made by one man?"

"Not a man. God did all that. God has always been and always will be. He is all-knowing and all-powerful, and He is everywhere all at once."

"Oh, stop. They ain't no one in the world like that. It ain't possible."

"Not for people, but for God, all things are possible."

Where is the pastor when I need him? Lord, give me the words.

"Stop arguing, Sue. Keep reading, missy. I like hearing all them words strung together."

Rachel continued to read until she heard Sylvia's soft snores. She looked at Sue, and they both turned to Sylvia. Head back against the rock wall, Sylvia's mouth hung open.

Sue reached behind Rachel. "Hey, wake up, sis. That's just plain rude."

As Sylvia rubbed her eyes, Rachel looked around. The sun was on the down side of the sky.

"Oh, my! I didn't realize it was so late," Rachel said. "I'm so sorry you two, but I need to head home."

Rachel shoved everything into her basket and crawled off the boulder. Sue scrambled after her.

"We gonna do this again maybe?"

Pleasure washed through Rachel. "I'll tell you what…I'll try to get back here again next Saturday. In the meantime, you should come to town, maybe attend the church service tomorrow morning. The pastor will be reading from the Bible, just like I did, and he'll talk about what he's read."

"Thank you, missy."

"You're welcome. I had fun. And please call me Rachel."

When all three were on the ground, Rachel pulled each sister into an embrace. "Good-bye, ladies. If I can't come on Saturday, then we'll just get together some other time."

The sisters nodded and smiled, then picked up their fishing gear and turned toward home. With a skip to her step and a song in her heart, Rachel thanked her heavenly Father for the afternoon she'd just spent, asking forgiveness for her selfish attitude before meeting up with the Manning sisters.

Rachel's prayer was interrupted by a sound off to her right. When she followed the noise, she came to a small opening in a pile of rocks. The whimper she heard told her it had to be a puppy.

She crouched in front of the hole and tried everything she could think of to coax the animal from its hiding place, to no avail. Then she remembered her uneaten snack and pulled out a piece of cheese.

Still on hands and knees, Rachel stuck her hand into the opening, calling softly to the animal as she moved. The growl sounded young and scared. She lay on her belly so she could reach farther. She was all the way up to her shoulder, holding the cheese out to the puppy, when she bumped some of the rocks. They moved, then collapsed, trapping her arm in the hole.

Unable to move her arm, Rachel struggled to move the rocks with her free hand. She succeeded only in making the rocks settle closer around her arm.

"Great. Now what am I going to do?"

As she lay there thinking, the puppy took the cheese from her fingers and then began licking them.

"You little rascal. Why couldn't you have come out before I stuck my arm in there?"

"Who're you talking to?"

Rachel twisted as best she could until she could see Luke sitting on his horse looking down at her. Heat rushed to her face at being caught in a very unladylike position.

"I was trying to get a puppy to come out of this hole."

"And he won't obey?"

"No."

Luke dismounted. "Get back and let me have a try."

"Uh, I can't. I'm stuck."

Luke stared at her for several moments, then laughed out loud. Her neck ached from trying to keep her eyes on him.

"Hush, Luke, you'll scare the dog. Now, instead of laughing, would you please get me out of here?"

Luke knelt beside her and began removing the rocks holding her captive. Rachel shook her head when she noticed his unwavering smile.

"I'm glad you find this so amusing."

"And I'm glad I was the one to find you. I would've hated to miss this."

Rachel made a face at him just as she pulled her arm loose. When she moved out of the way, he continued removing rocks until he could reach the critter that had caused so much commotion. Then he stepped back.

"That's not a dog, Rachel. That's a wolf pup."

"Isn't he cute?"

"You don't understand. That's a wild animal."

"He doesn't look wild. Look."

Rachel handed the pup another piece of cheese. It nearly took the tip of her finger with the morsel. She reached to pet its head, but when she heard a growl behind her, she jerked her hand back. Luke wrapped his arm around her waist and hauled her toward his horse.

"Luke!"

He pointed to an adult wolf. "The mother is back to claim her young." Luke's voice was just above a whisper. "We gotta go."

"What about my basket?"

Luke groaned and mumbled under his breath.

"What? What did you say?"

He continued mumbling, but none of it made sense.

"Luke, if you're not going to speak so I can understand you, then don't say anything at all."

He eyed her, finally saying "Women" loud enough for her to hear. He scared the pup toward its mother, then rescued her basket.

"All right, here you go. I'll walk you home so you don't get into any more trouble."

"Trouble." She rolled her eyes. "I'm no trouble."

"Then what do you call what I'm always getting you out of?"

"Predicaments."

"All right, then I'll walk you home to keep you from more unusual predicaments."

"Why, thank you, kind sir. Whatever would I do without you?"

Luke deposited Rachel at her doorstep and waited until she was inside. "Think you can stay out of any more predicaments?"

"I'll do my best."

He shook his head and began mumbling again as he walked away.

She laughed as she closed the door. Her idea to be alone today might not have worked out as planned, but she wouldn't trade a moment of it for anything.

SIXTEEN

Luke Mason couldn't believe his eyes. What were the Manning sisters doing at the annual church cleanup day? He'd been asking himself that all morning, but even he was less out of place than Sue and Sylvia. And since both his mother and the sheriff had asked him to help, he felt obliged to show for at least a little while.

He climbed down the ladder to greet the sisters. "Ladies, good to see you here, though I'm surprised."

"Yeah, me too," Sue said. "But the only way to shut Syl up was to come along."

Sylvia shook her head. "Oh, it's not as bad as all that. You said yourself you enjoyed coming last Sunday."

"You were here last Sunday? To the service?" Luke couldn't keep the shock from his voice.

Sylvia's head bobbed as she grinned. "Yep, and we'll be back again in the morning. Ain't that right, Sue?"

"Reckon so. I half wish that missy wouldn't have invited us. I'm guessing there's no more sleeping in on Sundays."

Sylvia laughed and gave Sue a shove. "Like you sleep in any morning."

Sue pushed her back. "Well, I could if I wanted."

"What missy?" Luke said.

"Huh?"

"You said a missy invited you to the service."

Sylvia looked around the church yard, then pointed. "Her. That nurse lady."

"Rachel?"

"Yep. That'd be her."

He clenched his jaw. "When did you see her?"

Sue squinted one eye, then looked at Sylvia. "Week ago, right? At the pond. We was fishing, and she showed up and started reading to us from the Bible. Then she invited us to come here."

Luke stared at Rachel. Any anger he felt had fled.

Sue patted his arm. "So what we supposed to be doing? They said there'd be some vittles here for those who showed up to work."

"Maybe that's a question you need to ask missy."

"Good enough."

Without another word the sisters strode to Rachel, and she gave them each a hug and led them to the bushes surrounding the building. Luke shook his head and returned to the top of his ladder to finish painting. The sooner he got done, the less chance he'd have to endure someone preaching at him.

From the corner of his eye, he saw Rachel working her way toward him, chopping weeds from under the bushes and hauling them to a pile not far away. As far as he could tell, she hadn't noticed he was there. He waited for her to get below him, then he dipped his brush into the paint and aimed.

A big drop hit her back. She paused but then resumed working. Luke dipped the brush and aimed again. A large glob splashed on her arm. She looked up just in time for another glob to hit her on the chin. She stepped back and wiped at the paint. Luke wasn't the only one laughing. Most of the men had seen what he'd done.

Rachel peered up at him with hands on hips. "All right, Luke, come down here and fight fair."

"I don't know what you're talking about, Miss Garrett."

"I'll just bet you don't. And since when did you start calling me Miss Garrett?"

"I was taught that was a sign of respect."

"Uh-huh." She looked around. "Where's your mother?"

Luke started to splash her with paint again. Just as he leaned out to aim, his foot slipped. The paintbrush slid from his fingers and hit Rachel on the shoulder.

Rachel ducked, then looked up at him. The shocked expression on her face made him burst into laughter.

"That was an accident."

"Right."

Rachel grabbed his brush, placed the handle between her teeth, and began climbing his ladder. All the workers around them were cheering her on, telling her not to let him get away with his antics.

"Now, Rachel, you know I didn't mean to do that," he said. "What you're thinking about doing is revenge, and you know that's not good Christian behavior. Think of the children who are watching."

Rachel continued her climb. He forced a serious expression on his face.

"All right, I'm sorry."

The look of determination on Rachel's face caused him to start laughing again.

Rachel didn't stop climbing until she was directly below him. Then she removed the brush from her mouth and smiled.

"You know my mother will be upset at having to get paint out of my clothes."

For the first time, Rachel hesitated.

"Go ahead, Rachel. I'll make him wash his own clothes."

Luke looked past Rachel and spotted his mother below. The smile returned to Rachel's face. She dunked her brush into his bucket and flung it toward him. A white streak hit his face and ran down his shirt with only a few drops on his denims. He couldn't believe she actually went through with it.

Amidst cheers and laughter, Rachel scrambled down the ladder.

Luke followed as fast as he could, only to find Rachel dipping her brush into a bucket on the ground. Paint dripping from the brush, Rachel stood ready for battle. Unarmed, it didn't take Luke long to make a decision.

"Truce?"

Rachel smiled and lowered the brush. Luke approached and stuck out his hand. Once he had hers securely in his, he pulled her close, then touched the end of her nose with the blob of paint on his finger. Rachel's mouth dropped open. He jumped back to avoid retaliation.

She wiped the tip of her nose. "Of all the dirty, rotten—"

"Truce, remember?"

"I do, but your memory's pretty short."

He smiled and waggled his brows. She finally laughed.

"I owe you one."

"That was a short truce." He held out his hand.

"I'm not falling for that again."

"Can I have my brush back?"

She looked around, then handed the brush to his mother. "Here, you give it to him. I don't trust him."

Everyone returned to their tasks. Everyone but Chad and Cassandra. The two stood together next to the church steps with no trace of amusement on their faces. Cassie's glower reheated the cheek she'd slapped the final evening they'd spent together. Luke gave her a slight nod, then climbed the ladder. Though he tried to focus on his work, he couldn't help but keep an eye on both Rachel and Cassie for self-preservation.

Rachel had never been to a house-raising before, and though it would keep her from reading to the Manning sisters for another Saturday, she was excited to take part in what appeared to be a big day. The party atmosphere that arrived with all the people added to her enthusiasm. The town's residents, along with many families coming in from the countryside, seemed to look for any reason to get together. The close friendships as well as the bright sunshine on the first weekend in May warmed her heart. The fact that Cade and Grace Ramsey would soon be moving into their new home added to her pleasure.

Dr. Barnes had told her that most of the residents would be at the house-raising, so he took the morning off, both to be on hand for any accidents that might happen and to be able to wield a hammer.

Before they got started, Pete Wallace asked for everyone's attention. "I'd like to introduce your newest neighbor. This is Max Payton. He bought Lyle Phipps's ranch. I hope you'll all make him welcome, especially since he's offered to help with the house-raising today."

The residents wasted no time introducing themselves. Cade shook not with his hand but with a hammer he extended to Max. Max took it with a laugh and walked with the men to the house. Though he looked to be in his fifties, he also looked strong and fit enough to lift a wall by himself.

While the men went to work putting up walls and a roof, the women set up tables for the meal they would have in a few hours. In a short time, the task was finished, allowing the women to visit before setting out the food.

Rachel spotted the Manning sisters sitting under a tree and headed their way. They hadn't missed a Sunday service since she'd invited them, or a church or town function for that matter. And without a doubt they enjoyed the food served at the church cleanup last weekend. Rachel had the feeling they hadn't eaten that well in some time. As she approached, she found them arguing over a catalog, one of Sylvia's fingers planted on one of the pages.

"I'm telling ya, that's one of them outfits them fancy ladies wear in big cities now."

"Ain't neither." Sue shoved Sylvia's hand away. "No fancy woman would wear something as silly as that. And look at that hat. Ain't no woman would be seen dead wearing something so ridiculous."

Sylvia looked up and waved Rachel over. She held the catalog out and pointed. "Tell her, missy. Tell my addlepated sister that big city women wear them kind of duds."

Rachel took the catalog and tried to keep from smiling. "No, Sylvia, your sister is right. This outfit is something people use when they're acting in plays." Rachel sat next to them. "See, it says right under the picture that it's a costume." She looked up to find them staring. "What?"

"Acting?"

"Plays?"

Rachel handed the catalog back to them. "That's when people dress up and pretend to be someone else. They do this on a platform, and other people pay money to watch them."

Sue tilted her head. "People get money for pretending to be someone else?"

"That's right."

"What'll you give me for pretending to be Sue?"

Rachel smiled. "Applause."

"Huh?"

Rachel clapped her hands together several times. "Applause. That's what people do to show they like something."

Sue made a face. "City folk sure are strange. I'll stick to the mountains where things is normal."

Rachel patted Sue's hand. "I understand. I'm partial to the mountains too." She stood. "I'd better get back and help put out the food. Let me know if I can help with anything further."

Sylvia stood with her. "I got a pot you can be sure to put out."

"You brought food?"

Sylvia headed toward their mule. "The preacher said to bring a dish to share. Folks was so giving last time, we thought we'd help this time."

Sue joined them. "Syl insisted we bring our best."

"Really? What'd you bring?"

Sylvia untied a sack and handed it to Sue. "Burgoo and hoe-cakes." She grabbed the handle of a pot and followed Sue to the tables. "Sue's just mad 'cause of how hard it is to catch them squirrels."

"Squirrel." Rachel swallowed hard. "I've…never…eaten one before."

"Oooo, you're in for a treat then." Sylvia thumped the pot on the closest table. "We cook them so long, the bones fall to the bottom and you only scoop up the meat."

Sue smacked her lips. "When do we eat?"

Rachel's appetite disappeared. "Around noon. I need to get to work. Have a good time, ladies."

"Why you call us ladies?"

Rachel stopped. "That's what you are."

Sylvia grinned and bumped Sue. "Least someone thinks so."

Rachel headed over to join Beth Barnes and Sadie Mason. "No smashed thumbs over there yet?"

Sadie stared toward the workers. Beth also turned to look at the men.

"I've heard a couple howls, but no one asking for a bandage yet." She motioned to the sisters. "They're becoming regulars."

"It's great, isn't it?" Rachel said. "They really are sweet, even though they're a little rough around the edges. I doubt they'd ever been to a town before coming to church a couple weeks ago. I hope they'll be made to feel welcome. They need to keep coming so they can come to know the Savior."

After giving her a quick hug, Beth started setting out the food. She tapped the pot already sitting there. "What's this?"

"Sue and Sylvia wanted to bring something."

Beth's brows rose but she didn't ask.

The three ladies talked until the men headed their way, each of the sweaty workers elbowing others out of the way to be first in line and claiming to have worked the hardest. They devoured a great deal of the food. Even some of the burgoo and hoecakes were eaten.

When Luke showed up to work, everyone teased him for waiting until most of the work was finished. He tucked his thumbs in his waistband.

"I'm only here to check your work."

The men moaned and flung bits of food at him. He laughed, then grabbed a quick bite before joining the men going back to work. The women dished up plates for themselves and enjoyed a long visit before needing to clean up. Rachel was about to get up when Sylvia brought her some of the burgoo and one hoecake.

"Sue thought you should try this."

She looked from Sylvia to the food. *Oh no.* "I'm sorry but I'm already full."

"Ya don't hafta eat much. Just try it."

And what if I get a squirrel bone? "All right."

Sylvia set the dish in front of her and waited. Rachel sent Beth a pleading look, but she only raised her brows and smiled. Some friend she was. Rachel picked up her spoon, scooped up a bite, and shoved it in her mouth before she could change her mind.

She paused, then smiled up at Sylvia. "I like it. It's very good."

Sylvia hefted the pot onto the table next to her. "Keep the rest."

The thought of seeing bones at the bottom made her shiver. "You should take the rest home so Sue will be happy."

Sylvia turned to look at her sister. "You're probably right. Wouldn't want you to have to come out tonight to patch me up."

Rachel waved good-bye to the sisters as they rode off. After the dishes were gathered and the tables put into wagons, the ladies lounged under the trees while the children ran off to play. The day was getting long when one of the boys came running from the back of the house.

"Come quick! William's hurt!"

Rachel jumped to her feet and followed the boy. "What happened?"

"He fell from a tree he climbed."

William lay moaning, and blood ran from his forehead. Rachel dropped next to him. "Don't move, William."

His bottom lip quivered, but the tears didn't fall until he saw his mother. Rachel looked at the boy who had come for help and asked him to run for the doctor, then she turned back to William.

"Do you have any pain, William, or did the fall just scare you?"

"My wrist."

Rachel lightly ran her hands over his arms and legs, checking for any broken bones. When Dr. Barnes arrived, Rachel moved back.

"He complained of pain in his wrist, and he has a cut on his head. Other than that, I couldn't find anything else wrong."

Several men had followed the doctor to check on William and now crowded close. Jim motioned them to move back, then looked at Rachel.

"Did you bring your bag?"

She ran to get it and brought it to the doctor.

"Go ahead and clean that cut on his head while I work on his wrist."

She opened the bag and reached inside. Something moved. She pulled her hand back and screamed.

❖ SEVENTEEN ❖

Luke Mason ran forward as the crowd moved back. A rattlesnake crawled from the medical bag. He drew his gun and shot, hitting it in the head. He knelt next to Rachel and grabbed her trembling hands, examining them for wounds.

"You all right? Did it bite you?"

Eyes wide, she shook her head. He stood, grabbed the snake, and threw it into the bushes.

Rachel stared at the bag as though she expected another snake to appear. Luke looked at Jim, and the doctor called her name. Rachel didn't respond. Jim touched her arm, making her jump.

"Oh, sorry."

Rachel went to work with a vengeance. Her hands moved quickly, though still with a slight tremor. Once William's forehead was cleaned and bandaged, she moved to help Jim with the wrist.

Jim touched her arm. "I've got this. Take her to my buggy, Luke. I'm almost finished and will join you soon."

Luke put his hand under her arm and helped her to her feet. Rachel's face was pale, and she never uttered a word as they walked.

"Here, sit in the buggy until Jim comes."

She did as told but stared straight ahead. He dipped his head trying to get her to look at him.

"Talk to me, Rachel. Are you all right?"

"I can't figure out how it got there." She finally looked at him. "How did a rattlesnake get in my bag?"

Jim and Beth joined them along with their two children. Jim put Emma and Tanner in the buggy, then tilted Rachel's face and checked her eyes. "How you feeling?"

"I'm fine. It scared me half to death, but I'm all right now." She shook her head. "The bag was closed when I brought it and when I ran to get it."

"What are you thinking?" Luke said.

"I just don't understand how the snake managed to get in there. I haven't opened it since I left the office yesterday, and it definitely wasn't there then."

Luke and Jim exchanged a quick glance. "That is odd." Jim had the bag in his hand and looked inside again. "I'd like to know the answer to that myself."

Rachel tried to smile. "No harm done."

"But there could have been," Luke said. "The only time the bag was out of your possession was here at the house-raising?"

"Yes."

"Did you see anyone lingering around here?"

"No. I didn't pay any attention."

Luke's mind whirled. Why would someone put a snake in Rachel's bag?

Jim moved next to him. "I'm going to take Rachel and my family home. Let me know if you find out anything."

"I will."

Luke looked around the area to see who remained that he could question. He doubted any of the men had seen anything, and not many women remained. Grace Ramsey sat next to Belle Kline on her porch. As he headed toward them, he saw Chad Baxter and Cassie Chatham walking together toward town. Chad glanced back at him, and Luke's suspicion of him ignited.

Rachel finished listening to Lucille Munroe's breathing and didn't like the faint rattle she'd heard. She'd have to let Jim know.

"I want you to stay indoors for a while and rest as much as possible."

"Mama always told me the best thing for good health was plenty of fresh air and running around. Guess the running part is out of the question, but fresh air never hurt anyone."

Rachel tried to look stern. "Maybe when you were a little girl, but in this case you need to stay out of the cool wind. Especially in the mornings and evenings. If I catch you outside, I'll tell the doctor you've been a bad girl."

"Why, that's no threat. Jim's too sweet a man to be mean."

"Then I'll just have to come over and sit on you to keep you in line."

Lucille's laugh ended with a brief cough. "Now that's scary."

Rachel winked. "Don't make me follow through on that threat." She put her equipment back in her bag, then sat back in her chair. "Tell me a little about your childhood. What were you like as a little girl?"

Lucille's eyes lit up. "I've been waiting for you to get done with all your nursing nonsense so we could get down to business." She shifted around in her chair. "I loved to run. Oh, but I loved to run. Mama said I went straight from crawling to running. There was this one time I had to use the privy something awful. Our house was up on a little hill, and the privy was at the bottom of that hill. I hiked up my skirt and was running down that hill just as fast as my little legs would carry me. At the same time, for who knows what reason, one of our roosters was running from some trees toward the barn. He was just as determined to get to that barn as I was to get to the privy. That dumb rooster cut right across my path. He got all caught up in my legs."

Lucille flailed her thin little hands to demonstrate her dance and tumble with the rooster.

"I'd try to step one way to get away from it, and it was right there. Then I tried to step the other way and there it was again. I managed to take several more steps before I finally lost my balance and tumbled down the rest of that hill with that dumb rooster still between my legs."

She laughed as she spoke.

"I finally came to a stop, and that rooster stood up and took off running toward the barn again, clucking and carrying on the whole way. After that tumble, I'd almost forgot what I was running down the hill for. But as soon as I stood up, I remembered. I took care of my business and headed back up the hill, laughing all the way. I was still laughing when I entered the house. Mama wanted to know what was so funny, so I told her. She didn't see the humor near as much as I did. Dumb rooster."

Rachel wiped tears from her eyes. She hadn't laughed so hard in a long time.

"Samuel and Edna used to love for me to tell them that story when they were young. They would laugh much like you are right now." Lucille reached over and patted Rachel's hand. "My Charlie would come into the room whenever they asked me to tell that story, just so he could hear it all over again." Lucille's face had taken on a faraway look as she traveled back so many years.

Rachel allowed her a moment to reflect. "When did you lose your husband?"

Lucille's eyes turned toward Rachel, but they still had that distant look to them. "The children were almost out of their teens when my Charlie died. We were working together out in the yard when he put his hand to his head as he looked at me. He said, 'I sure have an awful pain in my head right now, darlin'.' Then he fell to the ground and was gone." Lucille's lip trembled just a bit. "There's never been anyone else like my Charlie."

Rachel leaned over her and put her arm around the frail lady's shoulders as she placed a kiss on her forehead.

Lucille sighed and patted Rachel's arm. "I'm all right, dear. I love to tell my stories. Thank you, Rachel."

"No need to thank me. I love your stories and would sit here all day listening to them if I could. But as usual, I need to get back to work. I'll be back in a couple days to check on you and make sure you're better. Get some rest, now, so you can get well."

Rachel gave her one more hug. She'd never met anyone who was so frail yet had so much energy and strength of mind. She wished she could sit for hours and listen to Mrs. Munroe's stories of her life growing up. Maybe she'd do just that some Saturday.

Mrs. Chatham escorted Rachel to the front door. "Thank you so much for caring for and listening to my mother. She looks forward to your visits."

"Your mother is one of my favorite people."

Rachel bid her good-bye and hurried across the porch. She was running late, but then Jim should be used to her tardiness after seeing Lucille. She started down the steps, then the toe of her shoe caught on something. With the medical bag in her hand, she couldn't stop the fall. Her head and shoulder hit first followed by her hip and thigh. She flipped once and rolled down the remaining steps, landing in the dirt.

Rachel lay there for several moments to collect herself. How in the world had she managed to fall? Her shoe must have caught on her skirt. She rolled to her knees and pushed herself to her feet, then peered at the top of the steps. Nothing stood out as the cause of her fall. She shrugged and immediately grimaced from the pain in her shoulder. With slow movements, she reached for her bag.

Though each step made her grimace, the slow walk down the street helped her compose herself. She brushed off the dust from her dress before entering the doctor's office.

"I'm back."

Jim peeked out the door. "Good. Would you see what's wrong with Alex Graham?"

"All right."

Rachel called the boy and his mother into the second examining room. She bent to help him up onto the table. The pain in her shoulder and hip stopped her. She forced a smile.

"You look strong for your age, Alex. Why don't you see if you can climb onto that table for me?"

After two attempts, the boy managed to pull himself onto the table, then scooted to the middle.

"Good job. Now, what can I do for you today?"

"My ear hurts."

"Oh? Well, let's have a look in there, shall we?"

Rachel moved to the counter for the instrument she needed, then returned to the boy's side. From where he sat, the angle was awkward. She tried to adjust, but the move pulled at her sore muscles.

"Can you scoot down to the end of the table for me so I can get a better look?"

Alex slid down to the end. "How's that?"

"Perfect." She tugged a bit on his lobe as she peered in his ear. "Well, Alex, I can't tell what it is, but something's in there and needs to come out." She tilted her head and narrowed her eyes. "What'd you stick in your ear, young man?"

He looked everywhere but at her. "Nothing."

She put her hands on the table, one on each side of him. She bent to look into his eyes, then gasped.

Alex frowned. "You hurt too?"

"Miss Garrett, can I see you in my office?"

"Sure." Rachel looked at Alex and winked. "I'll be right back."

Jim closed the door behind her. "What's wrong, Rachel?"

"What do you mean?"

Jim eyed her for a moment. "You're walking and moving as if it hurts. So I ask again, what's wrong?"

Rachel sighed. "I fell down the steps at the Munroe house. I don't know how. I'm sure it was just clumsiness on my part."

"Did you hit your head?"

"Yes."

"Did you lose consciousness?"

"No."

Jim stared at her for several moments. "You have one of two options, Rachel. You can either stay and be examined by me or you can go to my house and let Beth do it. But make no mistake, you *will* be examined. With a fall like that, you could've hurt something and not realize it right away. The way you're moving tells me that's a possibility."

"I'm just sore, Jim. I'm not hurt any worse than that."

Jim crossed his arms and leaned against his desk. "Can you bend down and touch your toes?"

Rachel glanced down at her toes but didn't try to touch them.

"I thought not. Can you raise your arms over your head?" Again, Rachel didn't move. Jim's eyes narrowed. "So will Beth or I be examining you?"

"I can finish out the day."

"No, you can't."

She eyed her employer, clenching her teeth several times. "I'll ask Beth to do it."

"I'll see you tonight then. Good-bye, Rachel."

Jim opened the door for her and stepped around her to lead the way outside, opening that door for her as well. Pastor Robbins was riding by in his buggy. Jim flagged him down.

"Would you mind giving Rachel a ride to my house?"

"Not at all. Hop in."

Jim helped her into the buggy. "Make sure she goes into my house, not hers."

The pastor's brows rose. "All right." He looked between the two of them. "Anything wrong?"

"I hope not," Jim said.

The ride home was quiet. Rachel felt bad about that, but she didn't feel like talking. Much as she didn't want to admit it, Jim was right. She would have had a difficult time working the rest of the day. But he could have at least asked her instead of being so demanding.

The pastor pulled up to the Barnes home and helped her out. "If there's anything I can help with, Rachel, please ask."

Rachel managed a smile. "Everything's fine, Pastor. Just a slight case of hardheadedness. But thank you."

"All right."

After he drove away, she eyed her own house wishing she could escape inside. But she took a deep breath and knocked on the kitchen door before entering. Beth stood at the table kneading bread dough, her children playing with toys off in one corner.

Beth stopped kneading and wiped her hands. "What are you doing here, Rachel? Is everything all right? Is it Jim?"

"No, Jim's fine."

"All right, so Jim gave you the rest of the day off?"

Rachel hesitated. "Sort of." She took a deep breath and moved a few steps closer. "I need your help with something."

Beth left the table to stand right in front of her. "What is it, Rachel? What's wrong?"

Rachel let out a sigh and tried to step around Beth, then grimaced at the way her muscles rebelled.

Beth grasped her arm. "Rachel?"

"I fell down the steps in front of the Munroe house and I'm a little sore. Jim wants you to examine me to make sure I'm all right. I told him I was, but he wouldn't listen."

Beth glanced at the children. "Come on."

Rachel followed Beth to the small clinic at the other end of the house. Once inside the office, Rachel unbuttoned her blouse but had trouble getting it off. Beth stepped up to help.

"Oh my. Oh Rachel, your poor shoulder."

Beth helped her remove the rest of her garments, then examined the bruises.

"I can see where your body hit each step, Rachel, but your shoulder and hip look the worst. What about your head? Did it hit a step?"

"Yes."

Beth felt the side of Rachel's head. "You have a long narrow bump here. Did you lose consciousness?"

"No."

Beth checked Rachel's ribs and legs, then manipulated her arm. She retrieved a robe from a drawer and placed it over Rachel's shoulders.

"I don't think anything's broken, but you're going to be pretty sore for a while." She gave Rachel a gentle hug. "Would you let me fix you a hot bath? It should help with the pain."

"I don't want to bother you."

Beth frowned. "What are you angry about?"

"I'm embarrassed that I'm clumsy enough to fall down some steps, and I'm upset with Jim for not trusting my judgment. I told him I wasn't badly hurt."

"He's a doctor, Rachel. It's his nature to worry about someone in pain, especially his family and also his nurse, who is almost like family."

Rachel's eyes filled. Beth smiled.

"Come on. Let's get you soaking in some hot water."

They sat at the table while they waited for the water to heat.

"How did you fall, Rachel? Did you trip on something?"

"It felt like I did, but when I looked up to the top of the steps, I didn't see anything. Maybe my toe caught on my skirt or something." Rachel grimaced from another shrug. "I always knew I wasn't graceful, but I've never been so clumsy."

Rachel spent the remainder of the afternoon with Beth and the children and was reading to Emma and Tanner when Jim arrived from work. The children shrieked and ran to him. Jim scooped them up in his arms.

"I'm hungry." He pretended to take bites from them, causing more squeals. He finally set them down. "Run play in the kitchen for a bit. The grownups need to talk."

The children moaned but ran off as told. Jim sat across from Rachel, and Beth chose a chair between the two.

"Nothing's broken that I can tell, but she'll be pretty sore for a couple days. The bruises look awful, Jim. I had her soak in a tub of hot water for some time this afternoon and that helped."

"Good." Jim looked at Rachel. "I'm sorry if I came across as a tyrant, Rachel, but I had to be sure."

"I know. I understand. I guess I was just hoping you'd trust my judgment."

"Since when have doctors and nurses been good patients or been able to make an accurate diagnosis of themselves?"

"I have yet to meet one," Beth said.

"That includes you too." Jim made a face when Beth's mouth dropped open. He looked back at Rachel. "I do trust your judgment, Rachel, and I probably should have in this case as well. But I was worried about you. I get the impression you'd work yourself to death if I'd let you, even if something was broken."

"No more than you would."

"Touché. So are you still upset with me?"

"No. I'd probably treat you the same way. The only difference is, you wouldn't listen to me."

Jim laughed and stood, holding his hand out to her. She placed her hand in his and he helped her get to her feet. Before releasing her hand, he gave it a squeeze.

"I have to take care of you, Rachel. Since you've arrived, my practice has flourished."

"Now the truth comes out." She swatted his arm. "I'd hit you harder, but I'm afraid it'd hurt me more than you."

"Who knew a fall would work in my favor." Jim extended one of his elbows to her and one to his wife. "Let's eat. I'm starving."

That night Rachel lay in bed wide awake as she replayed the fall over and over. It didn't help. She still didn't have any solid answers. When she woke the next morning, moving her arm to rub her eyes produced a groan. Just taking a deep breath to yawn made her eyes water.

"Don't bother getting up. You've got the day off. Doctor's orders." Beth stood over her. "How you feeling?"

"Like I've been run over by a wagon pulled by six horses. Then they turned around and did it again."

Beth sat on a chair beside the bed. "That bad, huh? Jim gave me something for you to take if the pain's too bad. He'll be by here in a little while to check on you."

"I don't want any just yet. Maybe not at all."

"Rachel—"

She lifted her hand. "I know, and I'll take it if it feels any worse."

"Got a headache?"

"Just a little one."

Beth tilted her head and squinted one eye. "What aren't you telling me?"

"My ribs feel worse. It's hard to take a deep breath."

"Right side? Let me see."

Beth pulled the bedding down and lifted her gown. "Goodness, Rachel. Looking at you makes me want to cry."

Rachel started to laugh, then gasped. "Don't make me laugh."

"Sorry." Beth pressed gently on each rib. "I don't know, Rachel. One may be cracked. They sure are bruised. Like I said, Jim will be here soon, and I can have him take a look."

"Doesn't matter. Whether bruised or cracked, it'll take time to heal."

Someone tapped at the door but didn't wait for an answer. "It's me."

Jim entered, leaving the door open, and moved to the bed.

"Who has the kids?" Beth said.

"Sadie." He motioned to Rachel. "How bad is it?"

"Could be worse."

Beth snorted. "She can't take a deep breath and any movement makes her gasp."

"That good, huh? Did you take the pills I sent?"

"She's too much like you, honey. She refused."

Another knock sounded at the door. Luke entered. "You were right, Doc." He held out some string. "Some was still tied to the post. The rest lay on the ground beside the steps."

"What do you mean?" Rachel said.

"I had Luke go to the Munroe house and check the steps."

"And I found this string." Luke held it out. "Someone wanted you to fall, Rachel. Any idea who?"

Rachel's mind scrambled. Who...? And a name landed in her thoughts.

Beth touched her arm. "What aren't you telling us, dear?"

Rachel looked at her, then at Jim. "I've been keeping something from you. I guess I hoped it'd just go away, but..."

Jim stood quiet, waiting. She took a couple breaths.

"Back in Missouri, when I was still under Dr. Freeman's teaching, he sent me to a couple's home who were expecting a child. There was some trouble."

"What kind of trouble?" Jim said.

"The mother died in labor. The husband blamed me. It got so bad, my mother insisted I leave for a while." She looked from Beth to Jim. "That's the main reason I'm here."

Beth took her hand. "But he's hundreds of miles away."

Tears threatened. Rachel fought them as she shook her head. "No, he's not. About a month ago he showed up in town. He's been watching and following me, but he's never tried to hurt me."

Luke moved to the other side of the bed. "That you're aware of. Whoever did this did it in secret. How can you be sure it wasn't him?"

"Not only that," Jim said, "someone also put a nail in the rein and placed a snake in your medical bag. It could be the same man."

"You should've said something, Rachel," Luke said. "What's his name?"

"Michael Dunlavey."

"I'll check on him and also mention this to the sheriff," Luke said as he strode out the door.

Rachel peered up at Jim. "I'm sorry. I should have been up front about it when I arrived."

"Was there anything you could've done to save the woman?"

"No."

"Then you have nothing to apologize for. I've got to get back to work now, but you just plan on sleeping and relaxing today. We'll decide in the morning whether you feel up to working."

Jim leaned down to kiss his wife, then left. Beth squeezed Rachel's hand.

"It must have been bad if your mom asked you to leave."

"He threatened to make me bleed like his wife did."

"Oh, Rachel. You should've at least told the sheriff when you first saw him here."

"I know, but he hasn't done a thing except speak to me a couple times and follow me around."

"Following you around makes him look guilty. He'd have plenty of opportunity to place the nail, the snake, and the string." Beth tucked the bedding around Rachel's neck. "But don't worry about anything. Luke will figure it out. All you need to worry about is getting some sleep."

Rachel didn't figure sleep would come with so much to think about, but her lids grew heavy. Maybe she'd rest just a bit and try to get up later to help Luke.

EIGHTEEN

Luke Mason rode to the office to tell Sheriff Taylor what he'd learned from Rachel and discovered at the Munroe house. He hoped Morgan would let him look into Rachel's so-called accidents. He wanted to meet this Mr. Dunlavey. What kind of person would tie a string across steps to trip someone? Rachel could have broken her neck. Good thing she didn't because he had every intention of strangling her scrawny neck for keeping a possible life-threatening secret.

Minutes later, with Morgan's blessing, Luke headed to the hotel to see if that's where Michael Dunlavey had been staying since he arrived. He pushed through the door and crossed the lobby to the counter.

"Hello, Silas."

"Luke. What can I do for ya?"

"Do you have a Michael Dunlavey staying here?"

"Did. Said he was about out of money and left."

"Left town?"

"Don't think so. I saw him yesterday. Not sure where he's staying now, but most days you can find him sitting across from the doc's office."

Luke headed for the door then stopped. "What's he look like?"

"Tall. Thin. Hasn't shaved since he got here."

With a nod, Luke strode out of the hotel and down the boardwalk. A man sat across the street from the doctor's office, his chair leaned back on two legs against the building and his hat pushed low over his eyes as if he might be asleep. If the soiled clothes were any indication, he hadn't bathed since he arrived in town either.

Luke stopped in front of him and cleared his throat. When he received no response, he kicked one of the chair's legs.

"This better be mighty important."

"It is if you're Michael Dunlavey."

The chair thumped to the boardwalk, and the man bumped his hat back before looking up at Luke. "That'd be me. What of it?"

"You've been following Rachel Garrett around."

One corner of Dunlavey's mouth curled. "So she finally confessed to someone, huh? Did you arrest her?"

"For what?"

The man stood and peered into Luke's eyes. "Murder. She killed my wife."

"That's not the story she told."

"No doubt. Anyone would lie to stay out of prison or keep from getting a noose around their neck."

"So you thought you'd provide your own form of justice and try to kill her?"

"What?"

"You admit you've been following her?"

"Sometimes."

"And you take any opportunity you can to cause her to have accidents."

Dunlavey took a step back. "What? No! I haven't done anything to her. I've only been watching her to make sure she doesn't kill anyone else."

"Where were you yesterday afternoon?"

He pointed at the chair. "Right here. I fell asleep and she slipped away from me. I had to wait until she returned. Then she left right away with the preacher." Dunlavey crossed his arms. "You can ask most anyone in town. Someone was bound to have seen me sitting right there. Why? What happened?"

Luke shook his head. "You planning to stay in town?"

"For a while longer. Why? You planning to run me out?"

"Only if you give me a good reason. Have a good day."

"Wait a minute. Where's Rachel?"

Luke continued down the boardwalk.

"What accidents?"

Luke spotted Chad Baxter watching him before dashing into an alley. Luke ducked into the one nearest him and raced to the next street. But Chad was nowhere to be found. No matter. Luke knew where to find him, and when he did, Chad had some questions to answer.

"My goodness, Mr. Payton! What happened?"

Today was Rachel's first day back at work since her accident, and it was a busy one. She led Max from the waiting area and patted the examining table. As he slid onto the table, the doctor peeked inside the room, then entered.

"Max?"

"It's not as bad as it looks."

Jim motioned for him to remove his shirt. "I don't know, Max. It looks pretty bad. How much blood did you lose?"

"Plenty, but I got more."

Rachel helped him remove his shirt, revealing several cuts. She retrieved some bandages and first started cleaning the wounds. "How did this happen?"

Max shook his head. "From my stupidity. I needed cowhands so badly, I ignored my good judgment and hired a man who didn't seem trustworthy. I also ignored my other hands who told me to leave the man alone and let him sleep off his drunken binge from the night before. But I didn't hire the man to sleep, so I went to wake him up."

He winced when Rachel cleaned the deepest cut on his chest.

"It took some time, but I finally roused the man, only to have him leap from the bed and attack me with a knife. I would've tried to bandage the cuts myself, but they seemed a bit deep in some areas."

Jim nodded. "They are. The cut on your arm will only need to be cleaned and bandaged, but this big cut on your chest will need some stitches." Jim motioned next door. "I've got to finish with my other patient. Let me know when you finish cleaning the cuts and bandaging that arm, Rachel."

"I will."

When Max gasped, she paused in her cleaning. "Did you have the man arrested?"

"No. I haven't been to see the sheriff yet, and even so, as soon as the man saw what he'd done, he left in a hurry. I doubt the sheriff will be able to find him."

"But you do plan to report it, don't you?"

"Oh, I'll report it, but my main concern is to let the other ranchers know about him so they won't make the mistake of hiring him like I did. But I doubt he'll stick around and take the chance of ending up behind bars."

Jim returned and soon had the stitches in place and let Rachel bandage the wound.

"You'll have to go easy with the heavy stuff," Jim said. "Too much strain may open that cut again."

"Will bandaging it tightly help? I've got work to do."

Jim eyed the man in front of him for a moment. "It may help a bit, but you'll still need to take it easy or I'll be seeing you in here for some repair work. And if that happens, next time will be worse."

"Well, if that means more tender loving care by your nurse here, I just might do that anyway." He winked. "Why aren't you married to some nice young man who'd appreciate your nurturing ways?"

"Is that an offer, Mr. Payton?"

"My dear, if I were thirty years younger, it definitely would be."

Max stood and patted Rachel's arm. "Thank you, Miss Garrett. By the way, the work you do with the children at church is wonderful. Keep it up." Then he turned to Jim with his hand outstretched. "Thank you, Jim. What do I owe you?"

The men quickly settled up, then Max grabbed his soiled shirt and made a face. "I can't walk into the store wearing this. That poor lady in there might faint dead away."

"You're probably right," Rachel said. "Would you like me to walk you over there? You can wait outside while I get you another shirt."

Max put his arm around her shoulders and squeezed. "You're gonna make a great wife for some lucky young man someday."

Max and Rachel left the clinic and headed down the boardwalk. Just as Max was about to open the door to the general store, Sadie Mason exited while trying to manage an armful of packages and a basket of supplies.

Max grasped the handle of the basket. "Here, let me get that for you."

"Oh, Max, it's you. Thank you." Sadie gasped. "What happened to you?"

"While you tell her your story, I'll run in and get your shirt," Rachel said.

Max helped Sadie put down her purchases and motioned for her to join him on the bench next to the door.

Rachel envisioned the two as a couple. Then she scolded herself for mentally intruding on something that was none of her business. She found what she thought would be a good work shirt, guessed at the size, and made the purchase.

Luke stood beside his mother and Max, who was just finishing up his tale as Rachel exited the store. She handed him the shirt.

"What's this man's name?" Luke asked Max. "I'll tell the sheriff and we'll send out wires to other towns."

"Fred Ingram. He's not real tall, but he's a stocky one. I don't imagine many men would risk a fight with him."

"Like you did?" Sadie's voice held a hint of humor.

"Much as I hate to admit it, most men are a mite smarter than me." He winked.

"I doubt that," Sadie said as her face colored.

Luke reached for the basket. "Let me help you get home, Mother."

"I'll do that." Max stood and scooped up the packages. "I know you're busy, and my wagon is right across the road. I'll get her home safely."

Sadie took the basket from Luke. "I think that sounds like a fine idea. See you tonight, Luke."

Max stuck out his elbow for Sadie. She placed her hand in the crook, and the two headed across the street. Rachel no longer hid her smile. She looked up at Luke. His stunned expression changed to his usual frown as he watched them climb onto the wagon.

"That was nice of him," Rachel said.

Luke glanced at her before eyeing the departing wagon one more time. "Yeah, nice. Have a good day, Rachel."

His long strides carried him away in a hurry. She smiled again. It might take time, but Luke would get used to the idea of his mother with a suitor.

What is Mother thinking?

Luke strode down the boardwalk more confused than angry. Surely she couldn't be attracted to Max Payton. He figured she'd never be interested in another man after how much she'd loved his father. But if he were honest, he hadn't seen that gleam in his mother's eyes in a very long time. Not to mention that particular smile. He wasn't sure how he felt about the situation. He wanted his mother to be happy, but wasn't she happy the way things were? He certainly was, most of the time anyway.

He turned and looked one more time. They sure looked

comfortable together on that bench earlier. He'd have to keep an eye on things a little better. If they got to looking too cozy, he'd have to ask a few questions.

Just as Luke was about to continue to the office, he saw Chad hurry into an alley. Luke lit out after him, only to have him disappear once again. He'd managed to escape for the last three days. Chad needed to grow up and face Luke like a man. Luke had avoided questioning Chad and embarrassing him in front of his parents just in case he had nothing to do with Rachel's accidents. But if Chad kept evading him, he'd have to do just that.

He'd give him one more day.

NINETEEN

June had arrived in the form of a bright and sunny day. As Rachel hurried to work that Monday morning, she realized the last three months of her life were very much like the beautiful day. Her love for the town and the people in it knew no bounds. She said a quick prayer of thanks for God's abundant blessings, then hastened her steps so she'd have plenty of time to clean up the examining rooms before Jim arrived. She'd left them a mess Friday because she was worn out from the busy day.

Rachel pulled the key from her pocket, unlocked the door, and pushed inside. She hadn't gotten the door closed before someone grabbed her, clapped a hand over her mouth, and yanked her from the entrance. An arm went around her, clamping her arms to her sides. She dropped her medical bag to the floor.

She saw three men in the office in addition to the one who held her captive. One man stood at the window while the other two gawked, not even attempting to disguise the lust in their eyes.

"I'll let you go if you promise not to shout," the man holding her said.

Rachel couldn't respond as her heart threatened to explode.

The man shook her. "Do you promise not to scream?"

Rachel nodded, and the man slowly took his hand from her mouth. When she remained silent, he let her go.

"Where's the doctor?"

When she didn't respond, he grabbed her arms and gave her a shake. "When's the doctor coming?"

"H-he won't be in until much later."

When he released her, Rachel tried to back away and bumped into one of the other men. He took her arms in his big hands and held her tightly against him.

"Let her go," the first man said. When the big man didn't move, the first man clenched his teeth. "I said let her go, Spade."

Spade turned her loose and took a step back.

"It's getting awfully light outside, Quint." A man appeared from the back of the office. "We need to get moving."

Quint rubbed his whiskered chin as he paced several moments. Then he faced Rachel again.

"Are you certain the doctor won't be in for a while?"

Rachel's mind scrambled. If she said no, they'd just kill her and wait for Jim. She said nothing, and Quint grabbed her by the hair and shoved his face close to hers. "I asked if the doc was coming."

"Not until later. He has to visit some patients."

Quint glanced up at the ceiling, his jaw clenching several times. Still holding her hair, he pulled her close again. "Do you know how to remove a bullet?"

Rachel took a shaky breath. "I've assisted in many gunshot wounds. I might be able to do it alone, depending on where it is."

Quint pointed to the upper right side of his chest.

She nodded. "I should be able to take care of that."

The man released her hair and grabbed her arm. "Let's go."

Quint dragged her to the back of the office. Rachel tried to slow him. He stopped and spun to face her.

"Don't give me no trouble or I'll make you regret it."

"I'll need my bag and some supplies."

He scowled but turned her loose. "Hurry up and get what you need. We've got to go."

"My bag is by the door."

The man by the window bent and handed her the bag. Rachel bustled about, collecting what she thought she'd need. She'd just managed to deposit her tools and medicine in the bag before Quint had her by the arm again and pulled her out the back door of the office. He didn't stop until Rachel was standing next to a horse.

Rachel panicked all over again. She was about to tell him she didn't know how to ride when a cloth sack was dropped over her head. She started to reach up and pull it off but stopped when Quint growled at her.

"Leave it on or we'll have to tie your hands."

Rachel left it on. Someone lifted her onto the back of the horse.

"Hold on to the saddle horn."

She had only a moment to obey before they were on their way at a fast pace.

Luke Mason reined to a stop when Jim Barnes ran from his office and looked down both directions of the street. He nudged his horse toward him.

"What's wrong, Jim?"

"It's Rachel. She's not here." He looked down the street again. "She's always here early, but this time the door was locked and the office hasn't been straightened."

"I'll check her house."

Luke reined his horse around and galloped down the street, berating himself for not doing his job better. With all that had happened to her over the weeks, he should have kept a closer eye on her, even walked her to work.

He arrived at Rachel's house and pounded on her door and called her name. He kept at it until Beth came out of her house.

"What's wrong, Luke?"

"Rachel's not at the office. Do you have a key to this door?"

Beth had it in his hand in minutes. Once Luke had the door open, she followed him inside. They both looked around. Nothing.

Luke handed her the key and strode out. "I'm headed for the sheriff and then back to Jim. I'll have someone let you know what's happening." He climbed onto his saddle and turned the horse around.

"Luke?" Beth's frightened voice stopped him.

"I know, Beth. Just pray that she's okay."

❖ TWENTY ❖

The way Rachel's body ached, they'd been riding up the mountain for a week. In reality, she guessed it'd been closer to an hour. Maybe a little longer. Her arms felt like lead weights from holding on so tightly, not to mention her sore and numb bottom from sitting on a rock-hard saddle. And having to lean forward made her back throb. If only they'd allow her to see, it might help her to relax a little. And some fresh air sounded wonderful.

When the horses finally came to a stop, Rachel breathed a sigh of relief. Then someone's hands yanked her from the saddle and set her on her feet. The lack of circulation in her legs made them weak, and she would have collapsed if the hands hadn't steadied her.

The sack was pulled from Rachel's head and she took a deep breath. A rundown cabin sat in front of her surrounded and almost hidden by several trees. Quint took Rachel by the arm and forced her toward the cabin. He didn't stop until he'd yanked her across the main room and into a small bedroom in the back. On the bed lay a man bathed in perspiration. His eyes were closed and blood leaked through his shirt onto the sheet.

Quint handed her the medical bag and gave her a push toward the bed. "Fix him up."

She stopped at the side of the bed and felt the man's forehead. The

155

resemblance to Quint was unmistakable. Father and son. No wonder Quint was so demanding.

Rachel retrieved her scissors from the bag and cut away the soiled shirt. "I'll need plenty of hot water."

Quint left but was back soon. "I told the men to bring in the water when it's hot."

He hovered over Rachel's shoulder, watching everything she was doing. She bumped into him a second time and paused to look at him.

"You're going to have to move to the other side."

When the water arrived, Rachel cleaned the man's chest as best she could, then she washed her hands and the tools in the alcohol she brought along. Finally, she looked up at Quint.

"You'd better hold him tight. This is going to hurt."

Quint held the man by the shoulders, and Rachel took a deep breath. As she dug the tool around the wound feeling for the bullet, the man on the bed squirmed, then flung his arms and yelled. Rachel pulled her hands away. Quint cursed, then looked toward the door.

"Bear, get in here!" The man showed in the doorway. Quint motioned with his head. "Help me hold him down."

Bear lay across the man's legs while Quint adjusted for a better hold. Rachel tried again. Several minutes later, she found the bullet and pulled it out. Then she cleaned the wound and placed tiny stitches here and there before stitching the hole closed. She pulled wads of cloth from the bag and placed them over the wound before wrapping the shoulder to hold them in place. She finally sat in the nearby chair and rubbed her sore back.

"Is my son gonna live?" Fear radiated from Quint's eyes.

"I can't promise you that yet. He's lost a lot of blood. I'll have to try to keep him still so he won't reopen the wound, and he'll need plenty of rest to get his strength back."

Quint nodded, never taking his eyes from his son's face. Sympathy for him washed through her.

"I'd like to be taken back to town now."

Quint looked up at her. "You can't go back to town. You have to stay here and take care of my son." Rachel opened her mouth to protest, but the man's eyes hardened as he shook his head. "You're staying here." Then he stood and walked from the room.

Rachel sat in shock for several moments before following him out the door. The men quickly encircled her, all leering with grins on their faces. One man grabbed her.

"I'm first."

A gunshot went off, stopping all talk and movement.

"No one is to touch her while my son is sick." The men protested. Quint scowled. "Shut up!" The men fell silent. Quint pointed the gun at each of them. "You leave her alone until Tony is well. If one of you so much as touches her, you're dead. Is that clear?"

The men all nodded. Quint motioned her back inside the bedroom. "You can have her when Tony is well."

Rachel's mouth went dry and her legs weakened. She thought she might faint.

Quint entered the room behind her. "Is there anything you need?"

She nodded and forced her mouth open. "A drink of water."

"Stay in the room. I'll bring it to you."

Rachel returned to the chair by the bed, trembling all over. She couldn't remember having ever been so scared.

Quint came back with her water and handed it to her. "It would be best if you stayed in this room as much as possible. If you need something, ask me or Bear. I can't trust that the other men will leave you alone."

Rachel nodded and tried to take a drink, but her hands were shaking too much. She set the glass on the bedside table.

Quint squatted next to the bed and eyed his son. "How long before he's better?"

"Years."

Rachel had answered without thinking and was certain she'd made Quint mad. Instead, he chuckled.

"Keep your sense of humor, miss. You'll need it." He stared at her for a moment. "What's your name?"

Rachel stared back, sure she didn't want him to know but not sure she had a choice. "Rachel."

"Let me know if you need anything else."

He pushed to his feet and tromped out. After a quick check on the patient, Rachel looked around the room. The bare and dusty walls made it obvious the cabin hadn't been lived in for some time. A faded curtain covered a small window. Rachel rushed over hoping to escape. Nails were pounded into the corners. She grabbed the nails, jerking and wiggling them hoping to loosen them. They didn't budge. She pounded her fists on the sill and swallowed a scream, then sagged.

She dropped onto the chair, wanting to give in and cry. Instead, she laid her head on the bed.

Dear Lord, help me find a way to escape. Or if not that, please let me be found quickly.

Exhaustion ate at her resolve to stay awake. She was about to drop off to sleep when a noise at the door made her jump to her feet. One of the men stood leering at her. Bear appeared behind him, glanced at her, then cuffed the man on the ear, making him howl with pain. Bear reached in and closed the door again.

Rachel moved to the window and pushed back the curtains. She could see the setting sun's reflection through the trees on a small lake behind the house. Except for her situation, she would have loved the view. She continued to stare at the lake until the door opened. Quint stood in the doorway with a plate of food.

"That window won't open." When she nodded, he smiled. "I would have thought you odd if you hadn't checked." He entered the room and set the plate on the bedside table. "You better eat something. You missed dinner."

"I'm not hungry."

Quint lit the lantern and left the room. Rachel remained at the window, staring at the food for a moment before turning to look out at the lake again. She was trapped in a cabin full of men in the middle of nowhere soon to be enveloped in darkness.

Lord, help me!

To help her through the night, she tried to think of verses from the Bible. They wouldn't come. If only she had her Bible. She closed her eyes and then a verse came to her.

"*The Lord is my light and my salvation; whom shall I fear? The Lord is the strength of my life; of whom shall I be afraid.*" Another verse followed: "*Fear thou not; for I am with thee: be not dismayed; for I am thy God: I will strengthen thee; yea, I will help thee; yea, I will uphold thee with the right hand of my righteousness.*" Then came the verse she'd learned as a little girl, the one she said over and over when her brother died: "*God is our refuge and strength, a very present help in trouble.*"

Rachel repeated the verse and peace fought against her fear. God was in control. She'd have to find rest in that knowledge. She sat in the chair and begged God to help her through her ordeal, especially for protection from the men in the other room.

The man in bed moaned, interrupting her prayer. Rachel checked his pulse, then felt for a fever. He was hot but not enough to cause much worry just yet. She dipped a cloth in the bowl of water, now cool, and swabbed the man's face and neck. He calmed and fell back to sleep.

She dropped the cloth in the bowl, sat back, and prayed she'd see her family and friends again.

TWENTY-ONE

While Jim Barnes and Sheriff Morgan Taylor looked for clues inside the office a good part of Monday, Luke Mason searched on the outside for any sign of what might have happened to Rachel. Luke hoped to find wagon tracks leading from the back of the office, but none were to be found. All he could see were horse tracks in all directions. He headed to the back door and fingered the battered wood.

He opened the door. "Morgan!"

The sheriff appeared.

"Looks like someone broke in. It appears they used something to pry the door open, but there's nothing back here that looks like it could've been used for that."

Jim joined him and the sheriff at the back. "Some of my tools and medicine are missing."

Luke followed Jim and Morgan inside. "But no note about going to help anyone?"

"No, and she's never left the office quite like this before. She's waited until the next morning to get the rooms ready, but this..." Jim motioned around them and shrugged. "It's almost as if someone rushed through here knocking things down as they grabbed whatever they wanted."

"You think she was taken against her will?"

Morgan held up his hand. "Slow down, Luke. Let's not jump to anything too fast. Did you see anything outside that might tell us what happened?"

"No wagon tracks but plenty of horse tracks. But that's it."

Mr. Ashton entered the clinic. "Sheriff, someone stole from my store."

"Stole what?"

"Bags and cans of food mostly. Some flour, sugar, and coffee too."

Luke looked at Morgan. "You think maybe the bank was hit? Maybe Rachel saw them?"

"Let's go."

They'd just made it out the door when the saloon owner hollered. He joined them on the boardwalk. "A whole case of whiskey's been stolen."

Sheriff Taylor exchanged a glance with Luke. "Check the bank. If it's fine, meet me at the saloon."

Luke strode to the bank and checked the door before peeking in the front window.

"You thinking about breaking in?" Pete Wallace grinned when Luke spun around. "Glad to see you taking care of the place, Luke."

"You may not be thanking me once you're inside. Open up and let's make sure all is well."

Pete's smile disappeared as he pulled out his key. "What happened?"

"Not sure. All we know is that Rachel's missing and the saloon and general store have had items stolen from inside."

Pete opened the door and led the way to the safe. It appeared untouched. Luke looked around.

"I need to check the back door while you make sure nothing's missing." In minutes he'd rejoined Pete. "Back door's fine. How about in here?"

"Everything looks just the way I left it."

"Good. Look, Pete, I'm not sure what's going on but keep a gun nearby. I'm not sure these thieves are done yet."

"Will do. Let me know what you find out about Rachel. I'll help search if need be."

"Thanks."

Luke headed down the street to the saloon, but Morgan had already left and was checking the back door of the general store.

"The bank's fine, Morgan. What'd you find?"

"Both back doors look like Doc's. If the footsteps and horse prints are any indication, they hit the saloon first, then this store, and ended up at Doc's." He shook his head. "Looks like you may be right about someone taking Rachel. Let's see if we can round up some men to help search the area. We gotta find that little girl."

The desire to pray skittered through Luke's mind. Just as quickly he shoved it aside. He'd find Rachel with or without God's help. And he'd start with Chad Baxter.

Morning light filtered through the dirty window, and Rachel had never been so relieved. Other than her patient moaning most of the night, she'd been undisturbed. If God deemed to answer her multitude of prayers with a yes, she'd be found today and wouldn't have to endure another sleepless and fear-filled night.

Tony moaned again. As she'd done several times during the night, Rachel swabbed his face and neck with cool water, comforting him enough to allow him to rest awhile longer. She lifted the covers and checked his bandages. Blood tinged the cloth but not enough to cause alarm. She covered him again and paced, stopping every so often to peer out the window.

The men had been stirring outside the door, and soon the smell of frying bacon drifted through the room. Her stomach protested its lack of food. Rachel hadn't touched the plate Quint had brought her the night before. Just before he had gone to bed, he came in to check on her and his son, removing the untouched plate of food as he left. Shortly after that, she heard the sound of something being dragged across the floor. She had visions of one of the men hauling a bed in front of the door to block any possibility of escape.

The dragging sounded again, and Quint entered the room moments later with yet another plate of food, this one with hot eggs, slabs of bacon, and bread. He held it out to Rachel. She took it and placed it on the table before turning back to him.

"I, um…I really need to, ah…"

Quint finally caught on and motioned with his head. "Come on."

They walked through the cabin past the men shoveling food into their mouths. A few paused to stare, but she ignored them. Quint led her outside, then around the side of the cabin to the privy.

"How's my son?"

"He's running a fever, but that's to be expected. He's lost a lot of blood. He's got quite a fight on his hands right now."

They arrived at the dilapidated privy, and Rachel quickly ducked inside. When she finally came back out, Quint stood leaning against the wall of the cabin tapping his toe. He wasted no time returning to her side.

"Will he live?"

"That's up to him. If he's a fighter, he's got a good chance."

"He's a fighter," Quint said.

"When will you take me home?" Rachel asked as she walked back to the cabin with him.

Quint paused only a moment. "You won't be going back home."

Rachel stopped walking. "Then why did you feel it necessary to cover my head on the way here?"

"If you tried to escape, you wouldn't know which way to go. And if you did manage to escape, you couldn't give anyone directions here."

"And what reason do you have for keeping me after your son is healed other than to give your men some entertainment?" Even as the words left her mouth, the thought made her sick to her stomach.

"You've seen our faces and heard some of our names. If you were to be released, you'd tell the law all you've learned, and don't try to deny you'd do just that."

"And if I gave my word not to say anything?"

Quint smiled. "I wouldn't believe you. After all, you're a woman. I haven't known one yet who could keep from pouring out lies."

"I haven't lied to you yet." Then she remembered the one she'd told about Jim not coming into work right away.

"Your fate's set, little lady. You might as well get used to the idea."

Rachel stared him down several seconds before she turned.

"Wait. I want your shoes."

"My shoes?"

"If by some miracle you get away, you won't get far without shoes." He stuck out his hand. "Take 'em off."

Rachel bent, unlaced her shoes, and kicked them off. Then she continued to the cabin without him. She yanked open the door and walked right through the men without a glance as she headed toward the back bedroom. Most of the men stood. One of them grabbed her arm and pulled her toward him.

Rachel shoved at his chest and then jerked her arm. "Let me go."

"Not on your life," the man said with a grin. "I'm going to have me a quick bit of fun before Quint gets back."

Several men chuckled and some cheered him on. The man hooked one arm behind her, pulling her hard against him while he grabbed at the front of her dress with his free hand. Rachel fought his every move. He only laughed at her efforts, revealing a mouthful of rotten teeth. She slapped at his face, then clawed at it, her nails digging deep.

The man touched his cheek and saw blood, and his expression changed to anger. His fist landed on her ear, and lights flashed in her eyes. Before she could recover, his other fist caught her on her mouth. She landed hard on the floor, then was yanked back to her feet.

The man grabbed her dress front by the collar and jerked. The material just started to tear when Quint's voice came like the crack of a whip.

"Buck!"

All movement stopped and the room became deathly quiet. Quint and Bear stood in the doorway.

"Let her go," Quint said with a growl.

Buck dropped his arms. Rachel fell to her knees. The room dimmed. She crawled toward the bedroom. Every inch of her trembled. She made it to the bedroom doorway and pulled to her feet. Her legs refused to move farther. She dabbed at her throbbing lip and found blood.

Quint ordered Bear to grab Buck. Buck ran for the door, but Bear stood in his way and grabbed him around the neck. The two scuffled and grunted awhile before Buck finally quit struggling.

Quint strode within inches of Buck. "What'd I say about touching the girl?"

"I couldn't help it, Quint. She smells so good."

Quint backhanded Buck. "Not good enough." He pulled his pistol.

"No, Quint! I won't do it again."

"That's right. You won't." Quint pointed his gun at every man in the cabin. "Let this be a lesson about disobeying me." He turned back to Buck. "You get a two second head start."

"No, Quint. I won't run."

"Then I'll drop you right here."

Buck whimpered, then raced out the door. Quint aimed. Rachel ran across the room and grabbed Quint's arm. He swung his gun hand and caught Rachel's eye. She collapsed. Quint glared.

"Stay out of this! It's not your affair."

Quint ran out the door. Seconds later, a gunshot echoed through the cabin. Quint returned and pointed at one of the men with the gun barrel.

"Go throw the body over the cliff."

As the man left, Rachel rose and ran into the bedroom, slamming the door behind her. She sank to the floor and sobbed as she held her swollen eye.

Quint's voice seeped through the door. "The next man that touches her before I say they can will suffer the same thing. I command nothing less than complete obedience. Is that clear?" There was some mumbling. "Good. Now sit down. It's time we discuss tomorrow night. It might be a little more dangerous now that we'll have to make do with only four men."

As boots shuffled on the floor, the bedroom door opened and Quint walked into the room. He squatted down. "Sorry about hitting you in the face, but I can't have you interfering with how I handle my men. Don't do it again." Quint rose to leave the room but turned back one more time. "Get up and check on my son." Then he was gone.

Rachel struggled to her feet. She added more bandages to what was already there and wrapped them tightly to Tony's shoulder. She checked to see that his fever hadn't grown worse, then sank down onto the chair and let out a shuddering breath.

"Lord, help me get out of here," she said in a whisper. "Once Quint's son wakes up, they'll do unspeakable things to me."

Quint's voice rose again. Rachel moved closer to the door to hear what he was saying. Then Quint's voice lowered and she could catch only a few words here and there, but it sounded as though they planned to rob a stagecoach. She never heard where, only that it would happen the next night.

That bit of news set Rachel's thoughts going again about how to escape. With a robbery going on, there wouldn't be but one or two men left behind to watch her. Her odds of escape just got better.

While Quint continued to talk to his men, Rachel started plotting. Her patient moaned, and she absently swabbed his face. If she made it through the night, she'd give her idea a try.

TWENTY-TWO

Luke Mason knocked on the last door, glad to be about finished with the task Morgan Taylor had given him. After knocking on the door of every business and home in town, he was ready to do something a little more practical, like start his search for Chad Baxter. If he proved to be innocent, Luke planned to seek out Mr. Michael Dunlavey. Surely one of the two knew something.

The door opened. "Yes?"

"Hello, Mrs. Chatham. I don't know if you've heard what happened, but—"

"You mean about the nurse disappearing? Only a little. Where do you think she went?"

"We're not sure, that's why we're checking with everyone in town, to see if they've seen or heard anything." He paused. "How did you find out about Miss Garrett?"

"Chad Baxter came by to see Cassie. He mentioned Rachel's disappearance."

"Is Chad still here?"

"Ah…" She turned to look at the salon. "I think—"

Luke stepped inside the house. "I'd really like to speak to him, Mrs. Chatham. I won't be long."

"Well, I guess that would be all right."

"In there?"

Luke didn't wait to be escorted. He'd been in this house often. Inside the salon, Chad and Cassie sat together on the sofa. Chad jumped to his feet, fists clenched.

"What're you doing here?"

"Well, Chad, I could ask you the same thing."

Cassie stood and moved between them. "That's no longer any of your business, Deputy."

Luke raised his brows. "You're right, but I still need to talk to Chad."

"Then do it when he's finished here."

"I don't have the time. We need to talk now. I think Chad knows why, since he's the one who told your mother about Miss Garrett."

"You mean Rachel? Whatever happened to her, we know nothing about it."

"We? You mean you two do everything together? Like maybe putting a rattlesnake in a medical bag?"

Chad looked from Cassie to Luke. "What? No. We didn't do that."

"No? Then maybe you know something about Rachel's disappearance."

"Of course not."

"Of course not." Luke moved toward him. "Tell me where she is, Chad."

"I don't know."

Luke reached past Cassie and grabbed Chad by the shirtfront. "Where is she?"

"I'm telling you, I don't know. I just heard about it a little while ago."

Luke searched Chad's eyes and found only fear. He turned him loose. "If I find out you're lying, there's no place you can hide."

He strode from the house, his hands shaking. He'd wanted to pound Chad into the floor. Now he wasn't so sure. He'd decide once he found Mr. Dunlavey.

An hour later, Luke determined Dunlavey was no longer in town. Did he take Rachel with him? He found Morgan near the church.

"I've knocked on every door," Luke said. "No one knows a thing. What's been happening? Anyone helping in the search?"

"Half the town. They're off in every direction. Not very organized, but at least they're looking. If we don't find her by the end of the day, we'll get more organized and try again in the morning."

The searchers straggled in at dusk, all of them dusty, tired, and empty-handed. Most promised to be back to help in the morning. Luke went home long enough to check on his mother and grab a bite to eat. Beside herself with worry, Sadie was still with Beth Barnes and had been asked to spend the night. Luke returned to the office and looked for any kind of map of the territory and found nothing.

He dropped into the chair and ran his hands over his face. Helpless. He hated the word and especially hated the feeling, and yet he sat smack in the middle of it. Luke grabbed a sheet of paper and started drawing a map of the area from memory. At the very least, he could use it to help organize the searchers in the morning, plus it would help him put his own thoughts in order.

Sheriff Taylor arrived in the morning looking much more rested than Luke felt, but he praised Luke's efforts with the map. Morgan took it with him outside and separated the men into groups, using Luke's map to show each group where to start their search.

Morgan whistled to get everyone's attention. "I don't know how many men there are or even if they're from around here, but plan on them being dangerous. If you don't have a gun, see me and I'll make sure you're armed before you go out."

"Make sure you know what you're shooting at before pulling the trigger," Luke said. "We don't want Miss Garrett getting hurt by accident."

Morgan nodded. "Better yet, if you think you've found her, send someone in your group for either me or Luke."

Luke mounted his horse to look in his assigned area, and he could feel frustration riding with him. There wasn't a doubt in his mind someone had taken Rachel, and he had no idea if he was headed in the right direction. He didn't dare think about what they might have done to her or he'd lose his mind. His heart pounded at the thought of her being hurt or frightened, and his anger burned toward whoever had done this.

Luke gave himself a mental shake, knowing he had to keep a level head during his search. Emotion had never been a good guide in his profession.

The remainder of Tuesday dragged for Rachel. Quint had been in to check on her a few times, escorting her outside when necessary. He stared at her each time he entered the room. The last time he'd been in, he left the bedroom door open and didn't close it again until the men were ready to turn in for the night.

Quint's son was recovering faster than Rachel expected. Still very weak from blood loss, he slept the entire day, but his fever hadn't gotten any worse. Early the next morning, he opened his eyes and Rachel offered him some water. He managed a few small sips, then dropped off to sleep again.

About an hour later, Quint entered with yet another plate of food. "How is he?"

"Better. He woke up for a couple minutes early this morning."

"Why didn't you come and get me?"

"He was only awake long enough to take a sip of water. He's still running a bit of a fever and is pretty weak."

Quint stared at his son. "How soon can he travel?"

"You can't move him. It'd kill him."

"How soon?"

She glanced at Tony. "A week. Maybe more. A lot depends on him."

Quint took a deep breath and nodded. "You hungry yet?"

Rachel shook her head. Quint gave her a hard stare.

"Eat some of this." He set the plate on the small table. "I don't need no weak and fainting woman on my hands. I'll take you outside after you eat."

Quint left the door open again and tucked into his own breakfast. With shaking hands, she picked up the plate and managed a few bites. The food churned. She looked out the door. Quint was watching. She forced down a bit more, then had to set the plate aside before she lost what she'd eaten.

Minutes later, Quint led her out. She winced with each step, her feet getting more sore with each trip outside.

"Can I have my shoes?"

"You know better."

Rachel didn't try to argue. Since he'd shot Buck, Quint had grown hard and cold and much scarier than before. Back inside the bedroom, Rachel checked on Tony for Quint's sake, then nursed her tender feet.

She counted the minutes to the time Quint and his men would leave. The idea that someone would be robbed didn't sit well, but it would likely be the only chance she'd get to escape. Rachel spent a bit of time asking God for wisdom, protection, and guidance in her attempt to get away. But concentrating on her prayer wasn't easy, both because of nervousness and because she was confused about why God had allowed this to happen. While she tried again to focus her prayers, asking God to help her not to doubt Him, Quint entered.

"Your God can't help you, Rachel. You're here till *I* say otherwise. Your time is better spent taking care of Tony."

Rachel only stared at him without expression.

He shook his head and shrugged. "Some of the men and I will

be out for a while tonight. But I'm leaving Owen and Clark behind, so don't think you can get away."

After several horses left at a gallop, Rachel waited about half an hour, said a quick prayer, took a deep breath, and entered the main part of the cabin to face Owen and Clark.

❋ TWENTY-THREE ❋

Rachel entered the kitchen without so much as a glance in the men's direction. She opened every cabinet and dug around in all the drawers. There wasn't much as far as pots and utensils. She'd have to make do.

"What do you want?"

Rachel finally turned. Only one man sat inside the cabin. "Who are you?"

"Owen. And you haven't answered my question."

She paused, hoping to calm her pounding heart. "I finally got hungry. I was going to make some supper." Rachel turned her back to the man as she spoke, trying to keep her voice normal. "I don't see any meat. Do you have any around here?"

"Clark's out skinning a rabbit. He'll be in shortly." He pushed his chair back from the table. "Quint warned me you might try something while he was gone. If you're smart, you'll behave. I have permission to stop you any way I need to."

Rachel motioned to her feet. "Where am I going without shoes?"

She lifted the lid to a small bin, saw potatoes inside, and grabbed several.

"You gonna make enough for us too?"

After turning to stare at him for several moments, she finally nodded.

"I guess I can do that. Do you know if there are any carrots or some other vegetables around here?"

Owen pointed. "All we have is in that cabinet off to your left."

Rachel nodded and turned back to begin the meal. She hadn't expected the cabin to be so well-stocked, but now she'd be able to prepare a stew her captors couldn't resist. With every move she made, she could feel Owen's eyes on her. She hoped she wouldn't have to try to fight him off.

"Why aren't you afraid of me?"

She didn't turn around but answered truthfully. "I am. But Quint seems to trust that you'll obey him, so I decided I would too."

Clark came in then with the skinned and cleaned rabbit dangling from his hand. He stopped in his tracks when he saw Rachel. She returned his stare. His gaze moved to Owen, who shrugged.

"Give her the rabbit."

Rachel washed the meat, then cut it into pieces. Then it was time for the next step in her plan.

"This rabbit seems a bit tough. Cooking tough meat in whiskey helps to make it tender. Do you happen to have any around here?"

Perspiration broke out as she waited for their answer. Owen eyed her for a moment before he stood to open one of the cabinet doors over her head. He handed a bottle to her without a word, then returned to the table. He watched her pour some whiskey into the pot. After a few minutes, Owen lost interest and asked Clark if he wanted to play some cards.

For the next several minutes, Rachel continued with her cooking before taking her plan to the next step. She grabbed the bottle, carefully placed her tongue over the opening, and pretended to take a drink. She grimaced at the smell as well as the lingering taste on her tongue. She had to do it a second time, coughing and sputtering, to get the men's attention.

"What are you doing, lady?" Owen stood, shoving his chair back.

Rachel glanced over her shoulder before turning back to the

stove. "If you were in my position, Owen, wouldn't you want a drink?"

Several seconds passed before she heard the big man chuckle and walk up behind her. "Quint said you were probably a feisty one."

He reached for the whiskey, but Rachel grabbed the bottle before he could touch it.

"Get your own bottle."

She spoke with just the slightest slur. Owen turned toward Clark and laughed outright. He reached up and took down a full bottle, then returned to the table and settled down with shots of whiskey along with their card game. Rachel tossed a glance heavenward, saying a quiet thank you, then pretended to take another drink.

Amazed at how much alcohol the men could consume, Rachel kept dumping more whiskey into the pot to make it look as though she'd had just as much. Several minutes later, she fed them their meal, liberally laced with the whiskey in both the meat and the gravy. They didn't seem to notice as they shoveled the food into their mouths and washed it down with even more whiskey. Since she didn't sit with the men, neither was aware that she hadn't taken a bite of the food on her plate, though she continued her pretext of drinking from her own bottle.

The men drank and played cards close to another hour before they appeared ready to pass out. To Rachel, it felt like a lifetime. She had cleaned up the kitchen, dropping things now and then and giggling each time to appear drunk. When finished, she announced she was going to bed, leaving the door open enough to be able to peek out. Once she heard a loud thump on the floor, she knew it was time to go.

She stole a look through the crack in the door and saw not only their bottle lying empty, but also the one she'd been using. Both men were snoring, one with his head on the table and one on a worn-out couch.

She stepped out of the bedroom and turned to close the door as she'd left it. She tiptoed through the cabin, stopping when she saw that one of the men had shed his boots. Without hesitation, she sat and slid her feet into the boots.

After one more glance at the men, she opened the door just enough to slip through, thankful that the hinges didn't make any noise. Then she pulled it almost closed, unwilling to latch it for fear it would make a sound.

Rachel glanced around, then scooted behind the cabin toward the lake. In all the hours of gazing out the window, she'd noticed what appeared to be a small ravine leading away from the cabin. If she followed it downstream, she felt certain it would lead her to some kind of help, hopefully a home or a town.

Once she found the ravine, she ran as fast as the darkness and loose boots allowed. With each step, she prayed she'd remain free. She stopped now and then to listen for horses or voices before again running as fast as she could. She wasn't sure if the pounding of her heart was from the fear of being caught or from the exertion of running after going days with little food or sleep.

Bushes, vines, and scrub brush grabbed at her skirt, slowing her progress. The undergrowth tripped her often. Many times she lost her balance and fell. It wasn't long before her hands and knees screamed with pain as they took the brunt of the falls. Part of her wished for more moonlight so she could see better, but more light would give her captors the same advantage.

Another bush grabbed her, this one with long spikes that cut her hands, arms, and face as she fought to get loose. Her dress tore as she yanked free. Her skin stung from the cuts and scratches, but no way would she allow pain to slow her. Lack of sleep and nutrition was doing enough of that already. She'd stopped too often to catch her breath, but without the rest, she knew she wouldn't make it far enough from the cabin to keep the men from finding her.

Rachel dropped onto a large flat rock as she leaned against a tree near the water. The way she panted, it felt as though she had been running for days. Thoughts of her parents washed through her mind, and she wished that she could feel safe in their loving arms.

She didn't dwell there long. A noise like footfalls made her duck behind the tree. A deer trotted past, and the breath she had been holding came out in a gust of relief, scaring the animal into a run. Rachel's own scare put her feet into motion again, unwilling to rest until she got farther this time.

Time passed in a blur. Chest aching, Rachel stopped and dropped to her knees. She looked around and realized dim light gleamed ahead of her. The night had seemed to last forever, but now, seeing the first fingers of dawn approaching, it hadn't lasted long enough. She hadn't run far enough to keep from being found. No more rests. She needed to gain much more ground before the sun was all the way up.

Horrified at how fast the sun was rising, Rachel urged her feet to move faster. Minutes later, she ran out of the trees and into an open valley. She dropped to her knees and crawled along to keep from being seen. She raised her head and looked around for any sign of people or civilization. Seeing none, she continued crawling along the stream until the bank on each side rose. Limbs trembling and almost out of strength, she sought a good place to hide. She couldn't go much farther without some sleep.

Rachel crossed the stream where it was shallow and walked back to where there was a rocky overhang with tall grass growing over and around the opening to a crevice. As she crawled up under the overhang, the sound of hoofbeats thundered across the glade. Tears threatened. She moved as far back under the overhang as she possibly could and prayed yet again for God's protection.

TWENTY-FOUR

Luke Mason awoke Wednesday morning with a start. He swung his feet over the side of the bed and took several deep breaths to slow his heartbeat. He had to find Rachel today. Another nightmare like this last one and he wouldn't allow himself to fall asleep again.

The frightening dream of finding Rachel's body floating in a stream haunted him as he dressed and strode outside to saddle his horse. He focused on the stream. A small ravine flowed about a mile the other side of the Manning sisters' place. He didn't think anyone had looked for Rachel there yet. Sure, it was quite a distance from town, but he wasn't ready to rule out any area. After he let Morgan Taylor know his thoughts, he'd start there first thing.

It wasn't even daylight yet when he left the sheriff's office and set out toward the mountains at a trot, unwilling to risk his horse falling in a hole and hurting a leg. He'd ridden for close to an hour and stopped at the top of a butte to look over the valley below. He scanned the grassy valley and was about to give up and ride farther into the mountains, but movement caught his eye.

Luke leaned forward and squinted. Sure enough. The top of a head moved through the grass next to a small stream. He eased his horse down the side of the butte, then spurred it into a gallop toward the stream.

Before his horse came to a stop, Luke dismounted and ran to the top of the embankment. No sign of Rachel. No sign of anyone. He slid to the bottom of the bank and walked along the edge of the stream. Bootprints scuffed the mud. Too big to be a woman's, and Rachel didn't wear boots. He followed the tracks until they disappeared under a grassy overhang.

Luke lifted the grass and peered into the gloom. "Hello?" He reached into the dark and felt a crevice. "Hello?"

He scooted farther under the overhang and reached as far as he could. His hand touched something odd and he pulled back. He took a breath and shoved his hand in again. What felt like material brushed his hand. He grabbed a fistful and tugged.

A scream pierced his ears. A boot kicked him in the face and continued pounding at him. He grabbed at one of the legs and found bare skin. He pulled his hand back as if he'd been stung.

"Rachel! Is that you?" A whimper answered. "Rachel! It's me, Luke. Please come out of there."

"Luke?"

The name came in a whisper. He closed his eyes with relief.

"Yes, it's Luke. Come on out."

Ever so slowly, Rachel inched toward him. Boots were the first thing to appear followed by a torn and filthy skirt. When he saw her hand, he grasped it in his and helped her slide out of her hiding place.

He almost didn't recognize the bedraggled woman who stepped into the open. Her filthy hair hung in limp strands over her mud-streaked face. He pulled her into his embrace and held her close. Rachel wrapped her arms around his neck and buried her head into his shoulder.

As she sobbed, he bent close to her ear. "It's all right, Rachel. I have you now. I'll get you home."

He scooped her into his arms. She weighed almost nothing. The boots slid from her feet. He carried her to his horse, glancing around the area for movement or other riders. Then he mounted and wheeled his horse toward home.

Rachel's head dropped against his chest. He looked down. Her eyes were closed and tears streaked down her cheeks and temples. One eye was bruised and swollen, and her lip had been split. He pulled her closer.

Oh Rae, what did they do to you?

His throat ached as he fought tears. He dropped a kiss on her forehead. Even with the dirt all over her face and the grass and twigs tangled in her hair, she'd never looked more beautiful.

The ride back took almost two hours. Rachel woke twice after moaning and flailing her arms and legs. He almost dropped her the first time, but he managed to soothe her into falling back to sleep each time. As he approached the doctor's house, his mother and Beth Barnes were sitting on the porch. The moment they saw him they raced toward him. Beth stopped long enough to turn back to her daughter.

"Emma, honey, run inside and get your daddy."

Luke's arms were shaking. He decided to wait for Jim before dismounting. He didn't wait long. Jim came at a run. Luke handed Rachel to him and followed them inside to the clinic.

Beth had gone into the clinic but came back out. "Sadie—"

Sadie raised her hand. "I've got the kids. Go take care of Rachel."

Luke trailed Beth inside.

"Help me get her dress off."

When Luke heard Jim say that to Beth, he backed out of the room but stayed close to the door. He didn't want to miss a word they said.

"A weak pulse and pallid skin. What in the world happened to her?" Jim sounded worried.

"We need to clean her up so we can see the wounds better," Beth said.

"Right." Jim appeared in the doorway. "I'll send Sadie in to help you and take the kids to Pastor and Garnett Robbins to see if they can watch them for a while." He motioned to Luke. "Walk with me. I have questions."

"I need to let the sheriff know I found her."

"Can it wait a little longer?"

Luke blew out a breath. "Sure."

The questions waited until the children had been left with the pastor, then Jim unloaded. "Was she unconscious when you found her?"

"No. I saw her climb into a hole near a stream. When I tried to get her out, she fought me pretty hard."

"That how you got that bruise on your cheek?"

Luke reached to touch it and smiled. "Her boot caught me before I could stop it."

"Her boot? She wasn't wearing any shoes when you brought her in. In fact, her feet looked pretty beat up."

"She was wearing men's boots. When I picked her up, they fell off. I didn't bother retrieving them. But maybe I should go back and get them. Who knows? Maybe there's something on them that will help us figure out who they belong to."

"Won't hurt to check. Did Rachel say anything when you found her?"

"Not a word. Just fell into my arms and cried. Then she fell asleep." Luke walked along in silence, then had to ask the question uppermost on his mind. "Is she gonna be all right, Doc?"

"I think so. I'll know more after I get back, but I think rest is what she needs most."

"Good. I need to check in with Morgan, but I'll be back as soon as possible. We'll need to talk to her as soon as she's able."

Something pulled at Rachel. She just wanted to sleep. Tired. So tired.

Then she was cold. Someone had removed her covers. The men! They were finally taking what they wanted!

Rachel started flinging her fists as she screamed. "No! Stop!"

"Rachel!"

Her hands were grabbed. She tugged to free herself, then started kicking.

"Rachel, stop. It's us. It's Beth and Jim."

She stopped fighting and opened her eyes. The faces were blurry. She blinked several times. "Beth?"

Beth cupped her cheek. "That's right. You're safe now."

Rachel sat up in bed and was enveloped in arms. She had no control of her tears. They always seemed at the ready. But at least this time they were good tears. Once her head hit the pillow again, she wanted nothing but more sleep. Her lids fell closed.

"We have some questions for you, Miss Garrett."

Her eyes flew open at the man's voice. A badge gleamed above Beth's head.

"Do you feel up to answering them?"

No. "I'll try."

She looked around the room and saw Luke at the foot of the bed. He gave her a slight smile.

"Welcome home, Rachel."

There were those tears again. She let them run down her temples. Her lips trembled. "Thank you, Luke. Thank you for finding me."

He only nodded.

"Who took you, Rachel?" The sheriff took a step closer. "Do you know who it was?"

"No. I'd never seen them before."

"Them?"

"There were five of them. They were already inside the office when I entered."

"Why'd they take you?"

She hesitated and glanced at Beth, then Jim. "They needed a doctor."

"Then why didn't they wait for me?" Jim said. "Why'd they take you instead?"

"I told them you wouldn't be in for several hours."

Beth squeezed her hand. "Why would you do that?"

She just wanted to sleep. Why couldn't they do this later?

"Rachel?" Jim stood over her. "Why'd you tell them that?"

She fought to keep her eyes open. "I had to make a lot of quick decisions, Jim. When I think about them now after all that's happened, I believe I'd do the same thing again." She scooted up in bed to help her stay awake. "The first thought that flashed through my mind was that if they waited for you, they wouldn't need me, which meant they'd either kill me or just bring me along for their entertainment.

"I also thought you have a family to raise and I don't. And this town needs a doctor worse than it needs a nurse. So I told them you weren't coming in until much later. They would have killed you when they were through with you, Jim. They had no intention of letting me go. They even said as much."

He leaned down to squeeze her arm. "That was brave of you, Rachel. Foolish but brave. I just hate that you went through this."

"I know."

"Why did they need a doctor?"

"Gunshot wound. Quint's son had been shot."

"Quint?"

"The leader of the group."

"Were you able to save the son?"

Rachel nodded, smiling slightly.

"Do you think he'll make it?"

"As long as they don't try to move him. He was doing much better when I made my escape. I'm just afraid they'll risk leaving since I got away and all the movement will start him bleeding again."

Luke cleared his throat and her eyes went to him. "We need to get back to the group that took you. Would you tell us everything that happened?"

"I'll try." Her eyelids were so heavy. She wiggled a little further up on the pillow and pushed on. "As soon as I walked in the office door, I was grabbed and hauled inside. Quint had his hand over my mouth so I couldn't scream and only let me go when I promised to be quiet. When I told him Jim wouldn't be in, he asked if I could treat a gunshot wound. Then he dragged me outside, put a sack over my head, and put me on a horse."

"You didn't get to see where they took you?" Disappointment laced Luke's voice.

"No."

"But they took you into the mountains?"

"Yes. I'm sure of that because it almost always felt like we were going up, some places rather steeply. And when I escaped, I was always running downhill. But I have no idea what direction we went."

"Do you know about how long you were riding?"

"Forever." She tried to smile. "It seemed like a long time, but I'd guess around two hours or so." She closed her eyes as she remembered. "The cabin was almost completely surrounded by tall trees. It'd be hard to find unless you knew it was there." She opened her eyes and shook her head. "That thought didn't make me feel much better about my situation. Especially when I found out there were two more men inside."

"So there's seven men altogether, if we don't include the wounded son?"

"Was. Quint killed one for disobeying him. He had one of the men throw the body over a cliff."

"If there were so many men, how'd you manage to get away?" Morgan said.

"Three reasons I got away. God, whiskey, and plans to rob a stage-coach." Her mind felt as though she'd just finished one of those bottles of whiskey, she was so lightheaded.

"Whiskey and robbery?" Luke said.

She nodded. "I heard Quint telling the men about a stagecoach carrying a chest of money, and they were going to steal it."

"Where?"

"Quint started talking lower so I didn't get to hear much. But as he made his plans, I started making mine."

Beth shook her head. "But with whiskey? You don't drink that stuff."

"No, and I still don't. But in all my trips through the main room, I saw several whiskey bottles. I thought if I could get the men left behind to watch me to start drinking, they might pass out so I could sneak out. And it worked."

Rachel spent the next several minutes telling her audience about cooking a rabbit in whiskey and pretending to drink some of the liquid. There were several chuckles as she described her slurring of words and acting tipsy in an attempt to make the men think she was drunk. Rachel even managed to laugh about it.

"When I was sure they had passed out, I slipped from the cabin, found a stream, and followed it down out of the mountains."

Luke tapped the bedpost. "So I guess the boots you were wearing belonged to one of them?"

"Yes. Quint took my shoes so if I happened to escape, I wouldn't get far. As I left, I noticed one of the men had kicked off his boots, so I took them. They didn't fit well and I struggled to keep them on my feet, but at least the ground didn't tear up my feet."

Luke leaned forward. "Hold on. You said you followed a stream all the way down the mountain from the cabin?"

"Yes. It started at the small lake right behind the cabin."

Luke looked at Morgan. "If we follow that stream up the mountain, we can find that cabin."

The two men were out the door in seconds.

Jim moved to the other side of the bed and placed his hand on her forehead. "No fever." His hand moved to her wrist. "Strong. You're one tough little lady."

"I don't feel so tough. That was a rough trip."

"All those cuts, scrapes, and bruises prove that."

She grunted as she again fought to keep her eyes open. "There was very little moonlight to see by. Every time I tried to run faster, if the boots didn't trip me up, something else would and I'd take a tumble. I've never felt so clumsy. Plus I was weak from lack of food and sleep."

"They didn't let you eat or sleep?" Jim said.

Her eyes dropped shut as she shook her head. "They wanted me to eat, but I was so scared and nervous, my stomach rebelled. And I didn't trust the men enough to allow myself to fall asleep."

Beth took Rachel's hand in hers. "I know this might be a difficult question, Rachel, but did they do anything to you?"

She opened her eyes to look at Beth, then shook her head. "No, but some tried. Quint ordered them not to touch me until his son was well. That's the reason Quint killed that one man. He disobeyed."

Sadie moved next to Beth and leaned down to kiss Rachel's forehead. "I'm so happy you're back with us and all right. Don't fall asleep yet. I'm going to fix you a little something to put in your stomach." Rachel opened her mouth, but Sadie held up her hand. "Don't argue, dear. You won't win."

Sadie hurried from the room, and Beth tapped her finger next to Rachel's eye. "Is that how you got the black eye and busted lip?"

"Buck punched me when I scratched his face, and Quint hit me when I tried to stop him from killing Buck." Her eyes drifted closed and she took a deep breath. "I don't understand men like that. I hope Luke and the sheriff don't get hurt. Those men won't think twice about killing them."

"Then let's pray for them right now."

Jim's deep voice was quiet as he led the prayer, and the gentle drone lulled her to sleep.

❋ TWENTY-FIVE ❋

Luke Mason led Sheriff Morgan Taylor to the place he found Rachel, then they rode along the stream, following it up into the mountains as Rachel had described. Several times they had to ride away from the stream a short distance because the growth was too thick. Luke's mind wandered to Rachel and what she went through as she ran from her captors. To fight her way through the thick brush was bad enough, and his admiration of her grew with each step. He hoped the brush and brambles were all she had to fight off.

They rode over three hours before they came upon a small lake. Luke reined to a stop. "This has to be the lake Rachel described."

"I agree. Let's tie the horses back here. We don't want to risk being seen."

They dismounted, tied their horses to some branches, and pulled their rifles from their scabbards. Then staying within the cover of the trees, they followed the edge of the lake until they spotted the cabin. Luke knew a moment of disappointment when he didn't see any horses.

"No horses. You think they left?"

"Not sure. Maybe they're tied on the other side. Let's get closer."

They stole around the edge of the trees to the other side of the cabin. Still no horses.

"They may keep the horses farther away and we just missed them,"

Morgan said. "We still need to see if they're inside. Go to that side. When you're there, I'll holler and see what happens."

Luke made his way to the spot Morgan indicated, then aimed his rifle at the cabin when Morgan cupped his free hand to his mouth.

"You in the cabin, come out with your hands up." He waited several moments and shouted again. Still no movement or reply.

Morgan shot in the air one time. Nothing happened. He rose from his hiding place and approached the cabin. Luke did the same. They met at the front door. Morgan grabbed the latch and gave the door a push. They rushed inside. The place was empty. By the mess in the cabin, they had left in a hurry. Several spots of blood dotted the floor.

Luke and Morgan took their time going through the cabin looking for any clues to where the men had been or what direction they might be headed. The men had been thorough before they left. They took everything, even the food and whiskey they'd stolen. The only things Luke and Morgan found were evidence that Rachel had been there. Bloody rags were everywhere. The medical bag lay on the floor of the bedroom, its contents falling out in disarray. Luke bent and scooped the tools inside before picking up the bag.

Morgan motioned Luke to join him outside. "Let's see if we can find that body. Maybe we can link him to one of our wanted posters."

They both examined the edge of the cliff and even thought they might have found the spot where he'd been tossed. But after looking for several more minutes, Morgan shook his head.

"It's getting late. Let's head home before they end up getting the drop on us instead of the other way around. At the very least, we know where one of the hiding places is for this bunch of thieves. I doubt they'll be back anytime soon, but we can keep an eye on it."

Luke hated leaving empty-handed. A man as evil as Quint might want revenge, or at the very least he might try to get rid of Rachel as a witness. Luke had to stop him before either of those things happened.

Rachel woke with a start. Voices drifted into the room. A quick glance around reminded her she was safe. Beth Barnes sat in the chair next to the bed and smiled.

"Feel any better?"

"How long was I out?"

"All the rest of yesterday and all night. You know you upset Sadie for not staying up long enough to eat."

She yawned and snuggled deeper into the pillow. "I'll apologize later."

"I think she understood how tired you were. Besides, she's been busy entertaining all the people who've come to see you."

"I've had company?"

"None who've made it past Sadie. She's very protective of you."

Rachel smiled. "I guess I'll have to thank her later too."

Beth squeezed her hand. "Right now, I'm just thanking God for bringing you back to us."

Rachel adjusted her covers, glanced at the window, then the door, anywhere but at Beth.

Beth moved to sit on the side of the bed and leaned to look into her eyes. "Are you doubting God, Rachel?"

"No. A little. I don't know." Rachel stopped as her eyes filled with tears. "Why, Beth? Why did He let this happen? I was so scared."

Beth pulled Rachel into her arms when she began to sob, and the two women cried together. When their crying subsided, Beth laid her back against the pillows and took one of her hands in her own.

"I can't say that I know why this happened or even that I understand it. But you can't lose your faith in God because of it. Let it make your faith stronger." Beth sat silent for a few moments, then she pulled a Bible from the bedside table. "Remember Joseph and Job and Daniel and his three friends. I know you know their stories, Rachel."

Rachel gave a slight nod. She could use all the help she could get. Lack of trust didn't feel good, but the doubts continued to haunt.

"Even the blameless and faithful have bad things happen to them," Beth said. "But God rewards those who remain faithful through those bad times. I'm not exactly sure why each one of those men went through what they did, other than to be used as examples for us, to help us remain faithful through our difficult times. But Rachel, God brought you out safely, just as He did Joseph, Daniel, and his friends. Don't let Satan win this battle and make you doubt God. Let this experience help you grow stronger in your faith."

Rachel squeezed Beth's hand before smiling and closing her eyes. "You know, several verses about God's strength and promise of help went through my mind while I was being held captive, but I guess I didn't hold tight enough to them. Thank you for the reminder, Beth."

"You're welcome."

"And you're going to eat this before you fall asleep again." Sadie Mason moved from the doorway with a tray in her hands.

Rachel gave her a tired smile. "Hi, Sadie."

"My dear girl." Sadie set the tray on the table and sat on the bedside when Beth stood and left the room. "It's so good to have you back home again." She bent over and kissed Rachel on the forehead, then leaned back and peered into Rachel's eyes. "You still look so tired."

"I am. I'm starting to wonder if I'll ever get enough rest."

"Yes, well I'll let you get more once you eat every bite of this stew."

With a laugh, Rachel scooted up in bed and did as ordered. She didn't think she'd ever tasted food so good. She scraped the spoon against the bowl and savored the last bite.

Sadie took the bowl from her. "There's still a whole pot left. Would you like me to bring it in?"

"Don't tempt me."

Sadie's brows went up. "Goodness. You eat all that and you'll be worse than a tick on a dog."

Rachel slid lower in the bed, ready for more sleep. "That's a pleasant thought as I go back to sleep."

Sadie tucked the covers up to her neck. "I aim to please."

"She sure does." Luke tapped on the door as he entered. "She's been pleasing me for years." He moved to Sadie's side, put his arm around her shoulders, and gave her a squeeze. "You gonna let me question her now or am I going to be sent from her room again?"

Sadie made a face before smiling. "He's been wanting to ask you a few more questions, and I haven't let him wake you. Do you feel up to it, Rachel?"

"I'll try. Anything to help."

Sadie narrowed her eyes at Rachel. "Don't you let him tire you too much. I don't want to have to get after both of you. One child is enough."

She exited the room with the tray, leaving Rachel alone with Luke. He'd never looked so wonderful. She'd always thought him handsome, but now something had changed. More masculine. More…something.

"You sure sleep a lot."

"Only because they forced me to." Rachel had tried to sound upset, but the yawn that escaped messed up her plans.

Luke motioned to the chair. "May I?"

She nodded. As he sat, he produced her medical bag from behind his back.

"My bag!" She accepted it from him and took a quick peek at the tools inside. "I guess this means you found the place. Were the men still there? Did you get them?"

"No, but then we really didn't think they would be because of your escape. But at least now we know of the place. You were right. It was very well hidden. I thought about bringing your whiskey bottle back for you, but I didn't want to take the chance of it breaking on the way home."

Rachel shook her finger at him. "Thanks for the thought, but

I don't need any mementos of my time there. But thank you for returning my bag."

"My pleasure." He rested his forearms on his knees. "Do you really feel up to more questions or would you rather wait?"

"I'm all right."

"Good. First of all, did you catch any of the men's last names? Anything that will help us identify them?"

"No. At least not that I can remember. They only used first names or nicknames."

"I was afraid of that. Would you be willing to look at some wanted posters when you're feeling up to it?"

"I can either go to your office or you can bring them here. Whichever you prefer."

"Don't get in too big of a hurry. I don't want you to get sick. Mother would have my head."

Luke slapped his legs and started to stand, but then sat again. "One more thing. Just how bad was the man that was shot? I mean, since they had to move him, would they get far before they had to stop or was he well enough to make a long trip?"

"He was pretty weak from loss of blood. I can't imagine they'd get far with him if they wanted him to live, unless they had him on some kind of carrier or something."

"We didn't see any sign of a wagon or carrier. Only horse tracks."

"Then he's either dead or they're still nearby."

Luke nodded. "That's what I thought too."

He stared at her face for several moments. "How are you, Rae? And I don't want your standard 'fine' either. I had a pretty good indication of what you went through, both in the cabin and your trek down the mountain. Neither one looked easy."

Rachel smiled at the way he shortened her name. Only her parents and brother had ever called her Rae. "I really am fine. I went through a tough time when I first woke up, but Beth helped me through that."

"I heard Beth tell Jim that you had doubted God." He tilted his head. "But you don't now?"

"I was wrong to doubt Him. He was with me the entire time. I knew that then and I know it now. I was just upset that I had to go through such an ordeal at all."

Luke shook his head as he stared. "How can you forgive God when He claims to love you yet can put you through something so horrible?"

The anger in his voice made her soften hers. "I don't need to forgive Him because He's never wrong. And besides, I deserve so much worse because of my sins. I don't know why I went through that, Luke, but God had a reason. I'm just thankful that He brought me home safely."

Luke let out a loud angry sigh and stood.

Rachel reached out to him. "Please don't go."

He examined her face, then sat back down, but his nostrils flared. "God didn't bring you home, Rachel. I did."

She prayed for the right words and took a deep breath. "The countryside out there is pretty big, wouldn't you say?" She waited for him to respond, which he did with a grudging nod. "If it's that vast, how do you think you managed to find me?" Rachel let that sink in for a moment. "God led you to me, Luke. You were only the instrument He used to bring me home. And I thank you for being obedient to His will."

Luke's eyes blazed again. She reached her hand toward him and held it there until he took it in his. She grasped it tight. "Why are you so angry, Luke?"

With a quiet sigh, Luke gave a slight shake of his head. "You've just been through something awful, Rae, and you ought to hate God. You don't and that's great for you. But God took my father when I needed him most, and I can never forgive Him for that."

"The man I see in front of me is strong, honest, hard-working, kind, and fair. From what I can see, your father did his job. He raised and trained an incredible man, and then God took him home. You may feel you needed him, but evidently God didn't feel the same way."

Tears gleamed from the corners of his eyes as he stared at their hands. "But I was only fifteen. We had so much fun together, and I relied on him for everything."

She leaned a little farther and rested her hand on his knee.

"Maybe it was time for that young man to start relying on his heavenly Father instead of his earthly one." Rachel paused for a moment and Luke's eyes moved to hers. "Luke, God still loves you. He always has and He's never left you. In your anger, you turned your back on Him and tried to run from Him, but He's still right here with you, just waiting with open arms for you to turn back to Him. And the great thing is, you don't have to run all the way back because God is right here. You have only to turn around."

He released her hand and stood. "I've got to go."

"Luke!"

He stopped but didn't turn around. "I need to think, Rae. I'll be back to check on you later."

And then he was gone. Rachel felt like crying. She fell back against the pillows and asked God to help Luke through his struggle.

❖ TWENTY-SIX ❖

Rachel made it to Beth Barnes's kitchen on shaky legs and sat at the table for supper. She had just finished eating when Pastor and Garnett Robbins entered the kitchen door with Emma and Tanner. Emma crossed the room and stood in front of Rachel with her hands on her hips, looking every bit like her mother when she scolded someone. Rachel eyed her with as straight a face as she could muster.

"Where you been? You didn't tell me you were leaving. You didn't even say good-bye. You just left."

Rachel pulled Emma into her arms. "I missed you too, Emma, and I'm sorry about leaving without saying good-bye. I'll try to never let that happen again. All right?"

The little girl nodded before wrapping her arms around Rachel's neck and planting a kiss on her cheek.

Tanner approached, and Rachel pulled the little boy onto her lap before getting a hug from him. The pastor and his wife had waited patiently to welcome Rachel home, and they gave her hugs and kisses as well. Rachel choked up at the thought of how much she had come to love everyone in the room. She sent a silent thanks to God for His blessings.

Emma spied the cake on the table and hopped down from Rachel's lap to ask her mother for a piece. Tanner reached up and rubbed

Rachel's earlobe while popping his thumb into his mouth. Rachel couldn't think of a better way to end the day.

The warm feeling continued through the next several days as many of the town's residents dropped by to make sure she was all right. She'd come to love Rockdale and all its residents, and it seemed the feeling was mutual.

On Sunday, with the threat of rain looming, parents and children alike greeted her in the church yard. After she accepted an embrace from Max Payton, William Baxter ran up to her and gave her a hug.

"Do you have a lesson for us today?"

Rachel bent close to his face. "Would you like me to do another lesson, William?"

When he nodded, Rachel agreed, and the rest of the children cheered. She grinned at Beth Barnes and asked her to hold her Bible.

"All right, everyone, get into a line and follow me. You have to do everything I do and say everything I say."

When all the children were lined up behind her, Rachel walked away from the church, then started skipping. She looked back to make sure the children were all following the rules, then she swung her arms around in circles. She led them in circles, cutting through the line behind her, causing chaos and much laughter.

Then Rachel squatted while walking, flapping her arms, and quacking like a duck. The children followed right along, eliciting laughter from the watching adults. Rachel smiled in their direction and suddenly stopped. The closest children ran into her. But that didn't make her look away from Luke Mason, who stood with his mother and Mr. Payton. He wore an amused look on his face. Face flaming, Rachel led the children to the stump she always sat on for her lessons.

"Did you enjoy that?" Rachel received an enthusiastic yes. "Was

I a good leader?" She laughed when she heard a mixture of answers. "Finding a good leader to follow can be difficult. It's great when your leader has you do fun and happy things, but some leaders can make us do bad or harmful things. We have to be very careful about the leaders we choose to follow so they won't lead us into danger or evil. A good leader will be with us through everything and not run away at the first sign of trouble."

She leaned down and looked each child in the eyes.

"But who is the best leader for us to follow?" Rachel paused until she heard the answer she was waiting for. "That's right, Laura. Jesus is our best leader. God would never lead us into danger or tempt us to do something wrong, nor will He leave us when we find ourselves in trouble. We can trust Him to be a good leader because He would never lead us astray. And what did He give us for a guide?" Again she waited until she heard the right answer. "That's right! God gave us His Word, the Bible, and all we need to do is read and study it to know what is right and wrong. He calls for us to follow Him. Let's try to do that every day."

The children stood and hugged Rachel before running off to find their parents. Everyone hurried inside as the gray sky released the rain it'd been holding. She joined Jim and Beth, though her eyes kept wandering to Luke. Rachel sat and tried to listen to Pastor Robbins's message about the prodigal son, but Luke ended up being her focus until she'd missed most of the sermon.

"Brothers and sisters in Christ," Pastor Robbins concluded, "how many of us have taken the free gift from God for granted and run from Him? So many of us have been like that son and turned our back on the One who loves us. But just like that father running to welcome back his wayward son, our heavenly Father is waiting for us to come home to Him. Don't wait until you have almost starved yourself from His loving care. Turn back to the One who loves you unconditionally, and you will be welcomed with open arms."

The service ended with a prayer and closing song. But after

everyone was dismissed, Luke continued to sit in the pew with head bent over his Bible.

Rachel had no choice but to leave with the Barnes family, but her mind and prayers remained behind with Luke. As long as he continued to search, he'd find all the right answers.

Luke sat in the Robbins's living room. He'd just told the pastor about losing his father and all the anger and bitterness he'd felt toward God since then. All the while he talked, the pastor remained silent, only nodding from time to time. He never once made Luke feel condemned or that he disapproved of him. That gave him the courage to go on.

"Rachel told me that God never left me. That in all my running from Him and hating Him, He never left my side."

"Tell me, Luke, has your anger and bitterness toward God given you any happiness all these years? Any sense of peace?"

Luke shook his head.

"And after hearing Rachel tell you that God and His love have never left you, you now feel a longing, a sense of hope?"

Luke shrugged, then finally nodded. "I guess."

"You hadn't been a believer very long before you lost your father, but it only takes a moment in God's family to feel His abundant love for you. God's Spirit living within you is what makes you crave that relationship with your heavenly Father again. You've been disappointed with God, and now you're feeling disappointment without Him."

The pastor's words were right on target and they sank deep. The rumble of thunder in the distance echoed his unsettled heart.

Pastor Robbins leaned forward and rested his elbows on his knees, clasping his hands together. "Life is neither fair nor easy, Luke. The Bible tells us that over and over. God's own Son wasn't treated fairly while He was here on earth. But God's will is perfect, even when it's painful and difficult for us to endure. In spite of that pain, we need to trust God. He wouldn't put a hardship in our lives and then abandon us. He loves us too much for that. God doesn't always offer a way out of our difficulties, but He helps us through them. We need to remain faithful to Him and we'll retain that peaceful relationship with Him."

"And if we haven't remained faithful?"

The pastor leaned back and crossed his legs. "Rachel was right, Luke. God never left you through all of your anger toward Him. You may have felt alone all these years, but it was you who was running away, not God. Just as the prodigal son's father I spoke of today sat waiting and watching for his son's return, God is waiting for your return. And believe me, there will be much celebration in heaven when that happens. It only takes a humble heart to return to a full relationship with Him. Turn to Him, Luke, and you will feel that Fatherly love you crave."

Luke ran everything through his mind. "It's hard to believe God isn't angry with me. I haven't said or thought a nice thing about Him in years."

The pastor smiled. "'The Lord is gracious and full of compassion; slow to anger and of great mercy.' That verse is found in the Psalms. God wants a relationship with you as much as you do with Him, Luke. His love has no boundary lines, no limitations. He will welcome you back without any reservations."

"But there's still no promise that God won't disappoint me again, maybe put me through another heartbreaking loss."

"No. But He'll help you through it."

"So why put any of us through the hardships?"

"There could be any number of reasons. He could want to strengthen your faith. Or maybe what you learn from your experience could be passed along to help someone else. Sometimes you may never know the reason for a difficulty until you're with the Lord. But whatever the reason or problem, always trust that the

Lord knows best and will get you through. He'll never give you more than you can bear."

Luke sat quiet, still not sure he liked the answers he'd been given. Why would a loving God make His children miserable?

"I can see you're still struggling." Pastor Robbins took out a sheet of paper and began writing. When he finished, he handed the sheet to Luke. "Read over and study these verses. They may help. No, they *will* help if you'll let them."

Luke glanced over the Scripture references, then folded the sheet and tucked it in his pocket. He stood and held out his hand. "Thank you, Pastor."

"If you have any more questions—"

"I know where to find you." He smiled. "Enjoyed your message. I might have to come next Sunday to see if you're always that good."

Pastor Robbins clapped him on the shoulder. "Nothing like giving an old man a challenge."

Luke tugged on his hat and dashed out into the downpour. But even in the gloom of the day, he finally saw a ray of light for the first time in years.

TWENTY-SEVEN

The clouds that had dumped their storehouse of water all day finally moved on, revealing a sky bathed in freshly washed blue. Unable to stay inside any longer, Rachel stepped outside and let the sun warm her face. The muddy mess the storm left behind didn't deter her from her plans to work in Beth Barnes's garden. Besides, the weeds would pull much easier now.

Rachel returned inside to put on her oldest dress. Then she took off her shoes, hiked up her skirt, and waded into the garden. She smiled as the mud squished between her toes with each step.

She'd been working in the garden at least half an hour, tugging up the weeds and tossing them into a nearby bucket, and she enjoyed every minute. Some boys from down the street wandered toward her.

"Why you playing in the mud, Miss Garrett?"

Rachel stood and propped her fists on her hips. "Does this look like playing to you?"

One of the boys shrugged. "Kinda."

"Really? Well, come on in and start pulling weeds, then we'll see what you call what I'm doing."

They made a face and shook their heads, but neither did they leave. As she squatted to continue weeding, she asked what they were doing to fill their time now that they didn't have to attend school. Emma must have heard them. She came out and sat on the porch, watching and listening.

"It's the deputy."

At the boys' announcement, Rachel stood and turned to face him and wished something awful she wasn't covered in mud. She gathered up all the dignity she could muster and prepared for the certain onslaught of Luke's teasing.

"Hi, Luke." Emma's squeaky voice greeted him as she stood for a hug.

Luke bent for the hug and kissed Emma's cheek. Then he strolled toward Rachel and stopped at the edge of the garden.

"What in the world are you doing out there? Couldn't that have waited until it dried up?"

"No, it couldn't. This is the only day I have time to work in here. This Saturday, I intend to take Emma and Tanner again, so I won't be able to do any weeding then."

"I see." There was no missing the fact that Luke was trying not to smile. His voice held a hint of humor. "Well, if you have a minute, could I talk to you?"

"Sure."

She headed his way, lifting each foot all the way out of the mud before placing it down again. She looked up in time to see the shock on Luke's face before the grin took its place. She made a face at him.

"I'm barefoot because I didn't want my shoes to get muddy."

"Oh, but getting mud on your dress is okay?"

She looked down at it, then back at him and shrugged. "It's old." She finally made it out of the garden and stopped right in front of him. "Now, what was so important you had to take me away from my work?"

"First of all, I want to thank you for talking to me like you did earlier this week. It was something I needed to hear. You gave me a lot to think about, which led me back to church and a talk with Pastor Robbins afterward."

Rachel smiled and reached out to touch him, stopping right before she muddied his shirt. "I'm so glad, Luke. I was afraid I had pushed you further away. But I must say I was surprised to see you in church this morning. I'll bet your mother was pleased."

"She's been in the clouds all day. I've had to tie a string to her ankle so I can pull her down just to be able to talk to her."

Rachel laughed. "Will you be able to continue attending church, I mean, with your job and all?"

"I've worked it out with the sheriff. He's hired a part-time deputy who'll take those hours."

"You won't regret it. The pastor's messages are always inspiring."

"If today's is any indication, I agree."

Luke cleared his throat a few times and took a deep breath, avoiding her eyes the entire time. He scratched the back of his neck and tugged at his collar.

"Whatever it is, just say it and get it over with," she said.

He finally looked at her, then cleared his throat once more. "I also wanted you to know that I intend to walk you to work in the mornings from now on, so don't leave until I get here."

Rachel raised her brows to her hairline at this bit of news. "Oh really? When did all this come about? I don't remember agreeing to that."

She put her muddy hands on her hips, then removed them. She glanced at the damage to her dress before looking back up at Luke for answers. He crossed his arms and tilted his head.

"I decided to do it all on my own."

"I don't need your protection, Luke. Nothing like that will happen again."

"That's right. Nothing like that will happen again because I'll be walking you to work and checking the clinic before I leave. And you'll lock the door behind me and leave it locked until Jim arrives."

She tried to keep her voice calm. "You don't need to bother yourself. I'll be just fine."

Luke took her chin in his fingers and leaned down close to her face. "I intend to walk you to work every morning, Rachel, and you *will* be here waiting for me, even if I have to camp out on your door-step to see that you do."

Of all the arrogant nerve! Rachel huffed and pulled away from him, only to have him reach for her again and cup her face in both his hands.

"Please?" His voice had softened. "I couldn't stand the thought of anything like that happening to you again. Will you wait for me?"

Rachel's heart pounded at the way he held her with his face only inches from hers. Unable to find her voice, she nodded her agreement instead.

Luke dropped his hands. "Good girl."

And then he strode away, his whole posture showing pure confidence. Rachel narrowed her eyes at him, her chest still heaving from his touch, but also because he appeared to be gloating over his high-handed victory. She bent down, made a mud ball, and threw it at him.

The mud ball splattered squarely on his back. He stopped in his tracks and turned around.

"Well, that was rather immature, Rae."

Another mud ball hit him in the middle of his chest. He glanced down at it for a moment, then looked back up. Rachel stood with her hands on her hips and a smirk on her face. He deserved it.

Luke rubbed at the mud on his shirt as a menacing smile grew on his face. "Now you've done it."

He approached with measured steps. Her desire for flight took the place of fight. She squealed, turned, and ran, grabbing up more mud as she fled. She launched her mud at him, then grabbed one of the smaller boys, picked him up in her arms, and held him like a shield. The boy laughed, then screamed, then screamed to be put down.

Luke, grinning from ear to ear, stood in front of Rachel and the boy, mud dripping from each hand. "Put him down, Rae. He's not part of this. You started it. Now take your medicine like a big girl."

Rachel walked with the boy between them until she was near a tree, then she put him down and ducked behind the tree. When she didn't hear Luke following her, she peeked around the tree only to have a mud ball glance off her forehead with most of it ending up in her hair. With her mouth dropping in shock, she was almost hit by a second mud ball, jumping behind the tree just in time to avoid a glob in her face.

She decided to run for it and took off toward the garden again. She scooped up more mud as she ran, then turned and prepared to throw. The two squared off against each other, smiling ear to ear. Rachel threw first, only to have Luke drill her with a glob. He scooped up another handful. While he was bent over, Rachel unloaded again, hitting him on top of the head.

Before long they both were flinging mud without even taking aim. They were soon covered from head to toe, laughing so hard they could hardly stand up.

The children's laughter drew their attention. Luke and Rachel looked at each other and nodded in silent agreement, then began throwing mud at the kids. One glob came close to hitting Emma, who still watched from the porch. Her scream brought Beth from inside the house.

"Emma! What's gotten into you?"

"I almost was hit by that mud!"

"What mud?"

"Out there." Emma pointed at them.

Luke bumped Rachel. "Watch this."

Beth had just looked their way when the mud ball Luke threw hit her apron. The entire group went silent. Beth glanced down at her apron, then looked directly at Luke, her finger shaking at him.

"Luke Mason! You just wait until I tell your mother!"

They all hollered with laughter.

Rachel looked around at each mud warrior. Everyone was covered from head to toe. Only their eyes and teeth flashed white in the midst of all the gray.

Luke stuck out his muddy hand. "Truce?"

Rachel took his hand with her equally muddy one. "Truce."

He tilted his head and grasped her hand in both of his. "And you'll wait for me in the mornings?"

"Yes, Luke, I'll wait for you in the mornings. And thank you for your concern."

Luke closed one eye for a moment, then shook his head. "If you weren't angry about having to wait for me, then why the mud ball in my back?"

"It was the way you didn't ask. You *told* me to wait for you and you said it quite arrogantly. I just wanted to take you down a notch."

"And did you succeed?"

Rachel raised her chin, trying to be as sassy as she could. "I don't know, but I sure had fun trying."

Luke dabbed a bit of mud on the end of her nose. "You're a mess, in more ways than one."

"You're one to talk."

"By the way, have you forgotten about looking at the wanted posters?"

"Oh, I sure did. How about now?"

He smiled. "Or we can wait until we both clean up first."

She looked down at her dress, then at his shirt. "Right. Good idea."

"I'll change, then run to the office for the posters. That should give you enough time to get clean." He tipped his hat. "I'll see you in a bit."

Rachel called the kids to her and told them that if their mothers were upset about their clothes, to bring them by and she would clean them. Then she bid the boys good-bye before heading to her house. She looked around before hitching up her dress a bit and dipping her feet in a bucket that had filled with rain. Once they were clean enough, she entered the house, grabbed some fresh clothes, and headed to Beth's.

Before she made it to the kitchen, Beth said, "I already have the water heating."

"I'm sorry, Beth."

"No you're not." She grinned and shook her head. "Honestly, I don't know what got into Luke to do such a thing."

"He didn't start it, Beth. I did." She looked up to see Beth's mouth open in surprise. "But he deserved it!"

Beth laughed, then pointed at the room used for baths. "Get in there."

Rachel had just enough time to clean up and eat a sandwich before Luke arrived with the posters. She was pleasantly surprised at the change in him. Gone were the sullen looks and comments, replaced by a look of peace and happiness.

Rachel hadn't gotten far looking through the stack of posters when she came across Quint's picture. She held it up.

"That's him. That's Quint."

Luke nodded. "I already went through the stack while you were resting and came across this one as well as the next, which I believe is Quint's son, right?"

Rachel looked down and saw the face of the young man with the bullet, though this face looked much meaner than the one she saw in person. She nodded and gave it to Luke. "That's him. That's Tony."

"All right. Would you keep looking to see if you recognize any others? Like you said, most of them have nicknames, so I didn't find any others you mentioned."

Rachel flipped page after page. She'd grown weary when she came across Bear's photo. She slid it across the table.

"That's Bear. He seemed to be Quint's right-hand man."

Luke examined it for several seconds, then nodded and set it on top of Quint and Tony's posters. "Any others?"

Rachel continued through the stack and managed to find all but two of the men who had held her captive.

Luke reached across the table and squeezed her hand. "You did great, Rae. Morgan and I appreciate the help. We'll send wires to all the other sheriffs. We might actually find these men now." He stood, held out his hand, and helped her to her feet. "Allow me to walk you home?"

"You asking because you don't want another mud fight?"

He shrugged and smiled. "Something like that."

When they arrived at her house, he waited for her to enter. She closed the door and leaned against it with a feeling of contentment until she heard him yell.

"I didn't hear you lock the door."

She slid the bolt home.

"That's better. Goodnight, Rae."

"Goodnight, Luke. See you in the morning."

Luke couldn't remember having so much fun in a long time. He also couldn't remember a woman ever perplexing him as Rachel did. She was a mixture of sass, sincerity, determination, kindness, fun, and intelligence, and she delighted him like no other. Walking her to work every morning would be interesting, to say the least.

TWENTY-EIGHT

Luke Mason placed the basket of food in the back of the wagon and climbed aboard. "Thanks again for fixing us a picnic, Mother."

"You're welcome. Just have a good time. And say hello to Rachel and the children for me."

"Will do."

He flicked the reins and started on his way. After spending time with Rachel every morning the past five days, he didn't want a single day to go by without seeing her. Showing her the spot where he wanted to build a house was the perfect excuse to spend an entire day with her, even if he had to share her with Emma and Tanner. He pulled up in front of Rachel's house just as she and the children were coming out.

"You ready to go?"

She shielded her eyes as she looked up at him. "Go where?"

"To my secret spot up in the mountains. I told you I'd take you up there."

Emma started jumping up and down. "You have a secret place? Can we see it?" She turned to Rachel. "Can we see it? Please?"

Rachel's mouth opened and closed a few times, then she shrugged and looked up at Luke. "All right. Let me leave a note for Beth in case we get home late. Then I need to pack a bit more food so we'll have enough for you."

Luke put his hand over his heart. "I'm hurt, Rae. I can't believe you forgot about me."

"I didn't forget about you. But I thought you'd forgotten. You never mentioned the trip again, so I assumed it was off. If you'll get the children loaded into the wagon, I'll just be a minute."

He jumped down. "Don't bother with more food. My mother packed enough to feed us for two days. And don't worry about a note for Beth. I'll make sure you're home before dark. Let's get going. We have a long ride ahead of us."

He reached for Rachel's basket and placed it next to his before taking her by the waist and helping her up into the seat. He tickled the kids before placing them in the back on some blankets, and then they were off and ready for adventure.

They rode for over an hour, laughing and singing as they bumped and bounced along the kind of trail most people would have avoided. But Luke liked the privacy a rough road provided. The way Rachel wiggled, she was more than ready to get down and walk. She'd get her chance soon enough.

He turned the horses into a narrow opening of trees. Dark shadows enveloped them as the canopy of trees blocked out a good deal of the sunlight. The kids poked their heads between Rachel and Luke, and Rachel reached back and put her arm around them. They rode about another fifteen minutes before the sound of running water could be heard over the noise of horse and wagon. Just as suddenly as they plunged into the dark woods, they found themselves back in full sunlight, a small glade spreading around them with the stream running through the center and several trees scattered here and there. *Peaceful* was the first word that came to mind when he first found the place. If at all possible, it would one day be his.

Luke stopped the wagon to allow Rachel to look her fill. Her mouth had dropped open as she took in the scene in front of her.

"Oh, Luke, it's beautiful! I had a picture in my mind of what it would look like, but it didn't hold a candle to this."

Luke slapped the reins on the horse to move them under a large tree near the stream. Then he jumped down and helped Rachel from the wagon before scooping the kids to the ground. They immediately ran toward the stream, squealing in delight. Rachel was about to go after them when Luke stopped her.

"They'll be fine."

She sent him a look of doubt but stayed where she was. They grabbed the blankets and food out of the back of the wagon and laid them out under the tree. Then he motioned to the children.

"Shall we join them? Can't let them have all the fun."

The kids had found a place along the stream where a small shallow pond had formed, the water almost still. They were kneeling down looking at something when Luke and Rachel arrived.

Emma jumped to her feet. "Look, Miss Rachel!"

Tanner stood, revealing the mud soiling his pants. He took Rachel's hand, and pulled her to the water's edge. Luke peeked over their shoulders to see what had them so entertained. Tadpoles darted here and there along the water's edge. Tanner plunged his hand in trying to catch them. In the next second, he lost his balance and plunged headfirst into the water. He came up with a shocked look on his face, one that almost matched his sister's and Rachel's.

Luke reached down to help Tanner from the water. Tanner looked about ready to cry until Luke laughed. Then the boy grinned back at him. He pointed at the water from Luke's arms.

"That was fun!"

That was the start of a fun-filled morning. Luke taught them how to skip rocks on the pond, then they played a quick game of hide-and-seek. All too soon to suit the kids, it was time for their picnic and a quick nap.

They'd all worked up an appetite and fell upon the food with the fervor of a starving family, yet when they'd finished, they hadn't made much of a dent in all the food Sadie had put into the basket. With full bellies, the children were soon sleepy. Rachel read only a few pages of a book to them before they were sound asleep. She continued to stare at them while they slept. A gust of wind blew some locks of her hair across her face. Before she could push them aside, Luke reached and tucked them behind her ear.

"You're very good with children. You've proven that with these two as well as all those at church. The girls adore you, and I think all the little boys are in love with you."

Her face turned pink as she shook her head. "They like attention and I give it to them." She brushed some of Emma's hair from her face. "I don't know how to thank you enough for bringing us up here. I'm sure you had better things to do, but it's been great fun for the kids and very relaxing for me."

A yawn escaped, and Luke handed her a small blanket.

"You're welcome. Now why don't you lie down next to them and get a quick nap. I'd do the same, but I want to do a little fishing. My mother loves it when I bring home some fresh-caught fish."

She eyed the blanket. "You won't think I'm terrible company if I drop off for a while?"

"Not at all. Enjoy it." He pushed to his feet. "I'm just going to grab my fishing gear and I'll leave you in peace."

Luke lost track of time as he pulled in three large fish. One more ought to be enough to satisfy his mother. He'd never known anyone who loved fish more, and his father had always made sure she had a steady supply. Now that job fell to him. Not that he minded. Fishing brought him joy and peace, which was more than he could say about Rachel, though the feeling of joy didn't seem far away. The woman had gotten under his skin and he couldn't get enough of spending time with her even though she was a constant reminder of his lost faith.

Movement to his side grabbed his attention, and he reached for his pistol. A deer with two fawns wandered into the glade. He propped his pole between two rocks and skirted the glade in order not to frighten off the deer. He dropped onto the blanket and woke the two children before gently shaking Rachel.

She bolted upright. He put his finger to his lips before pointing. "Look over there."

Rachel turned, then gasped. "They're beautiful."

The three deer headed toward the water at a distance from them. The children quivered, and Luke had to remind them to remain silent so they wouldn't scare the deer away. They all watched as the deer drank their fill before walking back toward the trees. As soon as the deer disappeared, the children began jabbering with excitement, telling Luke and Rachel all about it as if the two adults hadn't seen a thing.

Luke was amused by it all, but Rachel listened with interest, exclaiming with them over all the wildlife they had seen on their outing. Again, Luke was struck by how considerate Rachel treated everyone. She listened to the person talking to her, giving each one her full attention no matter what their age. He'd first noticed it with the Manning sisters, how Rachel treated them as equals when many others avoided them.

The children paused long enough to take a breath, and Luke clapped his hands together.

"It's time to start heading back down the mountain."

The kids groaned as their shoulders slumped. Rachel pulled them into her arms.

"Just think, you get to tell your parents all about what you've seen. I'm sure they've never been here before and maybe they've never seen deer before. Especially baby ones."

"Yeah! Let's go."

Luke raised his hands. "Hold up. We still need to load the baskets and blankets in the wagon, and I need to retrieve all my fishing gear. Emma, why don't you help Miss Rachel with the blankets, and Tanner, how about you come help me carry my pole?"

As Tanner raced off to the pond, Luke helped Rachel to her feet, then leaned in close so only she could hear.

"I'm not so sure the parents will be as excited to hear their stories as the children are to tell them. They might be up all night."

Rachel chuckled. "Beth may never let me have them again." She touched his arm. "Did you catch a fish, Luke?"

"No, I caught three."

Rachel's eyebrows went up. "I'm impressed."

"Don't be. You three sleepyheads gave me plenty of time."

The children chattered all the way home. Neither Luke nor Rachel was allowed to say much of anything. They made it home right before dark. As the children bombarded their parents with stories about their day, Luke and Rachel waved their good-byes and made a hasty departure. The last thing Luke saw was Jim and Beth looking a bit stupefied. He laughed as he walked Rachel home.

At her door, he handed her the basket. She smiled up into his face, causing him to catch his breath at how beautiful she looked in the moonlight.

"Thanks again, Luke. That was a fantastic day. And thank your mother for all the wonderful food. Goodnight."

She entered her house, closing the door on a man who wanted only to have her come back out so he could pull her into his arms and hold her for hours.

TWENTY-NINE

The days turned into weeks, and nothing harmful had happened to Rachel. No accidents or attempts on her life. If it weren't for the residents getting sick or having accidents of their own, Rachel would almost call her life boring. Even Luke wasn't such a tyrant about her safety any longer. She'd gotten to walk to work by herself a couple times, and Jim had started letting her make house calls without him.

But along with the passing weeks came the heat, and today was no exception. The month of July dragged on, and the lack of rain or cool days became very wearing. Rachel left her house to find a gust of wind or even a whisper of a breeze, anything to help cool her down. She was just about to go around back when the Baxter kids stopped at the Barneses' house. Robin went inside and returned a minute later with Emma and Tanner in tow.

Robin saw her and waved. "Hi, Rachel. We're on our way to the pond to play in the water. You wanna come?"

Rachel eyed Chad. He probably didn't want her along. He hadn't said much of anything to her since she'd told him she only wanted to be friends. But he surprised her with a smile.

"Come on, Rachel. It'll be fun. And besides, Mother put plenty of food in the basket hoping you'd join us."

"Can you wait?" Rachel said. "I want to change into different clothes."

She ran inside and joined them minutes later. As they walked along, the group of eight chatted with excitement. Rachel and Robin took turns carrying Tanner whenever his small legs became too tired. Robin also carried a small bag and told Rachel she'd brought along her tablet and some pencils just in case she saw something she wanted to sketch.

William looked over his shoulder, then raced back to Rachel and took her by the hand, swinging it hard. "Are you going to get into the water with us, Miss Rachel?"

"I think I'll just sit on that big flat rock on the shoreline and dip my feet in the water. I don't know that I can trust you Baxters." Rachel winked and smiled. "I still haven't forgotten that snowball fight you got me into my first time at your house. How do I know you won't try to drown me?"

"It wasn't that bad," William said.

"You're right, it wasn't. But I'll enjoy just getting to watch all of you having fun splashing about."

The idea of swimming in the pond sounded wonderful, but she didn't think it was such a good idea with Chad and his brothers there. She also didn't fail to notice Chad's silence. Maybe he regretted his invitation. He had yet to say a word to her since he'd asked her to join them, though he did cast several looks in her direction. If only they could be friends. He was sweet and fun. At least he used to be.

Even Robin was more quiet than usual, but Rachel decided not to question her with so many others around. But once they reached the pond, Robin seemed to come out of it as she jumped into the water and splashed around with Emma and Tanner. While the older brothers were having a swimming race, William took over watching the two little ones so Robin could swim by herself. Then Chad climbed a tree and tied a rope to a large branch so they could take turns swinging over the water and landing with a splash.

Robin got out of the water and joined Rachel on the shore, wrapping a towel around her shoulders. They watched the boys with amusement as they each tried to see who could make the biggest splash. Emma and Tanner were content to sit and play in knee-deep water near the shore. Once again Robin fell silent and looked unhappy.

"Is everything all right, Robin? You seem unusually quiet today."

Robin cast a quick glance in Rachel's direction before turning her eyes to her lap, then out again to her brothers. Her mind seemed far away, and she didn't seem to want to talk.

"When did your parents let you start seeing boys?" Robin's voice was so soft and sad.

Rachel hesitated, not wanting to say the wrong thing and cause trouble with Robin's mother.

"It was probably different for me, Robin. From the time I was fifteen years old, my main thought was on nursing. I could never wait to get to the doctor's office to help out. Oh, I would notice an occasional boy's attentions and would give him some of my own in return, but it never really amounted to anything. Especially not enough to make me ask my parents if I could spend time with any of them."

"Oh." Robin didn't look any happier.

Rachel placed her hand on Robin's shoulder. "Is there someone special, Robin?"

The girl shrugged. "I don't know how special he is, but he's the first boy that's ever given me some attention."

"And you asked your parents if you could spend some time with him?"

Robin nodded. "They said they didn't like that idea."

"Did you have an argument with your parents about this boy, Robin?"

"Not really an argument, but they just wouldn't listen to my side of it. They said no and wouldn't change their minds." Robin grew agitated as she spoke.

Rachel rubbed her back to calm her and to lend comfort. "Did they give a reason for why they said no?"

"They said they knew of this boy and some of his friends. They weren't sure enough of him to allow me to spend time with him."

"Does he go to our church?"

"No, but I've invited him."

"So you met this boy through school?"

Robin nodded. "But I've run into him in town a couple of times this summer, and then he came by the house once not too long ago to ask if he could see me sometimes. That's when I talked to my parents about him."

Rachel repositioned herself so she could see Robin's face. "Robin, I've gotten to know you, your parents, and your brothers pretty well over the past months, and I think I can safely say that your parents love you very much and are just looking out for your well-being. If there's some reason they don't trust this boy, then you should wonder if maybe they're right. I really don't think they would keep you from getting to know a boy they trusted. Is this boy a believer?"

Robin's eyes dropped to her lap. "I don't know. I've never heard him even talk about God or Jesus." Robin looked into Rachel's face. "I know what you're going to say. God tells us not to be united with unbelievers. I remember Pastor Robbins saying that in one of his messages last year."

Rachel smiled. "That was exactly what I was going to say. But I was also going to add that we shouldn't even think about a relationship, especially a romantic one, with an unbeliever. We can be their friend and try to lead them to Christ, but it should be no more serious than that. They can lead us away from God." Rachel brushed some of Robin's damp hair from her face. "But it sure feels good to get a man's attention, doesn't it?"

Robin smiled shyly and nodded.

"Don't worry, Robin. God has someone special picked out just for you. So if someone or something is standing between you and a man you think of as special, then there must be a reason."

The two embraced then, and Robin's face looked much brighter than it had only minutes ago.

"Thank you, Rachel. I knew you'd be a good friend."

"Any time, Robin. I happen to think you're very special."

Robin's gaze moved over Rachel's shoulder and her smile widened. Rachel turned and her heart skipped a beat as Luke rode toward them.

Robin jumped from the rock and grabbed her bag. "Hi, Mr. Mason. I'm glad you were able to come by." She motioned to her bag. "I'm going over there to draw for a while. You two have fun."

Rachel gaped at Robin's retreating back. The little rascal. She'd have to remember to thank the girl later.

Luke slid from his saddle and took Robin's place on the rock next to Rachel. "At least if you throw mud at me now, I can jump in and wash off right away. And I can take you in with me."

"Oh, no you can't."

"Don't be so sure." Luke's eyes dropped to her bare feet cooling in the water. "That's all the farther you've made it, huh?"

"And that's all the farther I intend to go."

He continued to stare at her feet, and she pulled them from the water and tucked them under her dress.

"Well." Luke stood. "I'm going to join the Baxter boys so I can cool off."

He stripped off his shirt before removing his boots and socks. Then he launched from the rock and landed with a large splash. Several drops landed on Rachel. He turned and grinned.

"A little water never hurt anyone."

Then he swam with broad strokes toward Chad and his brothers. Rachel was glad of his distance. The sight of his bare chest had her heart beating much too fast.

The Baxter's antics became much more competitive once Luke joined them. She laughed often as some of them landed on their bellies with a slapping sound and came up roaring from the painful sting on their bare skin.

It wasn't long before Emma and Tanner wandered over to Rachel. She found a comfortable spot to lean on while the two children used her lap as a pillow for their nap.

In the meantime, the boys teamed up in some kind of wrestling match in the water. At first it was funny, but as the game wore on, the match between Luke and Chad became rougher by the minute. She knew men were competitive, but their game became more like a brawl. She wanted to yell at them and make them stop. Their fight moved her way. Even Chad's brothers stopped to watch, their eyes wide.

Luke finally shoved Chad away. "That's enough."

Chad's chest heaved. "Why?" He panted a few times. "Too rough for you?"

"You don't want me to get rough, Chad."

"I can take anything you wanna try."

Luke shook his head and waded from the water. Chad followed, splashing Luke all the way.

"Come on, Deputy." Chad sneered the last word. "Let's end this now."

Luke faced him. "What's your problem, Chad? We used to be friends. What happened to change that?"

Chad glanced Rachel's way, and her breath caught in her throat. Luke turned to look at her before he faced Chad again. He shook his head.

"I can't help you there, friend."

He left the water and approached Rachel. They exchanged a look. Soon all the boys followed Luke and rehashed their diving contest, and their laughs woke Emma and Tanner. When Robin arrived, they made short work of the snack Cora Baxter had made for them.

Luke glanced at the sky. "It's getting late. We should get the young ones home."

Chad stayed by Rachel's side as they walked back, often much too close and familiar, even putting his hand on her back. Uncomfortable with his attentions, she slowed her steps until she had Luke on her other side.

Chad huffed, glared at her and then at Luke, then stomped up to join his brothers.

"Sorry I ruined your day," Luke said.

"You didn't."

He motioned to Chad. "Well, I think I ruined his. I believe he's jealous of our friendship."

"I don't know why. I've never given him reason to think he and I would be anything more than friends." She stared at Chad's back. "I'm sure he'll get over it eventually."

"Maybe so."

"You don't sound convinced."

He smiled. "I know the way men think."

She looked at him when he didn't say more. "Well, do you plan to let me in on your secret?"

"Oh, no. If we'll never figure out women, I'm sure not going to help you figure us out."

Chad must have heard Luke laugh because he speared them with another glare.

Rachel took a deep breath. "All right, so a renewed friendship may take a while. A long while."

"He'll be all right. Every man has to deal with a broken heart at some point in his life. He got his opportunity early."

"Speaking from experience?"

He shrugged and smiled. "So I've heard."

She bumped him with her elbow. "You're being awfully secretive."

"Who me?"

She thumped him on the chest. "Stop."

He laughed again as they arrived at her house. "See you at church tomorrow?"

"I'll be there. Bye, Luke."

"Goodnight."

She closed the door and knew without a doubt that her heart had followed Luke home.

❈ THIRTY ❈

Rachel hopped out of Jim Barnes's buggy and climbed the steps to see Lucille Munroe. The last thing the poor lady needed was a cold. Rachel was glad Jim allowed her to tend to Lucille and prayed the medicine in her bag would help.

Mrs. Chatham opened the door only moments after Rachel knocked. "Thank you for coming. I've been so worried about Mother. She seems to be struggling to take a breath."

Rachel hurried down the hall and into Lucille's room. Her pallid skin almost matched the white pillowcase under her head. Rachel put her palm on Lucille's forehead and then her cheek before touching her wrist to check her pulse. Lucille opened her eyes and gave her a slight smile.

"It's about time you got here. It's been too long since we've just sat and talked."

Rachel dropped onto the chair next to the bed. "Why you rascal. You only got sick so I'd come sooner than usual."

Lucille gave a weak chuckle. "Don't hold it against me."

"Well, I won't stay and talk unless you take this medicine."

Lucille made a face. "Is it that awful tasting stuff?"

"It is, but you have to take it anyway."

"Oh, all right. But if I have to swallow that revolting remedy, you have to stay longer than usual."

Rachel grinned. "I guess that sounds fair."

She stood and, with Mrs. Chatham's help, propped Lucille up with another pillow and spooned the liquid into her mouth. Lucille screwed up her face while she swallowed.

"That's just plain awful. You tell Jim surely he can make that taste better."

"But that would defeat the purpose."

"What purpose would that be? Kill off all his patients?"

Rachel laughed. "No, but if the medicine tastes bad, the residents won't be so willing to give in to sickness."

"Humph. I think he just likes seeing our stomachs and faces turn inside out."

"Maybe so. I'll have to ask." Rachel returned to her seat and got comfortable. "All right, so how about you tell me something about when you were growing up? Or maybe something funny that happened after you were first married."

"Oh dear. I'm not sure anything funny happened when we were first married. We were so poor at first there wasn't much to laugh at even though we were happy. Charlie always found a way to make me smile though."

Lucille closed her eyes and Rachel figured the medicine had already gone to work making her sleepy. But then she smiled and opened her eyes.

"There was this one day that I'd gone into town to sell our eggs so I could afford to buy some flour. When I got back, there were all kinds of vegetables lying on our kitchen table, and my Charlie sat there with a smile on his face. He pointed at all the food and asked me to make him some soup. I asked him where he got all the vegetables. He said the neighbor kids gave them to him. I asked him why."

Lucille laughed softly and shook her head.

"He said he'd charged the children to use our gate to get to their garden. They could've gotten to it by going around our place, but because Charlie made a fun game of it, they kept going in and out of our gate giving him carrots, potatoes, onions, peas, anything that was ready to pick. When he thought we had enough for a couple meals, he ended the game.

"I always wondered if their mothers got upset when they found out how many vegetables they lost and if they ever found out why their gardens didn't produce that day. But I'm telling you, we ate like kings for a while. My Charlie was quite the businessman."

Lucille's last few words came out in a slur. Rachel stood and pressed her lips to the dear woman's forehead. She was warm but not alarmingly so. Rachel caressed her cheek, then pulled the covers up to her chin.

She turned to Mrs. Chatham. "If she doesn't improve, send word. Otherwise I'll be back in two days to check on her again."

As she left the house, Rachel said another prayer for Lucille's health. She paused at the top of the porch steps to look for anything that might make her trip, then descended and climbed into the buggy. The sun was beginning to dip low, the colors just starting to wash across the sky.

She rode along, enjoying the pleasant weather as well as her freedom after having everyone escort her everywhere. Although she enjoyed Luke's company, her lack of freedom got old fast. She turned the horse onto the next street and headed toward the office, ready for the day to end. Someone stood at the end of the boardwalk. She prepared to wave, then looked closer. She ducked her head inside the buggy, pressing it against the back, and tugged the rim of her bonnet lower, then slapped the reins to get the horse to move faster.

In front of Jim's office, Rachel hauled back on the reins and ran inside. "Lock the doors. One of Quint's men is in town."

She heard Jim yell something, but she ran back out to the buggy and headed the horse toward the sheriff's office, praying she hadn't drawn attention to herself. Once in front of the sheriff's office, she scrambled from the buggy and ran inside. The sheriff, Luke, and Cade Ramsey sat around the desk.

"He's here. One of Quint's men."

Morgan Taylor jumped to his feet and unlocked the case holding his rifles. Luke took her by the shoulders.

"You saw only one?"

Out of breath and her mouth gone dry, she could only nod.

"Where?"

She pointed. "Down at the end of the street. I passed him on my way here. I think he's headed this way."

"On foot?"

She nodded again.

Morgan handed Luke a rifle, then looked at Cade. "You willing to help?"

Cade reached for the other rifle. "What do you want me to do?"

"Keep your eyes open. More of Quint's men could be nearby."

Then he led Cade and Luke out into the street. When she started to follow, Luke stopped and wheeled around.

"Don't leave this office until it's all over, Rachel. Do you hear me?"

Rachel was trembling with fright, and she preferred to stay close to someone who would protect her, but she gave him a nod.

"You'll be all right," Luke said. "We'll get them. Make sure you lock this door behind me." Then he rushed out the door.

She locked the door and flopped down in a chair, her quaking legs unable to hold her any longer. She began praying in earnest for the three men, asking God to protect them while they risked their lives for her and others.

Luke caught up with Morgan just as he sent Cade to the roof of the bank. "Luke, you get into position at the restaurant across the street. I'm going to duck into the bank to warn Pete and everyone else to hide out in the back room."

While Morgan was in the bank, Luke scanned the street looking for the faces from the wanted posters that Rachel had identified as her captors. Morgan dashed out of the bank and into the alley next door.

Luke watched from behind a curtain hanging on the door of the restaurant as some men drifted toward the bank. They didn't come as one big group but rode into town from both directions, then scattered here and there along the street. As Luke waited for a signal from Morgan, he recognized some of the faces. He glanced down the street toward the sheriff's office to make sure Rachel was still out of sight before looking back at the sheriff.

As the men came together in front of the bank, all movement became hurried as all but two of them ran into the bank. Luke opened the restaurant door and inched onto the boardwalk. Morgan motioned to the men standing outside the bank. Luke nodded.

"Drop your guns."

The men responded by shooting at him. Luke rushed into the street and fired at the robbers as Cade shot at them from above. The two men fell to the ground. Luke jumped over them to follow Morgan inside. He paused to motion to Cade to watch the fallen men so they wouldn't follow and cause trouble from behind.

Luke ran inside the bank. Morgan lay on the floor, shooting at the other three robbers. Luke lunged to his left. A bullet whizzed past his ear. He fired at the men as soon as he landed. With nothing to hide behind, Luke lay out in the open as they returned his fire. Several moments later, the gunfire finally ended. Two of the robbers lay on the floor and the other dropped his gun and raised his arms.

Morgan jumped to his feet and grabbed the man, forcing him to the floor. He pulled out his handcuffs. "Luke, check the men on the floor."

Luke didn't move. He couldn't. Pain burned in his shoulder and radiated all through his upper body. Cade came in and took over holding the handcuffed man. Morgan approached through a haze, his voice sounding like a hum. The room dimmed. Luke slowed his breathing. He had to protect Rachel. If only he could get up.

Rachel sat inside the sheriff's office, cringing with fear. The gun-shots echoing through the town sounded louder than any she'd ever heard. When it finally ended, she breathed a sigh of relief. But it didn't last. What if one of the three men or any of the town's residents had been hurt? She jumped to her feet, then stopped as Luke's order to remain inside rang through her mind.

"Where's the doctor? The deputy's been shot!"

Rachel's heart stopped. Not Luke! She headed for the door. She didn't make it. One arm wrapped around her waist as a hand clamped over her mouth.

"Hello, Rachel."

A familiar voice growled in her ear. She tried to scream, but the man's hand pressed even tighter over her mouth.

"You only thought you'd seen the last of me." He breathed hard in her ear. "I told you your fate was sealed. You should've just accepted it. Running only makes it worse. Especially after you let my son die." He put his lips against her ear. "And you're gonna pay for that."

His tone sent a shiver through her. Rachel struggled with all her strength. Quint snarled and pulled her even harder against him.

"If you keep this up, lady, I'll have to knock you on the head. Now be still."

Rachel stood motionless, and Quint hauled her toward the back door of the jailhouse. Rachel's heart threatened to jump from her chest. She kicked and dragged her feet, then reached back to scratch at his face.

Quint spun her around and slapped her face, then grabbed her by the throat. "Stop struggling or you'll get my fist next."

His slap was hard enough to make her ears ring and her vision blur. He grabbed her around the waist and lifted her from the ground. In seconds, they were out the door and in the alley.

When Rachel saw Quint's horse, she thrashed about and tugged at his hands to free her mouth so she could scream.

Luke pulled himself up and leaned against the wall. He hated feeling helpless and lying on the floor made him vulnerable. He panted a few times to get his bearings, then glanced at the men inside the bank. He recalled the faces of the two men lying outside and again examined the faces of the three robbers inside.

He frowned at the big man in handcuffs. "Where's Quint?"

The man only grinned at him through his scruffy beard.

A feeling of panic gripped Luke. He pushed to his unsteady feet, grimacing from the pain, and headed toward the door.

Morgan moved to his side and grasped his arm. "You need to sit down, Luke. You're still bleeding from that gunshot wound."

Luke pushed away Morgan's hand and continued toward the door.

Morgan stepped in front of him. "Come on, Luke. Come back inside and wait for the doc."

Luke shook his head, his jaw clenching from the pain each step caused. "I've got to check on Rachel."

"I can do that. You need to see the doctor."

Luke shook his head again, more determined than ever to get back to the sheriff's office. "I've got to see her for myself."

Morgan sighed. "All right, but I'm going along." He turned to Cade. "Can you handle this for a while?"

"I got it."

Morgan supported Luke all the way across the street. As they climbed the steps to the office, the sound of a stifled scream came from the alley to their right. Luke and Morgan pulled their guns and raced to the alley.

As soon as Quint saw them, he pulled his gun and wrapped his free arm around Rachel's neck and yanked her back against him.

Rachel's eyes widened. "Luke!"

Quint pointed his gun at Rachel's head. "Keep quiet."

Morgan leapt back to the building for cover, but Luke remained in the open, Rachel's fear-filled eyes and her reddened cheek keeping his feet frozen to the ground. He knew the exact moment she noticed the blood on his shirt. Her eyes jumped back to his and filled with tears. Still looking into her eyes, he shook his head ever so slightly, hoping she'd believe he was fine.

The men stood facing each other, Luke's gun on Quint and Quint's on Rachel. Then Quint pointed his back at Luke.

"Back off and let me out of here before someone gets hurt."

Luke didn't move, and Quint cocked his gun.

Rachel moaned. "Luke, get back and let us go."

"He's not leaving with you, Rachel." Then he turned his eyes to Quint. "You can go, but you leave her here."

A harsh laugh came from Quint's throat. "Not happening, lawman. She's the only reason I came to this hole of a town. She's coming with me."

"Then you're not leaving."

"Then she dies right here."

Luke's heartbeat hammered in his ears. He wanted to pull the trigger on Quint, but just the slightest shake of the hand and he might hit Rachel. Quint grinned at him and adjusted his grip as he moved the barrel of his gun toward Rachel. Luke didn't have a shot. Panic set in.

Then Rachel wrenched herself from Quint's grasp and dropped to the ground. Luke pulled the trigger. Three quick shots went off. Luke fell to the ground, but not before Quint beat him there.

THIRTY-ONE

Rachel shoved Quint off her legs and scurried to Luke's side. She scrubbed the tears from her eyes so she could see. His eyes were closed. Blood continued staining Luke's shirt. She grabbed his shirt-front and ripped it open.

Luke moaned and opened his eyes. He stared at her several seconds. "You all right?"

She nodded and placed her shaking fingers over his mouth. "Don't talk."

She looked into his eyes for another moment, then examined the damage done by the bullets. The entrance of the gunshot just below his ribcage was small, but there was greater damage at the exit wound. The other bullet had grazed the skin on the opposite side of his body, though it was still deep and bleeding.

She turned to Morgan. "Get my bag from the buggy."

He ran off as she pressed her hands on the wounds to slow the blood flow. Luke had lost too much already.

Running footsteps entered the alley. Morgan returned with Jim, who dropped to his knees beside her. "You hurt?"

"No, but Luke has two gunshot wounds. One's a bad graze. Where I have my hands is where the other bullet entered and exited. He's bleeding hard."

Jim nodded and turned to the men crowding around. "Help me get him to my office."

Luke opened his eyes and grabbed Jim's arm. "Make sure Rachel's safe."

Rachel leaned her head down and touched her cheek to his. "Hush, now. Everything's fine."

"My wagon's right over here, Doc," one man said.

They lifted Luke from the ground, pausing when he groaned and passed out. Rachel kept her hands over the wounds. "Keep going. We've got to move."

They soon had him in the back of the wagon. Jim jumped in and knelt across from Rachel for the short ride to his office. Once there, they had Luke inside in minutes. Jim turned to one of the men.

"Go get Luke's mother and bring her here. Then go tell Pastor Robbins what's happened."

The man nodded and ran out the door. Jim turned to Rachel.

"Can you keep your hands there until I can get my tools ready?"

Rachel nodded without taking her eyes from Luke's face. He was so pale. Jim was soon beside her with his tools laid out on a tray.

"I'm going to start on the exit wound first since it's the worst, so I need you to go to the other side and help me roll him after we plug this side."

Jim was still working on repairing the damage to Luke's back when Sadie rushed into the room, her eyes filled with tears.

"How is he, Jim? And don't tell me to leave because I won't do it."

"In that case, take Rachel's place on that side so she can help me over here."

Sadie did as she was told, then focused on Luke's face. "Is he going to make it?"

"He's strong, Sadie, and that's what's important right now. He's lost a lot of blood, but I think he's strong enough to pull out of this."

Jim spoke calmly as he worked, and Rachel tried to take his words to heart even as she fought the tears burning her eyes.

They worked for another half hour, repairing all the damage they could find before closing and bandaging the wound.

Jim motioned to Rachel and Sadie. "Help me turn him back over."

When Luke was on his back, they began working on the entry wound. Beth arrived to help.

"Pastor Robbins took Emma and Tanner to his wife. He'll be here in a few minutes. Anything you need me to do?"

"Yeah, take a look at that graze wound on his other side. See if it needs surgery or if we can just clean and bandage it."

Rachel moved to the side to let Beth work while she continued helping Jim. Half an hour later they were finally finishing up. Jim stepped back.

"Go ahead and bandage the wound." He paused and Rachel looked up at him. "I think you just might have saved his life getting to him and staunching the blood flow as quick as you did."

She tried to smile but couldn't quite manage it, especially since she was responsible for the condition he was in. Once she had the bandages in place, her eyes went to Sadie. The poor woman sat staring at her son's face. Rachel went to her and put her arms around her neck, placing her cheek against Sadie's.

"I'm so sorry, Sadie."

Sadie leaned back. "Sorry? You saved his life. You have nothing to be sorry about."

The tears Rachel had held back started coursing down her cheeks. She shook her head. "I'm the reason he got shot. He was trying to protect me."

"Oh, my dear." She placed her hands on Rachel's cheeks. "That's his job. He's doing what he's wanted to do since he was a boy. I've no doubt in my mind he's only glad you weren't hurt." She put her arms around Rachel. "He's in God's hands, Rachel, and that's the best place to be. God will take care of him."

Rachel returned Sadie's hug, then moved to the other side of the bed to keep an eye on Luke and his pulse.

Beth stepped back into the room. "Since things seem to be under control, I'm going to relieve Garnett and take my kids home for supper. I'll stop by the restaurant and have them bring you some food."

Jim came in moments later with the pastor. "I need to go to the jail. One of the prisoners needs some help. Rachel, send for me if anything happens."

She nodded and continued her vigil with Sadie and the pastor. Jim returned about an hour later. He took one look at her and shook his head.

"Go home, Rachel. Get something to eat and some rest."

She looked him in the eyes and stiffened her jaw. "I'm not leaving, Jim. Beth had some food sent over. I'm fine."

"Have you had any sleep?"

She didn't say a word.

"I didn't think so."

"I'm not leaving."

He stared her down. She didn't flinch. He finally sighed.

"Would you at least take a nap? You can use my office or the couch in the waiting area. You've got to get some rest, Rachel. I don't want you as my patient again."

She relaxed and smiled. "I can live with that idea. I'll rest for a bit, then when I wake, I'll stay with Luke so you can go home. The town needs you rested more than me."

Jim returned her smile. "I can live with that idea."

Rachel managed only two hours of sleep, a nightmare of seeing Luke getting shot startling her awake. She rushed to the room he was in and found Sadie sleeping with her head resting on the bed and her hand on Luke's arm. Jim stood when he saw her and pulled her from the room.

"I'd hoped you'd rest a little longer. You won't make it through the night with that amount of sleep."

"I'll be fine. If he's resting comfortably like he is now, I'll just catch a catnap like Sadie's doing. I doubt she'll agree, but I'm hoping that I can get her to use your office for a few hours."

"She'll agree about as easily as you did when I asked you to go home." He pointed to the other room. "Beth brought some snacks if you get hungry."

"Thank her for me."

Rachel grabbed a slice of ham before joining Sadie at Luke's side. She stared at his face. She almost lost him today, and just the thought alone made tears well. She sniffled and Sadie raised her head.

"Now don't start that or you'll get me started."

Rachel wiped her eyes and nose. "I'm sorry. I just hate that he got hurt."

"It's the first time. Sure scared me. Brought back memories of when they told me my husband was killed."

"Do you feel like telling me what happened?"

Sadie looked at her for several seconds, then at Luke's face. "Gabe went after some bank robbers. They hid out in a canyon and waited for Gabe to arrive. They trapped him inside and shot until he died."

"Oh, Sadie, I'm so sorry."

"It was hard at first, especially when Luke turned bitter. But thank the good Lord I'll see my husband again." Sadie reached to touch Luke's cheek. "He feels warm."

"That's not unusual. His body's fighting right now. He should be better in the morning." Rachel eyed Sadie. She looked exhausted. "Why don't you go into Jim's office and get some sleep?"

Sadie shook her head. "I want to be here for Luke."

"You'll be more help if you're rested. You can take over for me when you wake so I can get some rest. Jim should be back by then."

Sadie finally agreed, kissed Luke's forehead, and left the room. Luke stirred a couple times during the night. Rachel managed to get a few sips of water into him. The fever hung on several hours. She bathed him with cool water whenever he seemed uncomfortable.

She stared at his tanned face and strong jawline and had to resist the urge to caress his cheek. The thought of leaving his side didn't sit well at all, but she'd need rest if she was to be of any help.

Sadie slept until five o'clock the next morning, so when Rachel was sent home, she didn't put up a fight. As she stepped out the door to walk home, Jim pulled up in his buggy.

He jumped out. "Great timing. Take the buggy home. Keep it until you're rested and ready to come back." He grasped her arm as she passed. "And make sure you sleep more than two hours this time. I mean it, Rachel."

She sighed. "I don't think that'll be a problem."

Rachel fell into bed exhausted and slept until almost noon. She dressed quickly, and when she was about to climb into the buggy to return to the office, Beth called to her.

"Come inside and get a bite to eat before you go back."

"I'm fine."

"You are now, but if you keep this up, you'll be Jim's next patient. Come in and eat with me and the kids."

Much as she wanted to be on her way, Beth's logic propelled her inside. She took the time to hug and kiss the children before taking a seat at the table. Once Beth sat, Rachel found all three staring at her.

"What?"

Beth had a slight smile on her face. "Did you look in the mirror before you left the house?"

"No. What's wrong?" She looked down at her dress, then wiped her hands across her cheeks and forehead.

Emma giggled. "Your hair is sticking out."

Rachel reached up and patted at her hair. "Oh, goodness. I was in such a hurry I never even thought to give it a good brushing."

They all shared a laugh before digging into the food. Once finished, the children ran off to play while Rachel stayed long enough to help clean up. She hadn't done much before Beth stopped her with a touch to her arm.

"Are you sure you're ready to go back to work already? You look a bit…well, weary."

Rachel smiled. "I'll fix my hair."

"It's more than that. You have dark circles under your eyes and you're pale."

"I probably don't look any more stressed than you do, Beth. We're all worried about Luke. But I've gotten almost six hours of sleep. I'll be fine."

Rachel returned to her house to brush her hair, then hurried back to the clinic. When she entered Luke's room, she stepped around Sadie and placed her hand on his forehead and then his cheek before moving to his wrist to check his pulse.

His eyes opened and he looked right into hers. She gasped and nearly came undone when he gave her a weak smile. Then his lids dropped shut again.

The urge to kiss him took her by surprise. She couldn't be sure when it happened, but she'd fallen in love with Luke Mason.

THIRTY-TWO

The next morning, as soon as Rachel walked in to check on Luke Mason, Jim Barnes told her that Morgan Taylor needed to see her at the sheriff's office. She glanced at Luke's room.

Jim smiled. "He isn't going anywhere, Rachel. Go see what the sheriff wants."

She trudged down and across the street, her feet growing heavier with each step. Quint and some of his men were inside, and she wanted no part of seeing them again. She took a breath and pushed through the door.

Morgan stood. "How's Luke?"

"I haven't seen him yet this morning, but he was better last night. Even managed to keep down some broth." She closed the door. "He's still very weak, but it looks like he'll be fine. It'll be a few weeks before he's his old self again, longer if he doesn't take it easy for a while."

"Knowing Luke, he won't want to take it easy for long."

"You're his boss. Tell him he can't come back to work for three weeks."

"I could tell him that, but it doesn't necessarily mean he'll slow down. You know him, Rachel. He can't sit still for long." He motioned to the chair next to his desk. "Have a seat."

"Is there something wrong?"

"Not really." He held the chair for her. "Please?"

She sat, and Morgan returned to his seat and leaned on his desk.

"I've wired the judge, but he said he wouldn't come until after I had you verify that the men in my jail are the same ones who held you captive." Morgan reached to touch her arm. "So as much as I know you don't want to see Quint and his men again, I have to ask you to go to the back and take a look at them. You won't have to stay long, but it's the only way the judge will make the trip."

Rachel's heart pounded. But if seeing them meant they'd never hurt anyone again, she'd have to overcome her fright.

"All right. Let's get this over with."

"Good for you. Luke told me you were full of daring."

"Is that what he's calling it now? I thought he'd dubbed me as insolent and sassy."

"Well, now that you mention it…" Morgan laughed as he stood. "No, I believe that boy has a great deal of respect for you. As does the town." He held out his hand. "Shall we?"

He opened the back door, and Rachel entered the cellblock. Quint rose to his feet and approached the bars.

"Well, if it ain't the princess." Quint wore an evil grin. "Nice to see you again, Rachel. Do I ever have great plans for you. Want to hear the details or just the highlights?"

Morgan stepped between them. "Watch your mouth, Quint."

Rachel took note of the sling on Quint's arm before glancing at the man on the cot.

"Why come into town to grab Rachel again?" Morgan said.

Quint's grin turned to a snarl. "It's her fault my son died. She's gonna pay for that." He reached through the bars for Rachel. Morgan grabbed his arm.

"Why blame Rachel for your son's death? He wouldn't have been shot if you weren't robbing someone."

"If she wouldn't have run, we wouldn't have had to move him. We hadn't gone five miles before he bled to death." Quint struggled to reach for Rachel again. "I wanted to watch you die the same way he did, slow and painful."

He freed his arm from Morgan and swung toward Rachel. She jumped back, and Morgan took her from the cellblock and sat her in the chair near his desk. She couldn't stop trembling.

"Are you all right, young lady?"

She nodded. "He wants to kill me."

"But he won't. He'll never be free again." He kept hold of her hand as he sat in his chair. "Can I tell the judge you recognized both men?"

She nodded again. "Quint's the one who grabbed me in Jim's office and he called the other man Bear." Her voice held a tremor. She glanced at the door to the cells. "What will happen to them?"

"That's up to the judge. But I know he doesn't take too kindly to men who kidnap women or shoot lawmen, not to mention trying to rob a bank. I imagine he'll be tough on them." He squeezed her hand. "You may as well know that those two will probably hang."

She shuddered slightly and didn't say anything for several moments.

"Am I done here? I think I'd like to leave now."

"Would you like me to walk you back?"

"Thank you, but I'll be fine."

She took her time returning to Jim's office. When she walked into Luke's room and saw him sitting up eating soup, she stopped, surprise stealing anything she could have thought to say. Her eyes filled with tears and she ran from the room. Her mind had been so intent on Quint's son that the sight of Luke looking so healthy flooded her with unspeakable joy and relief.

Luke loved the look of shock on her face. He looked at his mother. "Bring her back."

Sadie smiled and left the room. Minutes ticked by and Luke started to worry. Rachel finally appeared in the doorway, her eyes red-rimmed. He patted the side of the bed and waited for her to sit.

"Why the tears, Rachel?"

She wiped at her eyes. "I'm not sure. I guess you just caught me off guard. Maybe I'm just overly tired, but nothing's wrong."

"Are you sure?"

She looked about ready to cry again. She nodded and stood.

"Don't go. Stay and talk to me awhile."

"You need to rest."

"I'll rest in a bit. I promise." He patted the bed again.

Rachel sat and checked his bandages, pulse, and temperature. She had been avoiding his eyes, but he finally took her hand in his and their eyes met.

"Are you sure you're all right?"

Rachel bit her bottom lip as her gaze dropped to the quilt on the bed. "You just surprised me, Luke. I didn't expect you to look so good this soon. I mean, I'm glad you're doing so much better, but I really expected you'd still look pale and sick and such."

Luke rubbed his thumb on the back of her hand. "So you think I look good?"

Rachel's eyes popped back to his for a moment before dropping to the hand holding hers. She slowly brought her eyes back to his and returned his smile. She pulled her hand from his and reached for the bowl his mother had placed on the bedside table.

"Let me help you get more of this soup into you."

"Don't bother. I've had enough."

Rachel looked at what remained in the bowl and raised her brows.

Luke shook his head. "Don't give me that look. I really don't want any more. What I want is for you to tell me what happened when you went to the jailhouse. Mother told me you went to see Morgan earlier. So what happened?"

She tried to tuck the covers up around his shoulders. "Luke, you need to rest. We can talk about it later."

He again took her hand and waited for her eyes to return to his. "Something upset you. Now tell me what it was."

"Luke!"

"Rachel!" He did his best to imitate her tone and received the smile he sought.

"I wish you would rest."

"Not until you tell me what I want to know."

"No wonder you make such a good lawman. You won't take no for an answer."

"That's right. You'd do well to remember that. Now, stop avoiding the question and talk to me."

Rachel sighed, then told him everything Quint had said to her. With each disclosure, he grew more and more angry until he wanted to climb out of bed and beat the man with his bare fists.

She put her hand over his. "But it's all over now. They're in jail and can't do anything to anyone anymore." Rachel stood. "Now, I did as you asked. It's time you do as I ask. Go to sleep, Luke. You need to rest."

"All right. But I want you to do something for me. Tell Morgan I want to see him tomorrow."

Rachel's eyes filled with doubt.

He held out his hand to her. "Please? If you don't, I'll get someone else to ask him to come and see me."

"Oh, all right, I'll tell him. Now go to sleep!"

Luke smiled and closed his eyes. "Thank you, Rae."

Rachel gazed into his relaxed face. She leaned down to check for a fever and ended up brushing back the hair that had fallen over his forehead. The man had gone after robbers and ended up stealing her heart. And she didn't think she wanted it back. She checked his pulse, then made her way to the waiting area to let Sadie know of the errand Luke wanted her to run. Max Payton sat chatting with Sadie, but when she entered the room, he rose to his feet.

He gave her a quick embrace, then motioned for her to sit next to Sadie. "I was just telling Sadie that I hadn't heard about what had happened to Luke until this morning. She tells me he's doing much better."

"He is. He's back to being a rascal. He wants me to run an errand for him."

"What errand?" Sadie said.

"Only that I tell the sheriff he wants to see him in the morning."

"He'd better not be trying to go back to work already. I'll sit on him before I'll let him return this soon."

"I've already talked to Morgan about that very thing. He said he'd do what he could but that Luke has a mind of his own."

Sadie huffed. "Well, he didn't get that from me."

"Right," Max said. "And who was it that sprained her ankle because she wouldn't wait for help to paint her shutters?"

"She told you about that, huh?" Rachel said.

"No, I found out from Beth. And now I need to know something from you, Rachel. Sadie tells me she's doing fine, but she looks exhausted to me."

"She hasn't been home since Luke was shot, but I can't get her to go home and rest. If you can get her to go home for the night, speaking as a nurse, I think it would do her a world of good."

Sadie placed her hands on her hips. "Now wait a minute! I'll admit I went through a rough time at first, full of fear that I would lose my son the same way I lost my husband. But I'm much better now. Luke is healing quickly, and God has filled me with peace. But thank you for your concern."

Rachel put her arm around her. "Yes, you're doing great emotionally. It's rest you need."

Max nodded. "That's what I thought. Will you allow me to escort you home, Sadie?"

Sadie whacked Rachel on the arm. "Now see what you've done?"

"Yep, I got a handsome gentleman to accompany you home."

Sadie's face turned pink.

"I'll do better than that—I'll buy you supper first." Max put his hand over his heart. "Just for my own peace of mind." He extended his hand. "Would you do me the honor?"

A speechless Sadie accepted his hand and walked with him to the door.

Rachel couldn't help but smile. She prayed they would find happiness with each other...and that Luke would accept the relationship between his mother and the gentlemanly Max.

THIRTY-THREE

Rachel headed to Sadie Mason's house to check Luke's wounds. He'd been home only a few days, and Sadie was already complaining he was restless and that she had her hands full trying to keep him occupied. She claimed the only time he seemed content to sit quietly was when Rachel came around to check his wounds. He managed to coax her into staying long enough to play a game of checkers on two of those occasions. Today, Jim Barnes told Rachel that Luke could be her last stop for the day. If Luke learned that bit of news, there'd be no telling what he'd come up with to get her to stay.

She found him sitting at the kitchen table with something shiny in his hands. He stared at it so intently, he didn't realize she was there until she sat down. When he looked up, his eyes were moist.

"Would you like to be alone, Luke?"

He shook his head and sighed. He held the object out. "My mother just gave me this." The gold pocket watch had a hole through it. "My father was wearing this the day he was killed."

"I'm so sorry, Luke." His chin quivered briefly. "Are you all right?"

He looked at her and gave her a slight smile. "Earlier this summer I probably would've been furious, but I don't feel that kind of anger any longer. I think that's why Mother waited until now to give it to me. She knows I've become more at peace with losing him. I still miss him a lot, especially when I see things like this, but I'm okay with it now."

Sadie joined them then and made coffee before starting supper. They invited Rachel to stay. She accepted and helped Sadie finish preparing the meal. Luke never left the kitchen, and he and Sadie reminisced, telling Rachel all the stories they remembered. It ended up being one of the sweetest evenings Rachel could remember since moving to Rockdale.

During his recovery, Luke learned of the feelings growing between his mother and Max Payton. The man stopped by to check on them whenever he came to town, and he came to town often. It would take a blind man not to notice the way Max looked at Sadie. At first, Luke wasn't sure how he felt about it, but as his love continued to grow for Rachel, he became more understanding of his mother's need for that same kind of love. But he also wanted to protect her from getting hurt.

Luke decided it was time to find out just what Max was thinking. Since he didn't yet have Jim's permission to ride his horse, he hitched up the buggy and rode to the Payton ranch. He found Max standing by a corral.

"You got a minute, Max?"

"Sure do. Might even have two." He clapped Luke on the shoulder. "What can I do for you, son?"

Luke eyed Max. He liked the man. He was good and honest. But he wasn't sure he liked being called son.

"I won't beat around the bush. I'm wondering about your intentions toward my mother."

Max's brows rose for a moment, then he nodded. "You're the man of the house, and I appreciate that you're looking out for your mother." He crossed his arms and leaned against the corral fence. "I admire your mother very much, Luke, and with your permission, I'd like to get to know her better. I've been using your getting shot as an excuse to drop by, but now I'd like to come by just to spend more time with her. Maybe take her out to eat once in a while. She's an amazing woman. But I guess you already know that."

"I do. And I'm glad to hear that you know it too." He reached to shake Max's hand. "I think my mother would like to get to know you better too. I guess we'll be seeing more of each other."

Max smiled. "Thank you, Luke."

He turned to climb into the buggy but stopped at the sight of one of Max's hands riding into the yard. "Is that Michael Dunlavey?"

"Sure is."

"How long has he been working for you?"

"Let's see…I guess it's been four or five weeks now. Maybe more. Why?"

"Is he a good worker? You trust him?"

"I guess. He disappears for hours sometimes, but since he's always gotten his work done, I haven't complained. Is there a problem?"

Luke continued to stare at Dunlavey. "Not sure. If there is, I'll let you know."

He drove home, running all the new information of the day through his head. By the time he made it home, he was ready for a rest.

By the end of the week, Luke thought he'd lose his mind if he had to sit around any longer. He sat outside and waited for Rachel to come home from work to see if she'd take a walk with him. He couldn't stop his smile when he saw her come around the corner. Better yet was the smile she gave him when she saw him.

"Don't tell me, you're bored," she said.

"It's worse than that. You saved my life once. Now you've got to do it again. Take a walk with me. I've got to do something to save my sanity."

Rachel smirked and shook her head. "That was pitiful. I'm guessing it's Sadie's sanity I need to save, so in that case, yes, I'll walk with you. If nothing else, I can make sure you don't overdo."

"Use whatever excuse you want, just as long as you go."

"I'll go as long as you promise to stop when I say it's time."

"Deal."

As they walked down the road, they took turns telling stories of their childhood. Luke learned that Rachel's desire to become a nurse began after her brother died from a fall.

"It was my fault. I talked him into playing hide-and-seek in the loft. When he found me sooner than I thought he should, I pushed him. If I hadn't pushed so hard, he might not have tripped, or at least might have caught himself before going over the edge. I found out later that if he'd had help sooner, he might have survived. It wasn't long before I decided to become a nurse so I could help others."

"How sad. I'm sure that must've been a difficult time for you and your family." They were in front of the stable and he stopped. "Do you mind if I check my horse? I haven't been in there all day."

He went inside to give his horse some hay and a good brushing, but Rachel stood as far from the horse as she could. He waved her over. "Come closer. She won't bite."

"That's all right. I'm fine right here."

He tilted his head. "You're not afraid of horses are you? I thought you said your father ran a livery."

"He does."

"Then why are you afraid of horses? Didn't he let you work with them once in a while?"

"The closest I ever came to the horses was in a buggy or wagon hitched behind them, and Daddy always did the hitching."

"So you're telling me you were spoiled."

Rachel's mouth dropped open. He raised his brows. Her chin jutted out.

"I guess I was."

Luke held his hand out to her. "Come here. I want to show you that you don't need to be afraid of this horse."

Rachel's eyes went to his hand, then to the horse, then back to his hand again. He motioned for her to come closer, and she finally moved toward him. He grasped her hand lightly in his and tugged gently for her to step closer to the horse. When she finally took that step, Luke placed her hand on the horse's nose. Rachel tried to pull her hand away, but Luke grasped it tighter and guided her hand over the horse's nose.

"Oh! It feels so soft."

He released her hand, and she continued to rub the horse on her own.

"See, there's nothing to be afraid of. She's as gentle as they come. Would you let me teach you to ride?"

Rachel's head snapped toward him. Her hand dropped to her side and she took a step back. "No, that's okay. I don't need to learn that."

Luke reached for her hand again and gasped when the sudden movement caused a twinge in one of his wounds. Rachel stepped to his side.

"Are you all right?" She placed her hand over his that had gone to his ribs.

Luke looked into her eyes and smiled. "I like having you as my nurse."

She blushed and looked away as she took a step back. "I don't know why you offered to teach me to ride when you're not well enough for that kind of activity."

"It's not me who would need to get on the horse, Rae."

"But you won't be able to saddle it."

"No, but you could."

"I could not. I don't know how, and I'm sure I couldn't toss that saddle on her back anyway."

"You could with my help."

"Luke!"

"Rachel!"

His mimicry made her smile.

Jim came in at that moment but stopped when he saw them. "Am I interrupting?"

"Not at all," Luke said. "In fact, your timing couldn't be better. Would you mind helping Rachel saddle my horse?"

"You're not planning on riding are you, Luke? Because I don't advise that just yet."

"No, I'm not going to ride it. Rachel is."

Jim's brows nearly hit his hairline. "I'd be glad to help Rachel with that saddle. Just let me put up my horse and buggy first."

Rachel crossed her arms and tapped her foot. "I never said I would ride your horse, Luke."

"You never said you wouldn't either. Come on, Rachel, give it a try. I think if you did, you might find that you like it."

Rachel stared into his eyes. Just when he figured she'd decline, she agreed to try it.

She moved close as if to tell him a secret. "You know the last time you acted like this, you ended up with a mud ball in your back."

Luke gazed at her for a moment, then laughed.

"Are we ready to begin?" Jim said.

"You bet."

Jim quickly saddled the horse and offered to help her aboard.

Rachel looked at Jim, and Luke thought she might change her mind and back out. Then she finally nodded.

"That's probably the only way I'll be able to get up there."

Jim looked from the saddle to Rachel. "How about we move the horse next to our porch. That way Rachel will have an easier time getting on."

"You mean I have to go out where people can see me?"

Jim's shoulders shook in silent laughter, and Luke had to move so he couldn't see him any longer.

"Well, you can't ride in this little stable, Rachel," Jim said. "The horse will get dizzy walking in such a small circle."

"It'll be all right, Rachel. Come on."

Luke motioned for Jim to lead the way to the porch. Beth stepped out of the house.

"What's going on? Are you going somewhere else, Jim?"

"No, Luke's going to teach Rachel to ride."

"Oh, let me get Emma and Tanner. I think they'd like to see this."

She was back only moments later with her two excited children, and they made themselves comfortable in the chairs on the porch. Luke caught the scowl Rachel sent toward Beth.

Jim handed the reins to Luke. "Are you ready, Rachel?"

"No, but let's get this over with."

Jim stepped forward to help her mount the horse. "You don't mind if we watch, do you?"

"I don't think I have much choice, do I?"

"I guess not. Just relax and enjoy it. I agree with Luke—you just might find that you'll like it."

Jim helped Rachel swing her leg over the saddle by stepping off the porch. The horse gave a small step forward before Luke stopped it. Rachel released a small squeal as she grabbed for the saddle horn.

Luke looked up at her. "Sorry. Now, I'm just going to lead her around for a while until you get used to the feel of it. Sound all right?"

Rachel gave a little nod, and he gave her a smile of encouragement before heading down the street. Cheers from the children reached them as they walked away some distance before turning back to the house. Luke had to make the trip three times before Rachel would agree to take the reins and steer the horse herself, but only after Luke agreed to continue walking along beside her.

They had been at it for almost an hour when Jim told Luke to come and get him when they were ready to put the horse up for the night. Then he and Beth took their kids in to eat their supper.

Rachel was ready to get off, but Luke pulled the horse away from the porch before she could dismount.

"What're you doing? I thought we were quitting."

"We are, just as soon as you take one trip by yourself."

Rachel's eyes first went wide before narrowing. "No, Luke, I'm done. It's time to quit."

"Not until you agree to do it once by yourself." Luke began walking down the street again, but Rachel didn't let the horse follow him. He turned back. "What's wrong?"

"Aren't you tired yet, Luke? I mean, you aren't completely healed and you shouldn't be doing all of this."

"Yes, I'm getting tired, but I don't want to quit until you feel comfortable enough to ride a short distance by yourself. So let's get going."

Rachel shook her head. "Go sit down, Luke. I'll go by myself this time."

"Are you sure?"

She nodded and gave him a sweet smile. Then she heeled the horse gently and began a slow walk away from him. Luke stood and watched as she rode down the street a distance before turning the horse back. He knew she had gone by herself only because she was worried about him, and he couldn't have loved her more than he did right then.

Luke climbed onto the porch to help Rachel off when she stopped the horse alongside of him. She lifted her leg over the saddle to step onto the porch but lost her balance. Luke grabbed her to keep her from falling. The move caused his side to ache, but he loved the feel of her in his arms.

"Are you all right?" Did she realize just how close she came to getting kissed?

"Yes, thanks to you."

"You're welcome." He hadn't yet released her. "Did you have fun?"

"It had its moments."

Jim opened the door. "Oh, so you are done. Let me get the horse for you. We still have plenty of food left, so if you're hungry, just go on in. So what did you think, Rachel? Will you get back on again?"

"I might. It wasn't as bad as I thought."

"I suspected that might be the case," Jim said, then he left to put the horse up.

"Thank you for the lesson, Luke. Now go home and rest. I'm sure I made you overdo it, and I'm sorry about that."

"I'm fine. I'll be ready to do it all over again tomorrow if you feel up to it."

"I'll have to let you know about that. I can still feel that saddle even though I'm not on it any longer."

Luke laughed and turned to walk away, but when he heard Rachel call his name, he turned back.

Rachel touched his side though she looked into his eyes. "Are you sure you didn't overdo it today?"

Luke put his hand over hers and squeezed. "I'm sure. Good-night, Rachel."

Rachel woke the next morning and discovered soreness in muscles she didn't even know she had. She waddled over to have coffee with Beth and found her laughing.

"What's so funny?"

Beth pointed at her window. "I watched you walk over here."

Rachel slowly lowered herself onto a chair. "It's not funny, Beth. I haven't been this sore since I fell down those steps. I don't know how I'm going to do a lesson for the children tomorrow in this condition. I can hardly move, and I won't be able to talk through all their laughter."

"You could always get Luke to do it for you since it's his fault you're in this condition."

Rachel's eyes went wide. "That's a great idea. I just hope he stops by so I can tell him that because I don't think I can walk that far to go to him."

THIRTY-FOUR

Luke showed up Saturday afternoon to give her another riding lesson, but when he saw her attempt to walk, he gave her the day off. Rachel tried to give him a withering look, which only caused Luke to laugh.

She shook her finger at him. "If you want me on your horse ever again, you have to teach my lesson to the children tomorrow morning."

"I think I'm getting the worst end of this deal, but if it gets you on a horse again, I'll do it."

Rachel arrived with Luke Sunday morning and told the kids he was doing the lesson instead of her. When the children cheered, Luke examined her face to see if she was hurt by their reaction. But she only clapped along with them and then sat to listen.

The first hint of nervousness arrived when all eyes turned to him. He pulled a small bag from his pocket and showed the children several different kinds of leaves.

He held up one at a time. "Any guess as to what kind of tree this leaf came from?"

He continued through each leaf in his bag and let everyone guess. From another small bag, he pulled out a handful of different kinds of seeds, and again they went through the process of guessing each kind.

"Each leaf and each seed is different, and each one is special in its own way. God created each of the leaves and seeds just as He created each of you." He looked at each of the children sitting in front of him. "All of you are special in your own way and are very special to God."

That afternoon, Luke knocked on Rachel's door. "I held up my end of our deal. You ready to do the same?" He turned and pointed at his saddled horse.

She made a face, but then followed him outside.

Every evening for the next five days, Luke waited for Rachel to arrive home so she could continue her lessons. By Friday she had made significant progress.

"My muscles are no longer screaming at me nor am I ready to run screaming from your horse." She held out her hand and he took it in his. "Thank you, Luke."

"You're welcome. But you're not finished yet."

"I'm not?"

"Nope. You have one more ride to take. I'm borrowing a horse tomorrow, and we're going for a ride together. I'll be returning to work Monday, and as my nurse, you have to make sure I'm ready to ride."

"Well, if that's what it takes to get you being productive again, I guess I can manage."

"Don't sound so excited."

"Actually, that sounds like fun. I have to prove to you what a good teacher you are. I'd even challenge you to a race except that you're not ready for that yet."

"Oh, now that's a contest that has to take place one day."

She pointed her finger under his nose. "Don't get too confident."

He grabbed her finger. "We'll see."

He arrived at the stable early the next afternoon to saddle his horse and found Rachel inside.

"Anxious, are you? Great! Give me a minute and we can be on our way."

All the while they rode, he wondered if she'd yet figured out how he felt about her or if he should remove all doubt and just tell her. Lacking a good answer, he spent his time trying to keep her laughing. He loved to hear her laugh. Later they turned serious as they discussed their most recent studies and daily readings in the Bible.

The afternoon ended much too soon as he led Rachel to the stable and helped her slide off the saddle before leading his horse inside. He'd never considered himself a coward, but when it came to Rachel, all courage disappeared. Maybe getting back to work was the best thing for him.

Rachel followed Luke into the stable and stood quietly while he took care of his horse. When he'd forced her to ride with him that afternoon, he'd played right into the hands of Rachel and his mother. They'd struggled to find a way to get him away from the house long enough for Sadie and Beth Barnes to set up a surprise party for his birthday.

When he arrived early at the stable, she had been forced to hide his gift by shoving it behind some hay when he wasn't looking. Now she followed Luke out again, thanking him for the ride before turning toward her house.

Luke mounted the horse he'd borrowed and rode off to return it to its owner. Rachel waited until he was a good distance away, then went back to the stable to get his gift. She'd have to hurry to help Sadie finish preparing for the party.

She'd just retrieved the gift when she heard the door to the stable open.

"I saw you return to the stable, Rachel," Luke said. "Is everything all right?"

She spun around, hiding the gift behind her back. She hoped Luke hadn't noticed in the dark interior.

"What's behind your back, Rachel?" Luke headed toward her, his steps slow.

"I, uh…nothing."

"Rachel, what are you hiding?"

She'd never heard his voice so soft, so tender. She remained silent, her hand behind her back. But then he was standing in front of her with a smile on his face.

He held out his hand. "Hand it over."

"What?"

"Whatever you're hiding behind your back."

Rachel jutted her chin out with a smile. "No."

His brows went up for a moment, then he took a step forward. His breath caressed her cheek as he leaned closer. Her heart hammered as she prepared for his kiss. Then he lightly touched her arm and followed it down to her hand and grabbed the small box she held.

"What's this?" Luke whispered into her ear, causing a tingle to run over her skin.

After he took the box from her, he leaned back only far enough to look into her eyes. A second later he lightly touched her lips with his. It was all she could do to restrain herself from wrapping her arms around the neck of the man she loved.

Luke was smiling as he looked into her eyes. "I guess I should apologize for that, but I don't know that I'm all that sorry. I've been wanting to kiss you for some time now." He took a step back. "Are you upset with me?"

She smiled and shook her head. He stared at her several more seconds before finally looking down at the small box in his hand. His eyes went back to hers.

"What's this?"

"Happy birthday, Luke."

"Mother told you?"

"A long time ago."

"Why didn't you give it to me earlier?"

She shrugged. "It didn't seem the right time."

"Is now the right time?"

"Sure."

Luke tore off the bow and paper, then lifted the lid off the box. He took the gold chain between his fingers and pulled out the gold pocket watch. He examined the outside before flipping open the lid.

She didn't know what to think of the look on his face when he saw the picture of his father. When he finally lifted his eyes to hers, she could see the tears threatening to overflow. For the first time, she questioned the wisdom of her gift.

"Is it all right, Luke?"

"It's more than all right. It's wonderful. Thank you."

"Your mother found that picture for me. It seemed your father's watch signified an end to life. Maybe this one can mean the beginning of a new one."

Luke stepped forward and pulled her into his arms again. This time, he kissed her brow. Rachel wrapped her arms around his waist, and he held her close for a moment.

"Thank you, Rachel."

"You're welcome."

Luke leaned back and ran his finger down her cheek. "I'd better go. I need to get the horse back, and Mother is expecting me for supper."

"All right. I'll see you later."

The two left the stable together, but this time Rachel entered her house and watched for Luke to disappear completely before she left again for Sadie's house. When she came into the kitchen, Sadie rushed to her.

"My word, Rachel! I was beginning to worry about you two. Is Luke with you?"

"No, but he'll be here shortly. He's taking the horse back to its owner."

Rachel moved to the back of the kitchen behind all those already there to celebrate. She'd had her time with Luke. Now it was their turn to rejoice with him. Minutes later, when he arrived and was caught off guard, his eyes sought her out before giving her a warm smile.

It may have been Luke's party, but she was the one celebrating.

THIRTY-FIVE

Rachel hadn't been at work long Monday morning when Lucille Munroe's son-in-law burst into the office.

"Mother's sick. She's bad. You've gotta come."

Rachel's heart pounded as she and Jim Barnes raced after Aaron Chatham. They entered the elderly lady's room. The white bedsheets had more color than her face. Lucille's daughter Edna sat beside her bed, but stood and moved out of their way. Jim checked her pulse as he felt her forehead.

Lucille's eyes opened. "I told Aaron not to bother you. I don't need anyone fussing over me."

The effort to talk caused Lucille to cough. Rachel had heard that before and her concern grew.

Lucille looked from her to Jim. "I know what you're thinking, Doc, and I don't want you trying anything heroic to keep me here." She coughed again, much weaker this time. "I'm old and sickly and ready to go home."

Jim turned to Aaron, then to his wife. The couple had tears in their eyes. They looked at each other, then nodded to Jim.

Jim took Lucille's hand in his. "Would you like anything for your discomfort?"

She shook her head. "I'm all right. It's not so bad." She held her other hand out to Rachel, who took it as she sat down on the bed.

"Thank you for listening to my stories, dear. I know you had better things to do than listen to an old woman prattle on."

Rachel shook her head. "You have no idea how much I enjoyed those times, and I'll treasure the memories." The tears she'd fought streamed down her face.

Lucille gave her a weak smile. "Now, why are you crying, Rachel? You know we'll see each other again one day."

Rachel nodded, her throat aching. "I know, but I'll miss you until then."

The smile had never left Lucille's face. "Just go find some other old woman to nurse so you can hear some new stories. You've heard all of mine." Another cough shook her frame. "You've been a ray of sunshine for me, Rachel. Thank you."

Rachel leaned to kiss her cheek, then stood and moved away. Cassie rushed into the room, hesitated at the door, then hurried to her great-grandmother's side. Lucille grasped her hand.

"My dear girl. I hope you know how much I love you."

Cassie wiped at her eyes and nodded. "I love you too."

She tugged at Cassie's hand until her great-granddaughter leaned closer. "My hope and prayer for you is that one day soon you'll see what I've known all along…that you have a beautiful heart. You don't need to act proud and important for people to like you. Let them see the real you and they'll come to love you."

She patted Cassie's hand then she turned her eyes to her son-in-law. "Aaron." He approached and took Cassie's place on the bed. "You've been a dear man, a wonderful husband to my daughter, and loving grandfather. So caring and thoughtful. But there's one thing you've always fought me on, and I hope you'll soon change your mind."

Lucille's shaky hand reached for his. "I'd like to see you again one day too, but that won't happen until you believe in God's Son, Jesus Christ. He died for you, Aaron, just as He did for me, and He's just waiting for you to accept Him. If you do that, we'll be able to spend eternity together. If not, we'll be eternally separated. I've told you the steps to salvation numerous times so I won't go through them now."

Lucille coughed, but now she fought to catch her breath. With a rasp to her voice, she started again. "Trust in Him, Aaron. You'll never truly have peace until you do."

The speech and the coughing had completely worn the lady out and she closed her eyes. With her hand still within Aaron's, she fell into a deep sleep. Her breathing was so shallow, Rachel stepped closer to see if they'd lost her. Jim checked her and shook his head.

"She's only sleeping." He stood. "Rachel will stay and tend to her. I'll be back after I've checked on some of my other patients."

Cassie ran from the room. Aaron joined his wife on a small couch against one wall, their arms going around each other. Rachel occupied the chair next to the bed and began her vigil. It was getting late in the afternoon when she noticed Lucille's breathing had slowed and become even more labored. She called to the couple, who rushed to the side of the bed.

"I don't think it'll be much longer."

Aaron and his wife sat on the bed, each taking one of Lucille's hands as they stared into her face. Rachel moved to the background to allow the family a measure of privacy.

Ten minutes later, Lucille slipped quietly from them, having never again opened her eyes. When Rachel stepped forward and confirmed that she was gone, the couple leaned down and placed a kiss on her forehead before rising from the bed and into each other's arms. Then they turned to Rachel.

"Thank you for everything," Edna said. "You've been wonderful to my mother, and I appreciate all that you've done."

"You're welcome."

The couple slipped from the room, leaving Rachel with the body. She again sat down on the bed and looked into Lucille's face, taking in her peaceful expression. The floodgates opened then as she mourned the loss of the dear lady.

Rachel wept again at the funeral two days later. Luke Mason stood next to her, looking so handsome in his dark suit and hat, a string tie dangling at the neck of his crisp white shirt, a stark contrast to his tanned face. When she shivered from the cool fall air, he put his arm around her, lending not only warmth but comfort.

When the funeral had ended, she approached Mr. and Mrs. Chatham. After giving them both a hug, Edna pressed a small envelope into her hand.

"Mother wanted you to have this. Aaron found it tucked away in her Bible as he was looking through it yesterday."

Rachel opened the envelope and found the locket Lucille was rarely seen without. Also inside the envelope was a short note.

> My dearest Rachel,
>
> Wear this close to your heart and let it remind you that you are loved, not only by me and so many others, but most of all by God. Our friendship is proof of what can happen when two hearts meet. Remember, no matter what a day may bring, whether it be good or bad, He'll be there, loving you through it all.
>
> Your friend,
> Lucille Munroe

With tears running down her face, Rachel hugged Edna. "Thank you. I'll treasure this always."

She would have walked away then but Aaron touched her arm to stop her.

"You know how Mother loved to tell stories. Well, she'd written out the story about how she'd come to accept Christ as her Savior, along with all the verses she used to quote to me. I just wanted to let you know that as of last night, she'll be waiting for my arrival when my time comes."

His wife was smiling up into his face, her arms wrapped around his waist, and he smiled down at her before turning back to Rachel.

"Not only did she write out the references of all those verses, but she marked each place with a piece of ribbon, just to make sure I could find them. She had always recited the verses to me or read them to me, but I think reading them myself had more of an impact." He wiped the tears from his cheeks. "She was right. There is no other feeling of peace like what I have right now."

Rachel touched his arm. "I think Lucille would be the first to say that this is by far the best ending to any one of her stories. Welcome to the family, Mr. Chatham."

A week later, Rachel stared down into the grumpy face of local rancher Hank Willett, his frown making the creases on his face even deeper.

"I'm warning you, Mr. Willett, you've got to stay off that leg if you want it to heal properly."

"I ain't taking no orders from some bossy woman. Why didn't Doc come instead of sending this mess of frills?"

The last was said under his breath, but Rachel heard every word the elderly gentleman muttered.

"I'm only repeating what Dr. Barnes wanted me to tell you. He also said a man your age has no business climbing around the loft of a barn, that you have hired hands for that."

Mr. Willett's scowl deepened. "What's a city boy know about ranching?"

"He may not know a lot about ranching, but he knows that a broken leg won't heal properly if you don't stay off of it."

Mr. Willett crossed his arms and turned his head from her. From her previous rounds checking him, she knew he wouldn't say another word. She shook her head and pulled on her coat before grabbing her bag.

"I'll be back in a few days. Have a good day."

She climbed into the buggy ready to be home. Jim's horse seemed to know the way, so Rachel paid little heed, choosing instead to daydream. Her thoughts went to Luke and how close they'd become. Their interest in one another was now common knowledge to everyone in town. As she recalled the few kisses they'd shared, her hand went to her mouth. A lifetime of those wouldn't be enough.

The wheel of the buggy dropped into a large hole in the road, jarring her mind back to driving. Her medical bag had slid toward the buggy's doorway. She leaned down to pull the bag back to her feet and heard a bang. Searing pain ripped through her shoulder at the same time the horse let out a shrill neigh. As the horse tore down the road, the sudden surge of the buggy threw Rachel back. The buggy swayed from side to side. She tried to gain control by yanking on the reins. The horse didn't respond other than to shake its head and run faster before veering off the road.

The buggy bounced and bumped, tossing Rachel around. She grabbed the side bar and was just getting her balance when she heard another bang. The world went dark.

THIRTY-SIX

When Luke Mason heard the first gunshot, he reined to a stop. *Which direction did that come from?* He scanned the area and saw nothing. Before he could make up his mind which way to go, another shot went off. He spurred his horse into a gallop.

Minutes later, Jim Barnes's horse and buggy came into view. The horse raced across the clearing as the buggy rocked from one set of wheels to the other. Luke nudged his horse faster, but he didn't catch up before the buggy tipped over. The horse continued to run, dragging the buggy several yards before coming to a stop.

Luke launched from his saddle and grabbed the horse's bridle to keep it from running off again. He patted the horse's head until it calmed, then he moved to the buggy. Empty. Luke headed back to his horse, but he stopped when he noticed blood dripping from the horse's rump. The wound could have come only from a gunshot.

He mounted his horse and rode the direction the buggy had come from. A splash of white against the green and tan prairie grabbed his eye. He galloped over and quickly dismounted. The sight of Rachel's bloody face sent a chill through him. He stared at her throat and saw a pulse. He scooped her into his arms, climbed onto his saddle, and raced to find Jim.

What seemed like a lifetime later, Luke stopped in front of Jim's house and carefully stepped from the saddle. He climbed the porch steps and kicked at the door several times. Footsteps thumped from inside. Seconds later the door swung open. Beth's eyes went wide as she moved aside. His mother and Cora Baxter showed up behind Beth. They gasped, but Luke didn't slow as he carried Rachel inside.

"Jim here yet?"

"Not yet. I expect him any minute."

Luke laid Rachel on the bed. "This can't wait. I'm going after him." He stopped. "Help her, Beth. I think she's been shot."

He raced out of the house, his emotions running from fear to rage and back again. Who would shoot Rachel? And why?

He spotted Jim as he walked toward home. Luke stopped next to him. "Rachel's hurt."

Jim climbed up behind him. "What happened?"

"Looks like a gunshot grazed her temple, but she's also banged up pretty bad. I'm thinking the gunshot knocked her out and she fell out of the buggy."

"Gunshot? Who'd shoot Rachel?"

"That's what I intend to find out. I'll drop you at your house and go back to look at your horse and buggy, then follow the trail to where it happened. Where was Rachel visiting this afternoon?"

"I sent her to Hank Willett's place to check his broken leg."

"All right. I'll start at your horse and head that direction." He paused for a breath. "Your horse was shot too, and your buggy's wrecked."

When they stopped, Jim jumped from the horse and looked up at him. "I don't care about the buggy. That can be replaced. I thought all this nonsense was over. I sure hope you find out who's hurting Rachel and stop them."

He nodded. "I will, but I want to check on her first."

He trailed Jim inside and stopped in the doorway. All three women stood over Rachel, working to clean up her face. They'd removed her coat and dress, which lay in a heap on the floor near his feet. He crouched and examined her garments and frowned at the amount of blood. The entire left side and part of the sleeve was soaked. He grabbed her coat and found a hole. He stood and looked at Jim and the ladies.

"She was shot in the shoulder too?"

Jim didn't respond, but Beth and Sadie turned to him and nodded. The memory of his dead father raced through his mind as he backed out of the room. He could have lost her the same way. He still might.

He ran from the house, climbed onto his saddle, and galloped back to Jim's horse, his mind spinning. Just when he had started trusting God again, He allowed this to happen. Luke didn't know if he was more angry at the person who shot Rachel or at the unfeeling God who didn't care about those who loved Him.

Jim's horse still stood where he'd left it. Luke jumped down and unhitched the horse from the buggy, then slapped its rump. The horse would find its way back to Jim's. He'd send Cade Ramsey for the buggy later. Right now, he had to find the man who'd hurt Rachel, and that person better pray Luke could hold his temper.

He climbed back on his horse and followed the trail the wheels left in the grass. Rachel's medical bag lay intact along the way. He climbed down to retrieve it and tied it to his saddle before continuing on. He was just reaching the place where the horse pulled the buggy off the road when Morgan Taylor rode up to him.

"I heard about Rachel. You find anything yet?"

"Nothing of any help. Is she all right?"

"I didn't go by there to check. I came straight out to find and help you."

"All right, here's what I'm thinking." He pointed at the buggy tracks. "This is where the horse pulled the buggy from the road. That means Rachel and the horse were probably shot somewhere near here."

"Jim's horse was shot?"

"Only the rump. If I were to guess, the shooter was up high, possibly in one of these trees or in the nearby hills." Luke acted as though he held a rifle. "As he aimed down at Rachel, the bullet grazed the horse's hip on its way to hit Rachel. Make sense?"

"Sounds pretty good. Let's have a look around here and see if we can find something that might tell us who did this."

They split up. Luke scouted the cluster of trees and a quarter of a mile on either side while Morgan checked the hills. They met back up, each shaking their head, not even finding the spent shell casings from the rifle.

Luke faced Morgan. "I've been thinking. Someone's been after Rachel for some time now. Remember how that nail was found in the rein, then that snake was in her bag, and soon after that she tripped on that string at the Chathams and took a fall down their porch steps." He shook his head. "Those were meant to hurt her, but now someone's trying to kill her. What are the chances it's the same person?"

Morgan gave a low whistle. "Sounds reasonable. Who would hate her that much?"

"I don't know, but if we don't find him soon, he just might succeed next time."

"Agreed, but it's too dark to look any further. Let's call it a night and try again first thing in the morning."

Though he wasn't ready to give up, Luke nodded and followed Morgan back to town. The closer they got to Rockdale, the more distance he tried to put between himself and Rachel. He refused to run the risk of another painful loss.

Rachel moaned and tried to open her eyes, but her lids refused to cooperate. As something poked at her left side, her head throbbed. Another stab to her shoulder made her want to yell. Only a hiss came out. She finally got her eyes to open but saw only a blur. She blinked several times and tried again. Jim's face came into focus.

She worked to open her dry mouth. "What are you doing to me, Jim?"

He didn't answer, but her pain increased. She winced and moaned again.

"If this is the way you treat all your patients, then I think I'd better take over your practice for a while so you can work on your bedside manner."

"Well, that's a good sign. You're actually admitting you're a patient."

He dabbed something near her shoulders. She winced and hissed. "Ouch. That hurts." She looked Jim in the eyes. "What's wrong with my arm?" She could tell she was being ignored. "Jim?"

He gave her a long look, then took a deep breath. "You were shot."

Rachel stared at Jim as his words sank in. "Shot?"

She tried to replay the day in her mind. She remembered scolding Mr. Willett and leaving his home. She recalled some of the ride home and hitting a hole in the road.

A door slammed, and seconds later Luke entered the room. In his haste, he bumped into the doorframe and the nearby dresser. She was about to smile at him when she saw the expression on his face and then the look in his eyes. Moments later, he spun on his heel and dashed from the room. Sadie stood and hurried after him.

The look of fear, panic, even horror on Luke's face stuck with Rachel. Something in her heart told her she'd lost him. She stared at the door, willing him to return. The doorway remained empty.

"Rachel?" Jim grasped her chin and made her look at him. "I still need to take care of your head wound."

He turned her head, and she remained still while he went to work. In order to get through the ordeal, she forced her mind from Luke and back to getting shot. After she hit the hole, she reached to keep her bag from falling out of the buggy and then heard the bang.

"Who would shoot me, Jim? And why?"

Jim sighed. "I don't know, Rachel. I've been wondering that myself and haven't come up with any answers yet."

Exhaustion and pain dragged her mind into a daze, and she had trouble fighting the sleep pulling at her. Sadie returned to the room and sat on the chair next to the bed. Rachel examined Sadie's face for any sign of good news.

Sadie shook her head. "I'm sorry, but he wouldn't even talk to me."

Rachel couldn't stop the tears. Sadie leaned close and wiped them away, placing a kiss there instead. Rachel's eyes slid shut and she kept them that way, allowing unconsciousness to remove the pain.

THIRTY-SEVEN

Rachel slept through the night and woke when she felt pain in her arm. Hissing through her teeth, she looked up to find Jim Barnes standing at her shoulder.

"Oh, it's you again. Didn't you get enough of torturing me yesterday?"

Jim chuckled. "I didn't figure I'd get another chance like this, so I'm making the most of it."

Rachel groaned and hissed again when he moved her arm to check under her bandage.

Beth came in and smiled. "Good morning, Rachel."

"It was until your husband began torturing me again."

A sharp pain pierced her arm. She scowled at Jim, and he grinned at her.

"The sheriff is here wanting to talk to you," Beth said. "Are you up for it?"

She finally nodded. "I'll see him."

She was hissing again and saying ouch when Morgan Taylor entered the room.

He stepped to the foot of the bed. "Anything I can do?"

"Yes. You can arrest this man."

"All right, and what would the charge be?"

"Torturing his patients."

272

The two men shared a grin as Jim stood. "All done. I'll leave you two alone."

"You can stay," Morgan said. "This won't take long." Then he turned to Rachel. "Just tell me what happened."

"I'm not sure I know. I was on my way home from checking on Mr. Willett. The buggy hit a hole causing my bag to almost slide out. When I reached down to move it back, I heard a bang, felt pain, and the horse took off. The next thing I remember, I'm here."

"You don't remember getting shot?"

"Not really. Like I said, I felt pain in my shoulder. The bang must have scared the horse."

"It did." The sheriff moved to the side of the bed. "Luke told me the rump of Jim's horse was hit too."

"Oh, Jim, I'm sorry. Your horse won't want anything more to do with me. He'll see me coming and run the other direction."

"Where were you when the horse bolted?" Morgan said.

Rachel thought back. "Do you know that small cluster of trees next to the road, the one that has that big boulder near them?" When the sheriff nodded, she said, "I think I had just passed them."

"You didn't see anyone in or around the trees?"

"No, I didn't notice a thing."

"All right. Luke and I already looked around last evening, but we'll go check again. I may as well tell you, Rachel, that unless we find some evidence around that area, it's likely we won't be able to find out who did this to you."

Rachel nodded, then closed her eyes and prayed for sleep to take over quickly. She woke only an hour later. Cora Baxter sat next to the bed.

"Your turn to be the nursemaid?"

Cora smiled at her. "I volunteered to sit with you so Beth could get some work done. Can I get you anything?"

Rachel's eyes fell on the bedpan, and Cora rose to fetch it without a word.

"I'm sorry, Cora."

Cora shushed her and helped her take care of her business.

"Now, how about something to eat? Beth tells me you probably haven't eaten since lunchtime yesterday, and she wasn't even sure about that."

Cora left and returned minutes later with a bowl of stew and Beth right on her heels.

"It won't take both of you to get that into me."

But it did take both of them to help Rachel scoot up against the pillows. The upright position made her head throb, and she felt a little dizzy at first. She closed her eyes, waiting for the feeling to subside.

"Are you all right, Rachel?" Beth asked. "Are you dizzy?"

"I was but I'm better now." She opened her eyes to see her friend's worried face. "Really. Now go on back to what you were doing."

"You hate being a patient, don't you?" Beth said.

"More than I can say."

Beth patted her arm then left, telling them over her shoulder to call if they needed anything.

Rachel wasn't all that hungry, but she ate what she could just to please Cora, who held the bowl while Rachel used her good arm to hold the spoon.

"William's been begging me to let him come and read to you every day until you're well again. He said you've done so many lessons for them at church that it was time for someone to do something for you in return."

"Give him a hug for me and tell him I'd enjoy that. How about Saturday?" Rachel set the spoon down and shook her head. "That was very good, but I can't eat any more right now."

"Is there anything else I can do for you, Rachel? Anything I can get for you?"

"No, thank you."

"All right. Call out if you need anything. I'll be in the living room."

Rachel nodded and waited for her to leave, grateful for some time alone.

I don't know why all of this is happening, Lord. I can't understand why someone would want to hurt me, but I know that You're in control and that gives me a feeling of peace. And Luke. O Lord, Luke. I don't know how I'll go on without him. Please, Lord, get me through this without my heart breaking more than it already has.

The next time Rachel opened her eyes, Beth sat against the wall with her lap full of mending. Not giving away the fact that she was awake, she examined Beth until she had to smile.

"What are you grinning at?" Beth finally said.

"When are you due?"

Beth stared at Rachel for several seconds. "How did you know that? Jim doesn't even know."

"I don't know. There's just a certain look about you."

Beth gave her a skeptical look.

"When were you planning to tell Jim?"

"I hadn't decided yet, but I guess I'd better do it soon now that you know."

"I won't say a word." Rachel lay silent. "It's awfully quiet around here. Does Garnett Robbins have the kids?"

"No, Cora took them home. She's going to feed them and have Chad bring them back when they're finished." Beth eyed her for a few moments. "Were you looking for a distraction?"

Rachel shook her head. Beth gave her a look of compassion, and Rachel shook her head again before looking away.

"Don't, Beth. I don't know if I can stand that."

"All right, but I'm here if you need to talk."

"I know and thank you for that. So did Jim mention any of his patients to you?"

"He only talks about one," Sadie said as she entered the room. "Something about an obstinate nurse."

Beth stood and left the room, and Sadie took her place on the chair. The two eyed each other until Sadie stood and sat on the side of the bed.

"How are you, dear? And don't tell me fine. I want the truth."

The tears Rachel had kept at bay for so long filled her eyes. "It hurts. And I don't mean the wounds."

"I understand." Sadie grasped Rachel's hand. "He's still not telling me what he's thinking. He's not acting angry, he's just not talking."

"I saw fear in his eyes, Sadie. I can only guess that he's remembering what it was like to lose his father. He's scared."

"I thought the same thing. He's going to have to learn to trust God all over again. It'll just be a matter of time."

"I hope you're right. In the meantime, I'll keep praying for him."

"As will I. I read something this morning that helped, something I'd once memorized." Sadie tipped her head back and closed her eyes. "'Therefore being justified by faith, we have peace with God through our Lord Jesus Christ: by whom also we have access by faith into this grace wherein we stand, and rejoice in hope of the glory of God. And not only so, but we glory in tribulations also: knowing that tribulation worketh patience; and patience, experience; and experience, hope; and hope maketh not ashamed; because the love of God is shed abroad in our hearts by the Holy Ghost which is given unto us.'"

Rachel was smiling by the time Sadie finished. "Thank you for that."

"I'm glad it helped. Sure helped me."

Sadie stayed and chatted with her until Jim arrived to check her wounds. Then she said good-bye, promising she'd be back in the morning. Jim took his time removing her bandages.

"Beth tells me you didn't eat much today."

Beth entered at that moment and Rachel scowled at her. "I ate what I wanted."

Beth put her hands on her hips. "But you've got to admit that it wasn't much. You need to start eating better. In fact, let me get you a plate of food right now. You haven't had your supper yet."

And Beth sped from the room, leaving her husband grinning at Rachel.

Rachel made a face. "I know, I'm just not a good patient."

"I don't know of any person in medicine that is, myself included."

Jim finished his examination and put new bandages on her wounds. Beth returned with Rachel's supper. Jim helped her sit up a little more, then scooted out of the way.

"I think it's time for me to go home," Rachel said as she ate. "I've taken up enough of your time, and I need to get out of your way. I'm sure I can manage on my own now."

"We were hoping you'd stay here for a while," Jim said. "At least until they catch the person trying to hurt you."

Rachel's eyes went to Beth, dropping momentarily to her abdomen before going back to her face. Jim glanced at his wife and smiled.

"I know about the baby, if that's what you're wondering, and we don't think you'll be a strain on Beth. Like you said, you can probably start doing things for yourself now."

"Then why do you want me to stay?"

"If this person really means to harm you, and it's obvious he does, he could very easily break into your house and do anything he wants to you. We can't stand the thought of that and would sleep much better knowing you were here with us rather than by yourself over there."

Rachel eyed the two of them, trying to decide what to do. She finally nodded.

"All right, I'll stay. But I don't want you fretting over me, Beth. You've got enough to worry about."

"That won't be a problem. I'd worry more if you weren't here."

"I agree," Jim said. "And I know you're going to want out of this bed tomorrow, so I suggest that when you feel up to it, go with Beth to your house and pick out everything you want brought over for your stay here."

"All right. We can do that right after my bath." She ignored Jim's raised brows. "I want my hair washed too. And please don't say no. I feel filthy. Sadie said she'd be back in the morning, and I'll get her to help. We'll try hard not to get my wounds wet."

Jim shook his head at her. "You win." He was about to stand but then dropped back on the end of the bed again. "One other thing, and this isn't up for discussion. When you're well enough to go back to work, you'll no longer leave for work early until this guy is caught. You'll wait and go with me to the office and we'll prepare it together. You're easy prey when you're by yourself."

"All right. So when do I get to start working again?"

Jim shook his head as he walked away. Beth took his place on the bed.

"You do like to torment him, don't you?"

Rachel smiled. "It has its moments."

"Will you allow me to fret one more time, Rachel, and ask you to *please* finish your supper?"

Rachel rolled her eyes. "Nag, nag, nag."

Beth leaned over and whacked her on the leg. Rachel grinned and tucked into her plate of food again.

THIRTY-EIGHT

Luke Mason slipped into one of the back pews just after the service began. The only people aware he'd arrived were the pastor and Luke's mother. Sadie was at the front playing the piano and stared briefly. But before she looked away, Max Payton had turned and smiled.

Luke tried to keep his eyes averted from Rachel, but they continually slid in her direction. The strap around her neck let him know she wore a sling for her arm. Beth Barnes must have put Rachel's hair up this morning. He enjoyed the sight of her slim neck.

Luke forced himself to focus on what the pastor was saying, but by the time he managed to concentrate, he'd missed the entire message. He berated himself and slipped out just as quietly as he had arrived.

He went straight to the office. Work was one thing that could keep his mind occupied. When he arrived, someone sitting on the bench stood and joined him inside.

"What can I do for you?"

"Seen a still up in them hills." He pointed over his shoulder. "Big one."

Luke didn't bother sitting. "Where in the hills?"

He listened to the man's directions and thought he could find it. The man tipped his hat back.

"Ain't as easy to find as you think. But follow your nose and you should do all right."

Luke shook his hand. "Thank you. I've been after that thing for months."

He stopped by Morgan Taylor's house to fill him in, then headed home for warmer clothes. He entered through the kitchen door.

"Mother, can you pack me some food?"

When he spotted Rachel sitting at the table with his mother and Max, he stopped in his tracks. The two eyed each other in silence. Sadie turned in her chair.

"Why do you need me to pack food?"

Luke switched his gaze to his mother. "We just got some information on a large still in the hills. I'm going up there and scout the area. I may be gone through the night. It just depends on what I find." He headed toward his room. "I'm going to grab some more clothes. It's been getting colder at night."

Luke closed his bedroom door behind him and collapsed onto the bed. He had no idea running into Rachel would unnerve him so. He missed spending time with her. But as he thought back to the sight of Rachel's blood, he knew he couldn't go through another traumatic loss of a loved one.

He'd worked hard to find information about the person who shot her, but had come up with nothing. He reported everything to the sheriff but refused to talk to Rachel about his lack of findings. But he also refused to give up.

Once his emotions were under control, Luke grabbed some warmer clothes, shoved them in his saddlebag, and returned to the kitchen. He'd hoped Rachel would have left for home by now, but she still sat at the table. He picked up the canvas sack holding the food his mother put together for him.

"I don't know when I'll be back, so don't wait up for me."

He leaned down and kissed Sadie's cheek before heading for the door.

"We'll be praying for your safety."

He was reaching to open the door when he heard Rachel's voice.

"Be careful, Luke."

He paused but didn't turn around. "I will. Good-bye."

He rode hard up the mountain, passing the home of the Manning sisters on the way. This was the first time he didn't take the time to check on them. Maybe he'd have time on the way back. Thinking about them brought his mind right back to Rachel and he groaned. Everything seemed to remind him of her.

He stopped and sniffed the air. He couldn't smell any mash cooking, so he continued up the mountain. The man had said it would be hard to find but this was ridiculous. Then he spotted some tubing. He dismounted and picked it up, then followed a trail of trampled grass and broken branches through some thick brush. He ended up in a clearing. The still had been dismantled and moved again.

He threw the tubing into the trees, then returned to his horse and tried to follow the trail in the direction they were heading. It was slow going. He lost the trail several times but found enough to keep him going for hours. When he reached the rocks, he lost the trail for good.

He sat for several minutes looking all around him hoping to see movement, more tubing, anything. Why couldn't he catch these men? And how did they know right when to move? He reined his horse around and headed back down the mountain.

He swung by the Manning place but they weren't home. Odd. "Hello?"

He sat in their yard for several minutes, but they didn't show. If he wanted to get home before dark he had to get moving, so he heeled his horse into motion again. By the time he'd stopped by Morgan's, his mother was already in bed.

Unable to sleep, he paced most of the night. He'd fixed some coffee and was sitting at the table when his mother woke and came in.

"Didn't sleep last night, huh?"

He looked at her with eyes that felt filled with sand.

His mother sat next to him. "Why are you fighting it, Luke? What has you so scared that you won't go to the woman you love?"

He stared into his cup of coffee for a while, letting the thoughts run through his mind again. He finally turned to her. "I'm scared of losing her."

Sadie gave a very unladylike snort. "You've already lost her."

"I mean, I'm afraid she's going to die and I don't want to lose her that way. I don't think I could stand to lose another person I love like that."

"She might as well be dead for all that you're going through."

He inhaled sharply, and Sadie reached for his hand.

"You're acting as though she *has* died. You're mourning for her because you can't be with her, but it's through your own doing. I know that Rachel wants to be with you, but you're holding her at arm's length. Maybe farther."

She stood and poured a cup of coffee. "Do you realize that you're not trusting God? Your very actions say you think you could do a better job than He can. It appears to me that God wants you and Rachel together, yet you're fighting Him. This isn't much different than when you were angry and running from Him. You're turning your back on His decision and going your own way. I think if you'd give in and trust God and all of His decisions for your life, you'd be much happier and at peace instead of dealing with that ache you have in your heart."

She returned to the chair next to him. "Don't you realize how happy you'd be with Rachel, even if you had her for only a short time? I didn't get to be with your father nearly as long as I would've liked, but I wouldn't trade a moment of our life together, even if I'd have known in advance that he would die young."

She grasped his hand again and waited for him to look at her. "Trust that God knows what He's doing and that He'll give you and Rachel a long and happy life together. And if that's not the case, then trust He'll soothe your heartache if He decides to take her from you.

In your line of work, she could lose you on any given day, but she's willing to take that risk. How can you do any less?"

Head down, he sat in silence for several minutes. Then he stood quickly and kissed her cheek.

"Pray, Mother. Pray she'll take me back."

Then he ran out the door. He first stopped at the Barneses' home, but learned Jim and Rachel had left for work an hour ago. He was late for work, but that didn't stop him from heading to the doctor's office. When Jim told him she'd gone to run an errand, he left his horse and went in search of her.

He spotted her coming out of the post office across and down the street. She held some kind of paper in front of her as she stepped into the street. He headed her way. He saw a horse and buggy bearing down on her and called out to her as he started to run. Rachel looked up at him, then toward the buggy. Luke launched from the boardwalk and into Rachel, and they both rolled out of the way just as the horse and buggy raced past.

Luke lifted Rachel and wrapped her in his arms. "You all right? You hurt? Do I need to get Jim?"

"I'm fine."

He examined her face, then nodded and helped her to her feet and off the street. She took a step away.

"I can't even describe the horses, Luke. It all happened too fast."

"You don't have to. I saw who was driving."

He looked down the street, but the buggy was gone. Rachel grabbed his arm.

"Who, Luke? Who tried to hurt me just now?"

He was still in disbelief and it took him a moment to answer. "It was Cassie Chatham."

"Cassie? But why? I've never done anything to her."

"Actually, you have. You caught my attention and took me away from her. At least that's probably the way she figures it. I'm guessing she thinks if you're out of the way, she'll win me back."

She looked him in the eyes. "But I don't have your attention any longer."

Luke smiled, wanting very badly to kiss her. "Yes you do, more than ever." He cupped her cheeks with his hands. "I love you, Rae."

Tears welled in her eyes as her bottom lip trembled. Her eyes remained on his as she shook her head. He saw the doubt in her eyes.

"Talk to me, Rae. Tell me what you're thinking."

She reached up and took his hands in hers. "How do I know that you won't run if something like this happens again? How do I know you'll be with me through it all, no matter what?"

He raised her hands to his lips and kissed her fingers. "If I learned one thing during these last few weeks, it's that I can't live without you. I was miserable all this time. I ran because the sight of your blood scared me to death. It reminded me of losing my father, and I didn't want to lose you too. But Mother made me see that *I* was killing our relationship, not the shooter. Not Cassie."

He took a breath and looked her in the eyes. "I promise I'll never run from you again. Even if God decides to let us have only a short time together, that time will be precious to me, and I will treasure it forever in my heart."

Tears flowed freely as she smiled up at him, but she had yet to say a word. He leaned very close to her.

"Say it, Rae. Say the words that your eyes have been telling me for weeks."

She tugged one hand free and wiped at her tears. Then she took a deep breath. "I love you, Luke. More than I can ever describe, I love you."

Luke closed the distance to her lips and kissed her. He pulled back, only to lean in and kiss her again when he saw the look in her eyes. "Will you be my wife, Rae? Will you marry me?"

Rachel's lips parted in surprise and she stared into his eyes. He smiled. "I love you and want to spend the rest of my life showing you just how much."

A slow smile grew on her face, and he could stand it no longer. "Does that smile mean yes?"

She nodded. "Yes, Luke. I'd love to be your wife."

He sighed with relief. "When?"

"When?"

"Yes, when? I'd marry you tomorrow if you'd agree."

"Luke!"

"Rachel!"

She grinned and threw her arms around him. The crowd that had gathered cheered.

THIRTY-NINE

With Morgan Taylor at his side, Luke Mason knocked on the door of the Chatham house. As soon as Mrs. Chatham opened the door, Luke stepped inside before she could close it on him. Morgan followed on his heels.

"We need to talk to Cassie."

Mrs. Chatham looked first at Luke, then at Morgan. "Why?"

"She tried to run over Rachel Garrett with a horse and buggy," Morgan said.

"She did not. She wouldn't do such a thing. I don't think she even knows Rachel."

"She did. We have several witnesses." Morgan motioned to Luke. "He's one of them."

Her eyes went to him. "I don't believe you."

"Where is she?" Luke said.

Mrs. Chatham wrung her hands together. "I, uh...she's at a friend's house."

"Who's the friend?"

Footsteps descended the stairs. "Who was at the door?"

When Cassie saw Luke and Morgan, she turned and raced back up the steps. Luke ran after her and caught her before she reached the top. She screamed and swung at him. He grabbed her hand, led her back down the stairs, and held her still in front of Morgan.

"You're under arrest, Cassie," Morgan said. "You can't attempt to kill someone and think you can get away with it."

"I wasn't going to kill her. I just wanted to hurt her a little like she hurt me."

Luke wanted to shake her. "She never hurt you, Cassie. It was me that ended our relationship, not her."

"But you did it because of her."

"Let's go, Cassie," Morgan said. "We'll let the judge decide what to do about this."

Luke led Cassie down the porch steps and toward the jailhouse. Relief filled him that for the first time in many months, it appeared Rachel was finally safe.

The first snow of the season fell in silence, making everything look clean and white. Rachel and Emma and Tanner Barnes stood outside trying to catch the big flakes on their tongues. The darkened sky showed no sign of slowing the release of its white bounty.

Rachel scooped up a handful of snow and tossed it at the children. They squealed and tossed some back at her. Their playing was interrupted by a young man from the other side of town.

"Is Doc here? Mama sent me. She said she's about to have her baby."

Before Rachel could move, Emma ran inside and returned minutes later with her father in tow. Rachel trailed him toward the stable, but he stopped her.

"Stay here, Rachel. This is her fourth child, and she shouldn't have any trouble. Besides, this weather could turn stormy, and you don't need to be out in it with me."

He soon had the buggy hitched up and was on his way. Rachel dropped onto her back and showed the children how to make snow angels. They made their own on each side of her. When she stood, she could tell the temperature was dropping. She was about to suggest they go inside when a man rode their direction. She hustled the kids inside, then returned to face the man. She smiled when she recognized him.

"Mr. Farris! Good to see you again."

"The doc around?"

"No. Anything wrong?"

"I was riding past the home of Sue and Sylvia Manning. Sylvia ran out when she saw me and asked me to come for the doctor. She said something about Sue slipping off a boulder and hurting her side and her arm. I guess her head's bleeding pretty bad too. It's hard to say for sure. Sylvia was pretty upset."

Rachel's heart raced at the thought of those two women being hurt or upset. She looked up at him. "Thank you, Mr. Farris. I'll make sure the doctor gets up there as soon as possible."

He tipped his hat and rode off.

Rachel paced, trying to figure out what to do. Before long, she ran to the stable and stepped inside. Luke's horse stood in its stall munching on hay. With only a moment's hesitation, she led the horse out and had her saddled in minutes. She stopped at her house long enough to grab her medical bag, then climbed onto the saddle and urged the horse into a gallop.

Luke sat at the kitchen table staring at the papers in front of him. He'd drawn a map of the area and marked each place he'd found the remnants of a still. Except for the first one, they all circled or sat within a day's ride of the Manning residence. Luke shook his head at the absurdity of that thought. Those two women were too old, too sweet, to run a still and sell whiskey. Then again, the cider they gave him several months ago...

He groaned and ran his fingers through his hair, then over his face. He looked at the sheets one more time, then stood and walked away. He needed some fresh air to clear his head. Maybe a visit with Rachel would help. He could tell her his idea and see if she thought he was as crazy as he did.

When he opened the door and saw all the snow and felt the drop in temperature, he turned back long enough to grab his coat, then headed out into the cold. He ducked his head against the blowing snow and was almost to Rachel's house when he looked up to see her riding off on his horse. He ran after her.

"Rachel! Stop!"

He was still standing there gaping after her, when Beth Barnes stepped out of her house.

"Where's Rachel?"

Luke spun around. "She just took my horse!" Since Beth wasn't wearing a coat, he propelled her back inside the house. "Where was she headed, Beth?"

"I don't know. I saw someone ride up, talk to her, then ride away, but I don't know anything after that."

He paced. "Maybe she left a note."

He ran first to the stable. Seeing nothing, he entered her house and found a note on her table. He grabbed it up.

Sue Manning is hurt. I'm riding out to help her.

"The Manning place?"

Panic clawed at him. He had to find a horse and go after her. He ran out the door and down the street to the Baxter home.

The speed of the galloping horse unnerved Rachel, but she refused to slow down. The falling and blowing snow stung her cheeks. She ducked her face into the collar of her coat and nudged the horse to go faster.

Because of her reduced vision, she missed the fork in the road and had to turn around. Her heart hammered at the thought she might be too late. She found the right turn and raced down the next road. She leaned low, hoping to reduce the amount of wind slamming against her.

The next second, a gunshot went off. The horse reared, dumping her onto the ground.

FORTY

Luke finished saddling the Baxters' horse and raced out of their barn. He stopped at his house long enough to grab his rifle, then he spurred the horse out of town. He doubted Sue or Sylvia would hurt Rachel. They always acted as though they loved her. But after all she'd been through, he wasn't taking any chances.

He reined the horse to the left at the fork and prodded it with his heels to run faster. Then he heard a gunshot. He yanked back on the reins. The horse skidded to a stop. Luke slid from the saddle and scooted toward the trees for cover. Another shot went off. Luke looked to his right for the shooter. The snow blinded him. He crouched and made his way to the next tree. He still couldn't see anyone.

A gun blasted again. The bullet hit a boulder, and the ricochet left a loud ring. A scream followed the chime.

Rachel!

His heart pounding, Luke scooted to the next tree and peered around. Where was that shooter? He looked in the direction of Rachel's scream, trying to spot her. He saw her feet sticking out behind a large boulder and followed the route the bullet had probably come from. He squinted against the falling snow and thought he saw something move.

After a deep breath, he plunged forward as fast as he dared without making much noise. He stopped after about twenty yards and looked again. He rubbed at his eyes as he peered through the snow, then gave a short gasp when he recognized the shooter.

Rachel shivered as she lay behind the boulder. She'd thought she was safe after Luke arrested Cassie. Another bullet pinged against the boulder.

"Who's out there?" she yelled again.

Silence answered.

"Who are you?"

Frustration screamed through her. She had to get to Sue. She tried to crawl away, but another gunshot turned her back. She lay still. Whoever wanted her dead was finally going to get their wish. She clasped her fingers and started praying.

Luke looked around and realized he had no way to get to Joe Farris without Joe having a clear shot at him. His only two options were to talk the man out of killing Rachel or wait for the chance to shoot him from his perch.

He glanced at Rachel one more time, then took a deep breath. "Joe!"

Mr. Farris moved to the other side of the tree.

"Joe Farris! This is Deputy Luke Mason."

He waited for a response but received none.

"Give it up, Joe. You won't get away, and if you shoot Miss Garrett, you'll hang."

"I don't care."

"Why are you trying to kill her?"

"Because it has to stop."

"What has to stop?"

"She's killed too many people. Someone has to stop her."

"Who has she killed?"

"You know the answer to that."

"Remind me."

"My wife for one. And I talked to Dunlavey. He told me that nurse not only killed her brother but also Dunlavey's wife. Lucille Munroe was her latest victim, and I intend to make sure she's the last."

Help me, Lord. Give me the words.

"Rachel's not to blame, Joe. No one is. We may not understand why things happen, but we've got to trust that God will somehow bring good out of it, no matter how difficult it is to go through it."

"Nothing good came from my wife dying."

"Hadn't she been sickly for years? She's no longer hurting, Joe. You've got to believe she's in a better place."

He peeked at Joe to see if his words had any effect. Joe still sat in his perch, but now he was no longer looking at Rachel.

"And Mrs. Munroe had been sick for a long time. She told Dr. Barnes that she was ready to die, that she wanted to see her Lord and her husband again."

"What about Rachel's brother and Dunlavey's wife?"

"Rachel told me about her brother. That was an accident. They were playing and he fell." He took another breath. "She didn't kill her brother, Joe. She hasn't killed anyone. People die. That's a fact of life. All Rachel's ever wanted to do is help people, and that's all she's done since she arrived in Rockdale."

Luke took another look at Joe. "I understand your pain, Joe. I lost my father and lived in pain and anger for years. It's a horrible thing to go through, but life goes on if you let it. Let your life go on, Joe. I'm sure your wife would want that for you."

He stayed silent and waited to hear from Joe. He didn't have long to wait.

"All right. I'm coming out."

"Drop your gun first."

Joe threw the rifle to the ground and climbed down. Luke hurried toward him, wanting to get the gun before Joe changed his mind. He scooped it from the ground and tossed it farther away.

"Do you have any other guns, Joe?"

He shook his head.

"Drop to your knees." Joe obeyed.

With his rifle still pointed at Farris, Luke looked at the boulder. "You can come out now, Rachel." She didn't move. "Come to me, Rae."

Seconds later, Rachel stepped from behind the boulder. When she saw him, she came at a run and threw herself into his arms. He held her for several minutes before she turned to Joe.

"Is Sue really hurt or did you just say that to get me out here?"

Joe wouldn't look at her. "She's fine as far as I know."

Rachel took a step toward him, but Luke grabbed her hand and shook his head. She nodded and returned to his side.

"I forgive you, Mr. Farris."

His head jerked up and he stared as tears filled his eyes. "I miss my Clara."

"I know. I understand."

Jim arrived in a buggy. "Everything all right?"

"It is now," Luke said.

Luke took Rachel by the arm and turned her around to face him. "You know, I could arrest you for stealing my horse."

"I didn't steal it. I only borrowed it."

"You could have asked."

"If I'd have done that, you would've stopped me from coming."

"Without a doubt, and it would have kept you from getting into this predicament."

"This predicament helped you find out who was trying to hurt me."

He stared at her for several seconds, then shook his head. "Women! I'll never understand how females think."

He left Jim in charge while he rounded up the three horses. He returned with them and stopped in front of Joe, holding out a coiled piece of copper tubing.

"This yours?"

Joe licked his lips and looked away.

"You the one who's been running the still I've been chasing down?"

Joe shrugged.

"Who's been helping you?"

"I'm alone."

"I don't believe you. There's no way you can move and run a still by yourself." He grabbed Joe's coat. "Spill it, Joe, or I'll change my mind about having the judge go easy on you."

Joe looked up at him. "The first man ran off to join Quint's gang. Dunlavey's been helping me lately."

"Dunlavey?"

Luke thought back on what Max Payton told him about Dunlavey disappearing every so often. Now it made sense. He tied Joe's hands behind his back and helped him onto his horse. Then he walked Rachel over to Jim's buggy and helped her climb into it.

"Jim, will you make sure Rae gets home safe? I aim to marry that woman whether I can understand her or not, and I'm making you responsible to make sure she gets to the altar in one piece."

Jim laughed. "You couldn't find an easier task for me?"

Rachel whacked him on the arm. Jim winked and flicked the reins. Luke stood staring at the buggy as it rolled away.

"Hope you're as happy with her as I was with Clara."

Luke turned to Joe. "I'm already happy, Joe, and I hope I get to enjoy many more years of this very feeling."

FORTY-ONE

Rachel stood at the altar with her hand on Luke's arm. She could hardly look away from him; he'd never looked so handsome. Beth stood beside Rachel while Max and Sadie stood next to Luke. She leaned and smiled at them. They'd be standing at the altar as soon as her and Luke's ceremony ended.

She didn't have to look around the church to know it was filled to overflowing. Pastor Robbins stood and approached them, his smile wide.

"Are we ready to proceed?"

Luke looked around. "I think everyone's here, don't you?"

When his stomach rumbled, Rachel looked up at him. "You hungry? Didn't you eat anything earlier?"

He leaned down. "Nope. I was saving room for dessert later."

She raised her brows and made a face. She hated to admit it, but she'd had no part in the food preparations and didn't know what was being served. "What's for dessert?"

"Mud pie."

She whipped her head up to look at him. He grinned and waggled his brows. She burst into laughter. Without a doubt, their future promised to be wonderful and fun-filled.

1. At first, out of fear she'd lose her job, Rachel hid from the doctor the fact that she'd lost a patient. Have you ever tried to hide a past failure or mistake? Were you successful? How did it make you feel?

2. Luke's father was killed while chasing outlaws, and Rachel had several bad things happen to her throughout the story. Does being a child of God guarantee His protection? Why or why not?

3. Loss comes to everyone sooner or later. Compare how you dealt with a significant loss in your life with how Luke dealt with his. Has your perspective on life been altered because of your loss?

4. Rachel had some patients die while in her care. Those losses hurt, yet they didn't stop her from continuing with her desire to help others. Have losses or failures in your past ever changed or stopped any plans you'd made? If so, how?

5. Luke struggled with the question of why bad things happen to good people like his father and Lyle Phipps, the man gored

by the bull. He turned away from God because of his hurt and anger. Can you relate to his feelings? In what ways?

6. Is it okay to be angry with God and ask why? Why or why not?

7. After Rachel escaped from her kidnappers, she had a difficult time understanding why God allowed it to happen. How can surviving a trial bring you closer to God?

8. Luke became a lawman hoping to right wrongs and ensure that justice was done. Do you become frustrated when you see someone get away with evil actions? Why or why not?

9. Many people avoided the Manning sisters because they were uncomfortable with their odd behavior and lack of decorum. How important is outward appearance to you? Do you usually look past the surface or are you quick to make a judgment based on how someone looks?

10. Which character do you most strongly identify with? Why?

═══ About the Author ═══

Janelle Mowery is the author of several novels, including *When All My Dreams Come True* and *When Love Gets in the Way*, Books 1 and 2 in the Colorado Runaway series. When not writing, reading, and researching, she is active in her church. Born and raised in Minnesota, Janelle now resides in Texas with her husband and two sons, where she and her family raise orphaned raccoons, look at beautiful deer, and make friends with curious armadillos.

Visit her website at www.janellemowery.com

Other Books in the Colorado Runaway Series

Straight from the heart of the Old West,
*the **Colorado Runaway Series** is full of adventure, humor,*
and romance by award-winning novelist Janelle Mowery.

When All My Dreams Come True, Book 1

Bobbie McIntyre dreams of running a ranch of her own. Raised without a mother and having spent most of her time around men, she knows more about wrangling than acting like a lady. The friendship of her new employer awakens a desire to learn more about presenting her feminine side, but ranch life keeps getting in the way.

Ranch owner Jace Kincaid figures the Lord is testing his faith when a female wrangler shows up looking for work. Bobbie has an uncanny way of getting under his skin, though, and he's surprised when she finds a home next to his heart. But when his cattle begin to go missing and his wranglers are in danger from some low-down cattle thief, can Jace trust God, even if it may mean giving up on his dreams?

> *"You've got to love an author who helps you see, hear, smell, taste, and touch with her characters' senses—not to mention hope, fear, cry, and rejoice with them. Janelle Mowery takes her readers along for the ride."*
>
> —**Marcia Gruver**, author of the Texas Fortunes series

> *"Action, adventure, romance, intrigue—readers will find all of these and more in this beautifully written story."*
>
> —**Janice (Hanna) Thompson**, author of *Love Finds You in Poetry, Texas*

> *"Janelle Mowery's talent for spinning a memorable and satisfying yarn is flawless. With characters that will remain with you long after the last page is turned, this novel is a must-read!"*
>
> —**Kathleen Y'Barbo**, author of *The Confidential Life of Eugenia Cooper*

When Love Gets in the Way, Book 2

Grace Bradley wishes all she touches would turn to gold. Instead, it tends to tarnish...that is, until she finds freedom on the Double K Ranch. Grace is fleeing from the man her father chose to be her husband. But once her heart is captured by her new employer's best friend, and she finally understands the meaning of God's sacrificial love, she relinquishes her independence to save her loved ones.

Cade Ramsey contemplates running for dear life from the accident-prone woman he brought to his hometown. The trouble that trails her seems to latch on to him at every turn. But when Grace manages to win his calloused heart, he pursues her, praying he can keep her from following through on a decision that could ruin their lives.

An adventurous novel of faith, hope, and love in the Wild West.

To learn more about Harvest House books and
to read sample chapters, log on to our website:

www.harvesthousepublishers.com

HARVEST HOUSE PUBLISHERS

EUGENE, OREGON